Unconventional Ladies

A Regency novel inspired by P&P

Sydney Salier

Also by Sydney Salier

Unconventional

An Unconventional Education (Book 1) – A P&P Reimagining

The Denton Connection

Don't flatter yourself – A P&P Variation

Mrs Bennet's Surprising Connections – Prequel to 'Don't flatter yourself'

It's a Duke's Life – Sequel to 'Don't flatter yourself'. A P&P spin-off

Don't flatter yourself – Revisited – The alternate version of this P&P Variation

Surprise & Serendipity – A P&P Variation

You asked for it – A P&P Variation with a twist

Remember – you wanted this – A collection of P&P variations

To Michael

As always, thanks

My thanks also to all those lovely
readers on FF whose comments helped to
improve this story.

CONTENTS

1   Georgiana

Miss Georgiana Darcy waited for the last note of the sonata to fade before removing her hands from the keys of the pianoforte.

As was her wont when she was at Pemberley, she had been practising all afternoon. For her, the hours of practise were not a chore but a joy. She loved music, and after the last summer, it was the one thing that soothed her troubled spirit.

At the age of fifteen she was a shy girl. An old acquaintance had preyed on that reserve and fond childhood memories, to make her believe herself to be in love and agree to an elopement. She had been saved from that folly by the unexpected arrival of her brother, who had shown to her the calculating nature of George Wickham.

The shock of betrayal had made Georgiana even more withdrawn. Her brother and her new companion, Mrs Annesley, had both tried to help her regain her confidence, but it was a slow process.

A few weeks earlier, Georgiana could not bear it any longer, seeing her brother so concerned for her that she had encouraged him to accept an invitation from his friend, Mr Bingley.

The result of that visit was unexpected.

Like herself, Fitzwilliam Darcy was not comfortable in company, unless the company was comprised of family and close friends. In his case it was exacerbated by the fact that matchmaking mothers and their daughters had considered him their rightful prey for nearly a decade.

Mr Darcy was an excellent correspondent, who wrote to his sister frequently when they were separated. Now, for the first time, her brother's letters had been full of references to a young lady.

It seemed that Miss Elizabeth Mortimer was accomplished, beautiful, compassionate, delightful, educated, funny, gracious, humorous, intelligent, joyful, kind, lovely, modest, natural, open, perspicacious, questioning, resourceful, sensible, talented, understanding, vivacious, witty… the list only stopped because there was no adjective starting with x.

Although he did not say so, Georgiana suspected that her brother was head over heels in love. Only a man completely besotted could, and would, require virtually the whole alphabet to sing a lady's praises.

When she finished her practice, Georgiana's mind wandered back to her brother. She wondered how much longer it would take him to realise that Miss Elizabeth was perfect for him.

She was startled out of her ruminations when the butler entered the room, carrying a salver with a letter. 'An express from Mr Darcy has just arrived.'

Georgiana jumped up and rushed to collect the letter.

Mrs Annesley who had been working on some embroidery, looked up and watched her charge read the note. 'I gather there is good news,' she surmised when Georgiana's expression turned from pensive into a huge smile.

'My brother is getting married, and he wants me to come and meet his fiancée.'

'How wonderful. I am all anticipation to meet Miss Elizabeth.'

'How do you know it is her?'

'You forget, my dear, that you have related your brother's description of the young lady. I cannot imagine that he would be so effusive about one lady, and then plan to marry another.'

Georgiana laughed. 'You are quite right. But now that he has come to a decision, he plans to marry as soon as possible. We need to leave early tomorrow.'

Her face fell as she continued to read. 'It seems I have been invited by Mrs Mortimer to stay at Brook Hall, to give me an opportunity to get to know my new sisters.'

'Georgiana, I am certain that your brother would not allow you to stay with the family if he had the slightest concern about your wellbeing in their company. He must be certain that you will be at ease with your new sisters.'

'You are of course correct.' Georgiana tried to put on a brave face. 'And he does say that he will be at Brook Hall to welcome me, and to introduce me to the family.'

As she read further, her face brightened again. 'He says that if I feel the slightest discomfort after meeting them, Mr Bingley will host me at Netherfield.'

'See, you have nothing to worry about. Now, shall we see about our packing?'

~~~oo0Ooo~~~

The Darcy carriage was approaching Meryton. The closer they came, the more nervous Georgiana Darcy became.

'Stop fidgeting. We sent the outrider ahead to inform your brother of your arrival. I am certain he will be there to greet you and introduce you.' Mrs Annesley tried to calm her charge.

'Yes, I know. And my brother assured me that all the ladies are perfectly charming and amiable, and are looking forward to meeting me. But I never had sisters before. I simply do not know what to expect. I just hope they are not like the girls at school...'

Mrs Annesley, who had been watching the scenery out the carriage window, and had noticed that they had just passed through a gate, said, 'you should expect to exit the carriage shortly. I believe we have entered the grounds of Brook Hall.'

That news spurred Georgiana to look out the window. After a few minutes of driving through woods, the vista opened up and she spied a house reminiscent of Pemberley, albeit on a smaller scale.

By the time the carriage stopped in front of the house, the doors opened and Fitzwilliam Darcy exited in a hurry, followed a little more slowly by a slender lady of middle years.

When the door to the carriage was opened, and steps placed to help her exit, Darcy was on hand to assist his sister.

Georgiana could barely believe her eyes when she saw her brother. Where was the calm and controlled man she knew? Her brother was beaming at her, and as soon as she had her feet firmly on the ground
~~~

and straightened up to greet him properly, she found herself engulfed in a hug.

'Georgie, it is so good to see you. You made excellent time.'

'William, it is wonderful to see you too, and looking so well, but we are not alone.' While Georgiana was ecstatic that her brother looked happy, as well as happy to see her, she was worried about the impression they might be creating.

'There is no need to worry, my dear. Aunt Stephanie is family, and does not stand on ceremony with family. Come let me introduce you, you will love her.'

Darcy took his sister's hand and led her to the lady, who had looked on with pleasure at the warm greeting between the siblings.

'Aunt Stephanie, may I present to you my sister Miss Georgiana Darcy. Georgie, this lady is Mrs Mortimer, Elizabeth's mother.'

Georgiana curtsied, 'a pleasure to meet you, Mrs Mortimer.'

'I am very pleased to meet you too, my dear. But, since you are nearly family, you must call me Aunt Stephanie, like your brother does.'

'Thank you, Aunt Stephanie. I prefer Georgie to Georgiana, but will answer to both.' Georgiana smiled shyly.

Mrs Mortimer smiled and held her arms in a subtle invitation to give Georgiana a hug, but when the girl appeared too shy to respond to the invitation, she turned it into a gesture towards the house with one hand, while the other gently came to rest on Georgiana's shoulder. 'It is too cold to stay out here. Come inside and meet the girls.'

They had gone two steps, when Georgiana recalled her companion. 'Mrs Annesley,' she gasped.

Darcy looked chagrined that in his excitement to see his sister, he too had forgotten about the lady. He turned back to see that the lady had just exited the carriage with the help of a footman.

'Mrs Annesley, please forgive my thoughtlessness...' Darcy started to apologise.

'Never mind, Mr Darcy. I quite understand.' The lady smiled pleasantly at her employer.

Darcy performed the introductions and the party moved inside.

~~~ooO0Ooo~~~

As soon as the front door closed behind them, the sisters came streaming from the parlour, with Elizabeth in the lead.

Once Darcy had performed the introductions, the sisters insisted on showing Georgiana to her room, so that she could refresh herself after the journey. Before Georgiana knew what was happening, she was led up the stairs amid a group of happily chattering girls.

'William has been telling us so much about you.'

'What a wonderful sister you are.'

'Do you truly practice the pianoforte six or more hours each day?'

'Do you like riding? We can show you around the estate.'

A voice was suddenly raised above the babble. 'Quiet,' demanded Elizabeth. 'I am sorry, Georgiana, as you can tell we are excited and happy to meet you. But William also told us that you are shy, and I expect you would not be used to four sisters babbling at you all at once. If it is too much, just say so. We truly do not mind.'

Georgiana smiled helplessly. 'I am simply overwhelmed. William and I have always lived quietly…'

Kitty gave her a searching look. 'You were worried about being thrust into a group of strangers. Not certain if you were welcome, or possibly about putting a foot wrong.'

'How…'

'That is how I feel when I am amongst people I do not know well. It must be worse for you since you do not know us at all. But please, do not fret yourself. We do not expect you to be perfect. We each have our foibles, and we have learned not to judge.'

'What Kitty is trying to say is, just be yourself. According to William you are a rather nice person, and we are hoping to get to know the sister whom he knows,' Lydia could not help but try to help.

'I agree with everything my sisters have said, and here is your room. I hope you will like it,' added Mary.
~~~

In her excitement to meet William's sister at last, Elizabeth had forgotten about Mrs Annesley. Jane, realising her sister's faux pas, offered to escort the amused lady.

'Do not concern yourself, Miss Mortimer, I still remember being young and excited.'

They followed the chattering group at a more sedate pace. Mrs Annesley watched her charge carefully, but noting the goodwill amongst the sisters, thought it best to let Georgiana deal with them by herself.

Jane had noticed the look and said quietly, 'all will be well. As far as sisters go, you could not wish for better.'

'I believe you are correct, Miss Mortimer,' replied Mrs Annesley, content that Georgiana was in good hands.

~~~ooo0ooo~~~

Georgiana had refreshed herself and was changing into a clean dress with the help of the sisters, when she realised something.

'I thought you were sisters. But you, Kitty, call Mrs Mortimer mother, but Lydia calls her Aunt Stephanie...'

'We are sisters,' said Kitty.

Before she could explain, Elizabeth sighed. 'William obviously did *not* explain.'

'Men...' huffed Mary.

When Georgiana looked uncomfortable, Lydia managed to be first with the explanation. 'Please do not look so shocked. We can behave with perfect decorum in public. But we are at home now and you are almost family. At least you will be in a matter of weeks.'

'But to answer your question. The short version is that Lizzy, Mary and Kitty were adopted by Mrs Mortimer when they were young. Jane and I became her wards when our father died. That is why I call her Aunt. But since I think your brother is waiting for you, the long version of the story will have to wait till after dinner, when we can get together and chat all night if we can stay awake.'

Lydia gave Georgiana a hug. 'Do not worry, we rarely bite and then only someone who deserves it.'
~~~

'I am not worried. I am overwhelmed by your welcome. I am a complete stranger to you and yet you treat me like family…'

'We like your brother. Soon he will be our brother and that makes you our sister. We simply decided it was silly to treat you as a formal acquaintance for three weeks, and then change and treat you as family. We might as well skip the formal stage and go straight to family. It is more fun… for all of us.'

Georgiana was not yet certain about the fun part, but was willing to accept the welcome. Although… the enthusiasm would take a while to get used to.

<p style="text-align:center">~~~ooO0Ooo~~~</p>

2   Sisters

When she joined her brother, Georgiana was slightly bewildered by the sheer number of women in the house, each of whom was determined to make her feel welcome.

'Compared to the girls I met at that school, Lizzy and her sisters are rather unconventional, but, oh, so much nicer,' she enthused. 'I am so very happy for you to have found her.'

'Not half as happy as I am,' Darcy replied.

'And not half as happy as I am, since he introduced me to this delightful madhouse,' Richard said from behind Georgiana.

She whirled around and threw her arms around her cousin. 'Richard, what are you doing here?'

'I am well, thank you. And I am pleased to see you too,' he teased Georgiana.

'Richard, you know perfectly well that I am always pleased to see you, and I can see for myself that you are well,' pouted Georgiana. While she was generally shy with people, with her brother and favourite cousin she was outgoing. Richard in particular, due to his gregarious nature, encouraged her to be, at least a little, cheeky.

Darcy complained jokingly, 'I get a reprimand for greeting my sister like a loving brother in front of one person, and Richard gets a hug, without prompting mind you, and in front of eight people.'

Georgiana blushed at the reminder, but then laughed, 'but they are all family.'

'I should have known that the ladies would not need long to make you one of them.' Darcy smiled, feeling pleased for his sister. She had been lonely for far too long.

'Stop distracting me, brother. Richard, you did not answer my question.'

'I am here to see a very special lady,' her cousin replied, with a quick glance towards Jane.

Georgiana noticed the look but thought to tease her cousin. 'I know that you are my guardian and that you love me, but there was no need for you to come and protect me from these ladies. They do not seem so very ferocious to me.'

Darcy and Richard looked at each other and burst out laughing.

'Looks can be deceptive,' murmured Lydia.

Georgiana was confused and a little affronted by the reaction her teasing had caused.

'Forgive us,' chuckled Richard. 'But you only met your new sisters today, and in pleasant circumstances. You do not need me to defend you. Since you have obviously been admitted into their sisterhood, you have gained the staunchest defenders you could hope for.'

Richard, instead of reassuring Georgiana, confused her even more. She demanded, 'what do you mean?'

Before either of the men could answer, and possibly make matters worse, Mrs Mortimer stepped up to Georgiana and put an arm around her. 'Boys, stop confusing the poor girl.'

Georgiana was amazed when both answered in unison, 'yes, Aunt Stephanie.' Darcy answered cheerfully, while Richard replied a little sheepishly.

'Come sit with me and I will explain, Georgie,' offered Mrs Mortimer, before turning back to the gentlemen. 'I suggest you speak to Elizabeth and Jane, and let me enlighten Georgiana, rather than confusing her.'

Georgiana noticed peripherally that her brother and cousin had taken Mrs Mortimer's advice, to sit with the indicated ladies, while Mrs Mortimer led her to a sofa, and, after providing her with a cup of tea, began her explanation.

~~~ooOOoo~~~
~~~

'Do you have any specific questions that you would like answered immediately, or shall I tell you our story?'

'Can you tell me why my brother and Richard were laughing when I said that your daughters do not look ferocious? And why Lydia said that looks can be deceiving?'

'Because, unlike most young women, I ensured that my daughters could take care of themselves. In other words, they were all taught how to defend themselves, and each other, against physical attacks.'

'But is that not pointless? After all, men are usually much bigger than women.'

'Yes, men are bigger, but they are not invulnerable.' Mrs Mortimer took Georgiana's hand. 'Will it upset you very much if I tell you that the girls are capable of hurting or even killing someone who tries to hurt one of their sisters?'

'Truly? They can do that?' Georgiana asked. She looked around the room and saw five lovely and genteel young women enjoying tea and conversation. 'They do not look dangerous.'

'Yes, they can. Which is why Lydia made her quip.' She sighed. 'I do not believe that I will ever be able to teach that girl to refrain from indulging in persiflage.'

'But is there not a big difference between practice and doing something in earnest. Like, I enjoy to practice on the pianoforte, but do not feel confident to play in public. They may know how to do these things, but would they do so?'

'Again, yes, they would because they have already done so. Lizzy is still dealing with the consequences of killing two men.'

Georgiana paled. 'She killed… how?'

'Three militia men were attacking Kitty. Lizzy did not have a choice and she shot two of them. The third surrendered. I am grateful to your brother for helping her deal with the aftereffects.'

'Richard said they defend their sisters…'

'They do. He and your brother were present to witness what happened, but they were unable to interfere since they were too far away. The man who was threatening Kitty, was too close to the girls, and Richard could not get a safe shot. Whereas Lizzy was within a few yards.' Mrs Mortimer explained as she patted Georgiana's hand.

'You do not need to be afraid of them because of what they have done. They do not enjoy hurting people. They only did what was necessary to save Kitty.' When Georgiana still looked shocked and a little dubious, she added, 'are you afraid of your cousin Richard?'

'No. Why should I be? He is the gentlest of men.'

'He is also a soldier who has killed… In the defence of our country.'

After a moment's thought, understanding lit up Georgiana's face. 'I had not thought of it that way.' She tilted her head questioningly. 'Richard said that they would defend me…'

'Since you are now their sister, they will defend you, should you be in need of defending.' Mrs Mortimer smiled encouragingly at the young girl. 'But the problems in this area have been taken care of, and you should not need defending. Now, are there any other questions, or would you like to hear the story of how we came to be a family?'

'The girls were going to tell me after dinner… but it might be easier if just one person told the story.'

'Very well, I shall give you the outline, and the girls can fill in the details.'

Mrs Mortimer provided Georgiana with the background of the sisters. How she had come to adopt the middle girls, after witnessing the neglect by Mrs Bennet, because she judged the girls not pretty enough and thought Elizabeth a hoyden, due to the girl's less feminine interests. Why Jane and Lydia had come into her care, after their father's death, and why even they had chosen the name Mortimer instead of Bennet.

Georgiana was horrified. 'How could Mrs Bennet consider marrying Jane to that horrible man, and then reject her favourite daughters just because she suddenly had a son?'

'In regard to the first part of your question, I suspect that Mrs Bennet was desperate. The estate is entailed and she was about to lose her home. She is not a particularly accomplished woman and feared having to live in poverty.'

'As to the second, I do not know. At the time, Lydia was chafing at the restrictions I placed on her, since she had been spoiled by her mother, and wanted to get back to the life she had known. Maybe Mrs Bennet thought that the girls would be better off with me, and the only way to convince Lydia, was to reject her outright.'

'You are very charitable to attribute those motives to the lady.' Georgiana was unconvinced.

'As I said, I do not know her true motivations, and therefore, until I know, I suspend judgment. For me it is irrelevant. The girls are here with me and we are happy. At least Mrs Bennet has calmed enough that when we encounter her in public, she is polite and civil to everyone.'

'It must have been difficult for them,' hazarded Georgiana. 'But from what I can tell, everything has worked out for the best. Even for my brother...'

~~~oo0Ooo~~~

Dinner was held back a little to allow Georgiana and Mrs Annesley to have time for a bath, to wash off the dust from travelling.

Mrs Annesley was reluctant to intrude on a family dinner, until she was assured that Mrs Taylor and Miss Martin were considered family in this rather unconventional household.

Georgiana was surprised to find that the dining table in the family dining room was round rather than rectangular, until Kitty explained that as a child, she had developed a fascination with King Arthur and the knights of the round table. Mrs Mortimer had indulged her by commissioning a round dining table for the family. 'It makes seating for a casual family dinner much easier.'

Mention of King Arthur led to a lively discussion of books.

Darcy, who was seated between his sister and Elizabeth, was pleased when Georgiana was drawn into the discussion by Kitty, who was sitting next to Georgiana.

Eventually, and reluctantly, Darcy and Fitzwilliam took their leave.

As he said goodbye, Darcy asked his sister, 'will you be comfortable here amongst all these ladies?'
~~~

'I will be perfectly fine, brother.' Georgiana smiled at him. 'You know that I always wanted a sister. Now that you have gifted me with five, I am looking forward to getting to know them.'

'That is the spirit,' interjected Richard who gave Georgiana a hug. 'I expect that by tomorrow, no one will suspect that your name is Darcy rather than Mortimer.'

<div align="center">~~~oo0Ooo~~~</div>

The girls changed into their nightclothes and congregated in Jane's room, since it was furthest from everyone else, and their chatter would not disturb the other residents.

Elizabeth had collected Georgiana, and on the way commented, 'there is one excellent point about living in a house full of women. Since there are no men around, we do not have to worry about traipsing through the corridors at night in a robe.'

They joined the other sisters and they were soon engaged in pleasant conversation, with the sisters telling Georgiana about growing up in a home, where they were encouraged to be the best that they could be.

Something that had struck Georgiana earlier in the evening made her curious. 'It seems excessively peculiar to me that my brother acts like he had known your family all his life.'

'In a way he has. Would you believe that Mother once rescued your brother when he was stuck in a tree?'

'My brother stuck in a tree? I cannot credit him even climbing a tree, much less getting stuck in one.'

'Admittedly he was but eight years old.'

Since Georgiana had not heard the story before, Elizabeth related the tale.

'That explains much,' laughed Georgiana. 'Not just about William, but also Richard. Both of them are usually extremely protective of me. But this time, William just handed me over to you and told me to have fun.'

'Are you having fun?' asked Kitty.

'Yes, I am. I have never had sisters before.' Georgiana became thoughtful. 'I think I can understand why William is so incredibly relaxed and cheerful here. Even though he did not remember her until she reminded him, simply the fact that he knew her as a boy and she helped him, while also keeping him out of trouble, makes him trust her, and by extension, the whole family.'

After chatting a while longer, the day spent travelling caught up with Georgiana. When she was getting too tired to continue, Elizabeth reassured her. 'You cannot possibly learn everything about us in one evening. There will be plenty of time on other nights.'

Georgiana reluctantly went to bed.

<p style="text-align:center">~~~oo0Ooo~~~</p>

3   Discoveries

Georgiana had thoroughly enjoyed the time spent with her new sisters and was pleased to discover that it was an almost nightly ritual for the sisters to come together for a chat before bed, and even more pleased, when she was asked to be part of the group.

Over the next week, she slowly learnt more about her new sisters.

'Lizzy, earlier this year, William told me about the ball at Aunt Matlock's, when you helped him hide from Miss Bingley. Did you know that he has been looking for you ever since?'

'He mentioned that when we met.'

'Did he tell you why he wanted to meet you?'

'Come to think of it, he did not say. Do you know?'

'Yes, I do. Do you know that you were the first woman who did not chase him? He said you seemed friendly and cheerful and prodigiously amused that he was hiding from the hounds. But you did not solicit an introduction on the strength of the help you provided. You smiled and walked away.'

Georgiana giggled. 'No woman had ever walked away from William.'

'So, I was a novelty?'

'You most certainly were.'

'In that case he was lucky the other ladies did not know that he would be interested in them, if only they pretended not to be interested in him. He might have married years ago.'

'I am glad they did not know. But why *did* you walk away? I may be biased, but I think he is one of the most handsome men in the country.'

'Because I was but seventeen years of age, and felt that I was much too young to consider marriage. At the time, even the most handsome face could not tempt me. It still would not tempt me if he did not have intelligence and a wonderful personality as well.'

Elizabeth's comment left the younger girls in a thoughtful mood, considering their future.

~~~ooO0Ooo~~~

Another evening Georgiana noticed that Kitty was sitting a little off to one side with a sketch pad.

When she requested to see the sketch, Georgiana was amazed that with just a few lines, Kitty had managed to capture each of their likenesses. 'This is wonderful, Kitty. Although I can draw and produce a reasonable likeness, I need my subjects to hold still. Yet you have perfectly captured each of us while we were speaking and moving about.'

Kitty smiled, pleased at the compliment, and explained, 'I am just the opposite. I find that I cannot produce a still life. Do not misunderstand, my masters have taught me enough that technically I can paint anything, such as a bowl of fruit or a landscape, but it is always lacking something. I need my subjects to be animated to produce a good likeness.'

'Whereas I cannot paint at all,' added Lizzy.

Mary giggled. 'I remember the time when mother complimented you on painting a recognisable hippopotamus, when you had tried to paint Phoenix.'

'Mary, you promised not to repeat that story again.' Elizabeth laughed with chagrin.

'I promised not to tell strangers about your lack of talent. Georgie is family, not a stranger.' Mary defended her indiscretion, still laughing.

'Please forgive us,' she added to Georgiana, 'but occasionally we have to bring Lizzy down to earth. Since she is inclined to think entirely too well of herself, we have to ensure she does not think she is perfect.'

Elizabeth struck a haughty posture and exclaimed in mock offense, 'I am perfect. I am the perfect me.' She too dissolved into a fit of giggles.
~~~

'Although I have to admit that Mary is partly right. Many things come very easily to me, and sometimes I forget that others do not have the same advantage. While it is salutary to my humility that I cannot paint, I do envy Kitty her ability. There are times when I would love the ability to capture a perfect memory.'

'Like the view from Oakham Mount,' suggested Kitty. 'You know, I was quite put out when James gave you that painting.' She blushed.

'Why, Kitty. Do tell. Are you interested in James?' asked Elizabeth, suddenly concerned.

'I simply admire his artistic ability,' protested Kitty, realising she had given away a secret which she had cherished for years.

Mary, who was closest to her younger sister, put an arm around her shoulders. 'Of course, you do. We quite understand,' she reassured the girl, while thinking that Mrs Mortimer needed to invite the cousins again.

Georgiana, sensitive to Kitty's embarrassment, kicked Lydia's ankle, when the youngest sister looked like she would offer one of her famous remarks.

Lydia initially looked offended, but when Georgiana gave her a pointed look, she grinned and quietly commented, 'I see that you have appointed yourself to be my conscience. It could be worse I suppose, since you do not have the training to kick hard.'

'Maybe I had better learn.' Georgiana raised an eyebrow.

'Why is everyone always picking on me?' Lydia sighed theatrically.

<p style="text-align:center">~~~oo0Ooo~~~</p>

While Georgiana was busy getting to know her new sisters, Jane was much occupied getting to know her suitor.

After agreeing to allow Richard to court her, she initially opted for conversations in the parlour, or for strolls through the garden.

'What are your plans for the future, Colonel. Will you remain in the army?'

'That will depend on what happens with us. I had always planned on remaining in the army until I found a wife. Being married to a soldier is not the kind of life I would wish on a woman I cared about.'

'If you do leave the army, what are your plans?'

'My mother has a small estate about half-way between Cambridge and Newmarket, which she promised to me. It is ideally suited and located for breeding horses.' He grinned at her. 'I may be giving up the cavalry but I refuse to give up horses.'

'I gather that you like riding?'

'Yes, Miss Mortimer. There are few other things which I like as well.' He hesitated a moment, but thought it best if they were honest with each other. 'I noticed that you have an excellent seat, and that you handled Hermes beautifully. I do not know many women, who can handle a stallion as competently as you did.'

Jane blushed. 'I gather you also noticed that I was riding Hermes astride.'

When Jane had learned to ride, she had insisted on riding side-saddle, so as not to give her mother cause to suspend her lessons for learning hoydenish ways. But since coming to live at Brook Hall, she too had opted for riding astride, since she considered it safer and more comfortable. Although on the day in question she had worn an ordinary dress, rather than her riding habit with the split skirt, the pelisse did cater for her new riding style, and had kept her legs properly covered.

'I did, and I must congratulate you on your dressmaker. Your pelisse preserved your modesty and propriety. I hope you will introduce Georgiana to her. She too prefers to ride astride.'

'You do not object to the impropriety?'

'Miss Mortimer, I am a pragmatic man. I want the women I care about to be as safe as they can be. I always considered riding side-saddle to be unsafe and an unnecessary strain on the horse.'

Jane laughed. 'Of course, you would consider the comfort of the horse.'

'My horses have usually been more reliable than many men I have known, especially in the *ton*. So, yes, I care about their comfort.' Richard grinned back at her, although there was a serious undertone in his reply.

Jane was momentarily speechless. There was a quiet intensity about this man, which was so very different to Mr Bingley. In comparison, even the officers of the militia, whom she had met in recent weeks, seemed like boys playing at war, while this man had seen the worst that life could throw at him.

'So, you wish to breed horses,' Jane stated, getting back to the original topic. She was not yet ready to delve too deeply into the feeling which Colonel Fitzwilliam roused in her.

'Yes, but not just horses. I hope to have a large family… with the agreement and cooperation of my wife, naturally.'

'How many children are you hoping for, Colonel?'

'A dozen or so sounds about right to me.' Richard grinned at Jane's shocked expression. 'But I am willing to reconsider…'

Richard shrugged, his expression turning melancholy. 'I only have one brother, Darcy only has Georgiana, who is much younger, and our cousin Anne is an only child. It would have been nice to have to have several siblings. Did you not find it a benefit to have four sisters?'

'Partly. But for much of my childhood, only Lydia and I lived at home, and at the time she was very self-centred. I cannot blame her for that, since Mrs Bennet encouraged Lydia in her behaviour. But I am determined that I will not allow any child of mine to be favoured above others.'

'I had not thought her spoiled. Precocious maybe…'

'She has greatly changed for the better since we have come to live at Brook Hall. Mother would not tolerate tantrums.' Jane smiled fondly at a memory.

'I was exceedingly pleased when we discovered that Lydia had acted out the way she did out of boredom. Once she had learned that it was acceptable to use her mind, she became insatiable about reading, and we discovered that she has a remarkable sense of humour.'

'Yes, I heard some of her remarks…' said Colonel Fitzwilliam with a sly grin.

Jane blushed. 'We are still working on her discretion. I am afraid it is a slow process.'

~~~oo0Ooo~~~

At last, on Sunday after services, Darcy was able to get some time alone with Georgiana, by the simple expedient of taking her from church to Brook Hall in his own carriage.

'How are you feeling?' he asked, looking at her carefully.

Georgiana understood the look and the question he was truly asking.

'I am well. Truly well. The girls are amazing, and Elizabeth is exactly the kind of sister I had hoped for. She is incredibly accomplished in many ways, but she is imperfect enough to not make me feel inadequate. Are you not glad that I insisted that you should accept Mr Bingley's invitation?'

Darcy smiled at the thought of Elizabeth.

Georgiana decided to be polite, and think of that smile as a man in love, rather than a besotted fool. But polite or not, for the first time, that she could remember in recent years, her brother looked truly happy.

'Yes, Georgiana, I am very grateful to you.' Darcy turned serious again. 'There is something else I thought we should talk about. Did anyone mention that Wickham was in the area?'

Georgiana lost her own happy smile. 'Yes, Elizabeth told me that one of the men she shot was George. To think that he could have made me believe I was in love with him...'

She took a deep breath to calm herself again, and was grateful that Darcy gently squeezed her hand which he had taken hold of. 'I admit that I was glad to hear he was dead. Part of my distress since summer, was the thought that he might use his knowledge to threaten you. Now I feel like a great weight has been lifted off my shoulders.'

'I believe he got what he deserved.' Darcy's mood changed when he added. 'Richard was most impressed with the ladies' performance.'
~~~

That comment restored Georgiana's mood. 'I suppose only a soldier would be impressed by a woman who shot a man. But Lizzy said that you have been very supportive of her as well.'

'How could I not be. She protected her sister. It made me think that she would protect you just as fiercely. It only made me love her more.'

'Thank heaven you have developed some sense. I would have been most displeased with you if I had missed out on all those wonderful sisters.'

Darcy just shook his head in disbelief at his sister's changed attitude.

<center>~~~oo0Ooo~~~</center>

'You are corrupting my sister,' Darcy teasingly accused Elizabeth later that afternoon as they strolled through the garden.

'Not at all. We are just providing her with an excellent example of what an unconventional education can achieve.'

'Pray tell, what special advantages can such an education give you?'

'It allowed me to catch a very desirable husband. One who had escaped all those insipid ladies of the *ton*.'

'Touché.'

'If that is what you wish…' Elizabeth smiled mischievously as she wrapped her arms about his waist, looking like an invitation to be kissed.

Darcy, ever the gentleman, obliged.

<center>~~~oo0Ooo~~~</center>

4   Wedding

Lord and Lady Matlock arrived on Saturday and were hosted by Mr Bingley. Louisa Hurst, although a little flustered to have such noble houseguests, did her brother proud. Bingley was pleased that his sister at last was stepping out of Caroline's shadow.

Lady Matlock, after greeting her son and nephew looked around, and not finding the person she was looking for asked Darcy, 'where is Georgiana? I thought you had sent for her?'

'She is staying at Brook Hall, getting to know her new sisters. If I were not so very pleased with the effect which they are having on her, I could almost be jealous. The last two weeks I usually have only seen her in company with one or more of the Mortimer ladies.'

Lady Matlock laughed. 'I should have known that Stephanie would take that girl under her wing as well. I look forward to seeing the improvement in Georgiana.'

'If you feel up to it, we have all been invited for dinner at Brook Hall. Then you can see for yourself how much more confident Georgiana has become.'

'I would be delighted to have dinner with my old friend,' replied Lady Matlock.

'I too would like to see my niece,' Lord Matlock said pointedly. 'Thank you for asking...'

'You are very welcome, Uncle,' Darcy responded with a smirk.

<p align="center">~~~oo0Ooo~~~</p>

Georgiana was waiting with the Mortimer ladies to greet Lord and Lady Matlock. She waited impatiently, but politely for Mrs Mortimer to welcome her guests, and introduce her three youngest daughters, before rushing to her aunt and uncle to give each of them a hug.

'I am so very pleased to see you. Is it not wonderful that William has found his perfect match? Did you know that they first met at your ball?' she gushed.

'Who are you? You look like our niece, but Georgiana is an excessively shy girl…' Lady Matlock teased her niece, but the fond smile spoke of her great pleasure that Georgiana seemed to have overcome her problems from the previous summer.

'Aunt Susan, were you not the one who kept telling me to be more confident and outspoken?' Georgiana mock pouted.

'Be careful what you wish for,' came the almost expected sotto voce comment.

Everyone turned towards Lydia, who gave them an unrepentant grin. 'Did I say that aloud? Oh dear…'

After a moment of stunned silence, Lady Matlock broke the tableau by a quiet chuckle. 'Yes, I can see why Darcy thought it a good idea to have Georgiana get to know her new sisters,' she said to no one in particular.

She turned to see Darcy, who had quietly greeted his beloved while his relations were preoccupied, standing next to his fiancée. 'Elizabeth, I am very pleased that you managed to coax Darcy out from behind his pillar.' She gave Elizabeth a hug and added, 'and please, I would like you and your sisters to call me Aunt Susan.'

'Thank you, Aunt Susan. But you are wrong, I did not do any coaxing. I only ever saw William hiding behind a pillar once. And that was a special occasion,' Elizabeth defended her fiancé.

'If you say so, my dear. I am simply happy that my favourite nephew has found his perfect partner.'

Richard too had used everyone's distraction to greet his special lady. He now presented her to his parents. 'Mother, Father, I know that you are already acquainted with Miss Mortimer, but I am pleased to inform you that she suffers from insanity. She has agreed to allow me to court her.'

Jane looked as shocked as his parents, but for different reasons. 'Colonel, I do not suffer from insanity… I thoroughly enjoy it.'

Lady Matlock laughed at the quip. 'This evening is full of surprises. I have always wondered if there was a woman on this earth, whom Richard could love more than the army.' She hugged Jane. 'I hope you will give him a chance. I believe he can learn to be an adequate husband.'

Jane felt a slight tremble in Lady Matlock from the suppressed emotions of worry and relief. A look of understanding passed between them. Lady Matlock had been terrified of losing her son in battle. Now there was hope he would remain safe, and she felt immeasurable gratitude towards the young woman.

Jane, being more diffident than Elizabeth, had worried about her reception by Richards family. She was relieved to be acceptable to Lady Matlock, whatever the reason.

'I think the training he received in the army will stand him in good stead,' Jane said with a twinkle in her eyes. 'He is used to taking orders.'

'I hope someone gives the order to roll over and play dead...' muttered the embarrassed gentleman.

'That was supposed to be my line,' complained Lydia.

<p style="text-align:center">~~~ooo0Ooo~~~</p>

The day of the wedding started off grey and with a light drizzle. Elizabeth was slow to wake up, since Mrs Mortimer had insisted that she drank a special concoction that would allow Lizzy to sleep the night through.

Ever since the day of the attack on Kitty, most nights Elizabeth had woken up screaming because of horrific nightmares.

After the first two nights, Mrs Mortimer suggested that Elizabeth should sleep in the Mistress' suite, since it was buffered from the rest of the family wing. While it did not help Elizabeth, at least she did not disturb and upset her sisters.

This morning Mrs Mortimer brought her a tray with tea and a light repast, to tide Elizabeth over until the wedding breakfast.

'How are you feeling today?'

'Rested, excited, but a little fuzzy.'

'Breakfast and a nice hot bath will cure that.' Mrs Mortimer smiled encouragingly at Elizabeth. 'I shall leave you in peace and get ready myself. I will be back in an hour to assist you. If I can fight my way past your sisters, that is.'

~~~ooO0Ooo~~~

While Mrs Mortimer did not have to fight her way through the sisters, Elizabeth was grateful to have the use of the Mistress' suite for this occasion.

Elizabeth had always thought her room, and the rooms of her sisters to be very generously proportioned, but the rooms of the suite were significantly larger. Not only that, the suite consisted of a sitting room, a bedroom, a dressing room and a bathing room.

This morning she needed all that space, since Mrs Mortimer, all the sisters, new and old, as well as a maid were ready to assist Elizabeth to get dressed and fix her hair. It was pandemonium until she suggested that some of the girls should help Jane to get ready, since she was the bridesmaid.

The girls took the hint, and all but Georgiana left to help Jane.

Georgiana justified her remaining, by pointing out that each of the main participants now had three assistants. 'I am glad that none of them seem upset that you singled out Jane.'

'Since Richard is standing up with William, Jane was the logical choice. The others understood my reasoning. As a matter of fact, Mary made the suggestion,' Elizabeth explained while she was sitting at the dressing table, allowing Tilly, Mrs Mortimer's personal maid, to style her hair under Mrs Mortimer's direction. Georgiana was passing the pearl-studded hairpins to Tilly.

When Mrs Mortimer was satisfied, Elizabeth was at last allowed to don her gown. Elizabeth was very pleased with the dress, which was a pale green silk with a few touches of white lace and some darker green ribbons to set off the simple and elegant style. The same ribbons were woven through her long curls.

~~~ooO0Ooo~~~

The girls, together with Mrs Annesley and Mrs Taylor, had gone ahead in the Darcy carriage, which he had sent to help ferry all the ladies.

Mrs Mortimer let them have a few minutes head-start while she spent the time with Elizabeth and Jane.

'Are you ready for your new life, my dear?' she asked quietly, trying to suppress the moisture in her eyes. The girl who had captured her heart on Oakham Mount all those happy years ago was ready to fly the nest. While she was pleased that Elizabeth had found a good man to love, and who loved and respected her in return, it was still painful having to let her go.

'Yes, I am. At least I think so.' Elizabeth took Mrs Mortimer's hands and looked at the woman who had been her true mother. 'Thank you... for everything...' She did not elaborate, since they both knew that Elizabeth did mean *everything*. Everything that Mrs Mortimer had done for her and her sisters for more than eleven years.

'It has been my absolute pleasure. And remember, I will always be here for you if you need me.'

Jane watched this scene with mixed emotions. While she had become close to Mrs Mortimer in the years that she had known her, she also knew that there was a special bond between her sister and the lady. But now she could also see the pain which the separation was causing both of them.

While she was a little envious of that bond, Jane realised that she was well on her way to having such a connection with a certain gentleman. Jane felt better when she noticed the envy disappearing.

~~~oo0Ooo~~~

The carriage with the three Mortimer ladies, accompanied by Miss Martin, who was determined to protect her star pupil until she was safely married, arrived at the church.

Footmen had been busy, spreading out matting to ensure that Elizabeth could get into the church without getting muddy, despite the damp ground. Now they were standing by with umbrellas.
~~~

Once they were handed out of the carriage, Jane led the way into the church, followed by a proud Mrs Mortimer with Elizabeth on her arm. Miss Martin brought up the rear.

As soon as they walked into the church, Elizabeth and Darcy only had eyes for each other. No one who saw them could be in any doubt that theirs was a love-match.

The spell was broken momentarily when Mrs Mortimer kissed Elizabeth's cheek and gave her hand to Darcy, who acknowledged the lady with a smile and a nod of thanks.

Once Mrs Mortimer took her place amongst her daughters, the ceremony proceeded as per usual.

Mrs Mortimer peripherally noticed that the Gardiners had managed to arrive just in time for the wedding, and were sitting with Mr and Mrs Phillips. Her own brother had accepted the invitation, but an accident the previous week prevented him from attending.

Even though Darcy and Elizabeth had invited only a few people other than family, the church was nearly full with neighbours who had come to wish the couple well. The wedding party was too focused to notice a quietly weeping lady hidden away at the rear of the church.

The wedding ceremony was over quickly and the vicar presented Mr and Mrs Darcy to the assembled congregation.

<center>~~~ooo0Ooo~~~</center>

As per Elizabeth's and Darcy's request, the wedding breakfast was only attended by family and their closest friends.

The food and the company were excellent. The speeches were short and generally confined to good wishes for the couple. Except for Colonel Fitzwilliam who gave advice full of inuendo, which made not only the bride blush.

When Fitzwilliam finished, Darcy stood up and thanked everyone for their good wishes. He finished by telling the Colonel, 'thank you for all that advice, Richard. It will be my pleasure to reciprocate at your wedding…'

Richard groaned, 'I had not thought of that.'

~~~ooOOoo~~~

A small convoy left Brook Hall in the early afternoon. Even though highway men had not been an issue in the area for some time, everyone agreed that it was a more convenient way to travel. After all, accidents can happen even to the most experienced and well-equipped travellers.

The Darcy, Matlock and Gardiner carriages, followed by two carriages with servants and luggage, made their leisurely way to London, where they each went their own way.

The journey passed pleasantly for the newlyweds, who at last were free to indulge in passionate kisses, although the chilly temperature and the uneven road prevented them from getting carried away.

When they arrived at Darcy House, Elizabeth was pleasantly surprised by the tastefully elegant décor. Darcy introduced her to the butler and the housekeeper, Mr and Mrs Carter, who were pleased to welcome their new Mistress.

The couple opted for dinner in their private sitting room after refreshing themselves.

Claiming weariness from the travel, they decided on an early night...

~~~ooOOoo~~~

Elizabeth slowly drifted towards wakefulness, and relished the feel of the warm body next to her. For the first time in weeks she felt relaxed and well rested.

She sighed contentedly. The sound caused her husband to pull her closer and nuzzle her neck. 'Good morning, my love,' he murmured. 'Why the sigh?'

Elizabeth turned to face Darcy with a smile. 'Because, for the first time since the attack, I have not awakened during the night with nightmares. You make me feel safe.'

'I am pleased that I am useful to you as a dreamcatcher.' Darcy responded to the smile with one of his own.

'I already caught my dream...' murmured Elizabeth as she reached for her husband.

It was several hours later before they were ready to leave their rooms.

~~~oo0Ooo~~~

29
~~~

5   Lady Catherine

Elizabeth and Darcy spent a few relaxing days in Darcy House, rarely leaving their chambers.

On the odd occasion, when they did come out, Elizabeth was pleased to explore her new home and becoming better acquainted with the housekeeper and the rest of the staff, while Darcy attended to some business letters which he deemed urgent.

Although they were not receiving visitors, they had agreed to have dinner with Mrs Mortimer's brother, since his injuries had prevented him from attending the wedding and meeting Darcy.

Darcy was in the foyer, waiting for his wife to finish the last-minute touches to her toilette, before going out to dinner, when there was a peremptory knock on the front door.

The footman had barely started to open the door, when it was pushed wide, and Lady Catherine stormed into the house.

'Ah, Darcy, there you are. You are just the person I wanted to see. Nephew, I have come because of a most outrageous story in the newspaper.'

'Good evening, Aunt Catherine. Are you well?' Darcy greeted her politely and pointedly, while wondering how to get rid of his aunt in the shortest possible time.

Lady Catherine ignored his courtesy. 'There was a scurrilous report about you marrying some country nobody. I know this cannot be true, since you will marry Anne. But you cannot ignore this report. You must speak with the editor and get them to print a retraction and an apology.'

'Why would I want to do that, Aunt Catherine?'

'Because some people may believe the story to be true. I will not have this.'

While Darcy and Lady Catherine were focused on each other, Elizabeth had come down the stairs and walked up to Darcy.

'My apologies for taking so long,' she addressed her husband. 'Will you introduce me to our guest?'

Before Darcy had a chance to accede to her request, Lady Catherine cut in. 'Darcy, what is this? Do you not know that it is bad form to entertain your mistress in your own home?'

'Aunt Catherine, this lady is my wife and I will not tolerate for you to insult her.'

'Your wife? No, this must not be. This is a travesty of the highest order. I insist that you have this marriage annulled immediately. You cannot pollute the shades of Pemberley with this... this... this person. I will not stand for you marrying anyone but Anne.'

'That is not your decision to make, Aunt.'

'But you and Anne have been promised to each other since you were in your cradles. It was your mother's and my dearest wish to combine the great estates of Pemberley and Rosings.'

'Neither my mother nor my father ever mentioned such an engagement. The first time I heard of this supposed attachment was from you, after both my parents were dead and unable to refute you.'

'But the Fitzwilliam name deserves, nay demands, a spouse from the first circles.'

'In that case, you had better hope that Anne is agreeable to marry a man who meets your exacting criteria. Such as, take her to live a long way from Rosings, leaving you in charge of the estate. Which is your true wish.'

'I was not speaking about Anne, but of you.'

'You forget, I am a Darcy, not a Fitzwilliam. But you have come at an inconvenient time...'

Lady Catherine cut in. 'I will not be put off. You will speak to me now and resolve this issue to my satisfaction.'

Elizabeth had listened enough to the Lady's ranting. 'Lady Catherine, you may be William's aunt, but since you are discourteous enough to arrive without warning, you will have to take second place to my uncle, with whom we are engaged to dine.'

'How dare you insult me like this. I will not take second place to some jumped-up tradesman.'

'You are obviously uninformed. I would never call the Viscount Middlebrook a jumped-up tradesman.'

'Neither would I. But I was speaking of your uncle…'

'So was I, Lady Catherine. William and I are to dine with my uncle, the Viscount Middlebrook. Now… since we do not wish to be late, you must excuse us. Goodbye, Lady Catherine.'

'Goodbye, Aunt Catherine.' Darcy nodded at his aunt, before giving a final instruction to the butler. 'Carter, please ensure that Lady Catherine leaves, and does not re-enter the house.'

They left a still spluttering Lady Catherine standing in the foyer.

'You were magnificent,' Darcy complimented his wife when their carriage pulled away.

'Should we have mentioned that the Gardiners are also joining us?' giggled Elizabeth.

~~~ooO0Ooo~~~

The couple had an enjoyable evening with Elizabeth's family.

The Viscount was gracious, but teasing, when Elizabeth introduced her husband. 'What is the secret of the Darcy men, that they always seem to attract exceptional women? While your father was a good enough man, Lady Anne was special. But she never gave me a second look…' He sighed theatrically.

His wife interjected, 'never mind my husband. He is being crotchety because he is confined to the house, and does not have a chance to admire all the latest debutants.' She indicated the Viscount's splinted leg.

Elizabeth laughed. 'It seems you still have an eye for the ladies then.'

'An eye is all I have these days, since that blasted stallion spooked, and nearly took my leg off,' the Viscount mock complained.
~~~

Elizabeth posited. 'I believe there must be a secret competition in this family. Is it, about who can ride the most spirited stallion, or is it about who can get the most interesting injuries? I can never tell.'

'Perhaps it is a combination of both,' her uncle was diverted by the impertinent question.

'How do you keep score though?'

Before he could answer, dinner was announced.

~~~ooO0oo~~~

When they returned home, Mr Carter informed them that Lord Matlock was waiting for them in the library.

'Good evening, Uncle, to what do we owe the unexpected pleasure of your company?'

'Good evening, Darcy, Elizabeth. I needed some peace and quiet after listening to my sister rant for two hours straight. Since your house is in walking distance, I sought the refuge of your library. Particularly since Catherine let slip your orders to refuse entrance to her.'

'Uncle, as much as we enjoy your company, you know you cannot stay here indefinitely. As a matter of fact, I suspect that if you stay here for too long, and leave Aunt Susan to deal with your sister, your wife's ire will be much worse than your sister's.' Darcy grinned at Lord Matlock.

The gentleman groaned, 'at least Susan's voice is not as shrill as Catherine's. But I was also hoping that you or Elizabeth might have a suggestion how to deal with my sister in this situation.'

'She only my aunt, but she is *your* sister. Which means she is your problem, not mine.' Darcy looked at his uncle's hopeful expression and added, 'why do you not use the *Head of the Family* line and tell her that she is in the wrong, and that abusing my wife will only be to her own and Anne's detriment.'

'I was hoping to avoid that, but I suppose I could threaten her with a complete break with the family if she does not contain her displeasure. She hates being thwarted, but her attitude is becoming an embarrassment to the family.'
~~~

~~~ooO0Ooo~~~

A few days later, Darcy noticed a little snippet in the gossip column of the newspaper.

Reliable sources have revealed that a certain Lady dB is no longer a welcome member of Lord M's family, due to her objectionable attitude to the latest member of the family. Lord and Lady M, on the other hand, are delighted with their newest niece. Lord M was heard to comment that Mrs D is worth ten of his sister.

Two days later, the same reporter added another titbit.

Lady dB was refused entrance to her brother's home. It seems Lord M was serious in severing the connection.

~~~ooO0Ooo~~~

Lady Catherine returned to Rosings in high dudgeon. The nerve of her brother to take the side of this little upstart against herself. It was not to be borne. She had never been denied anything, and she was not going to allow it now.

The last few days had been a miserable experience for Lady Catherine.

First and foremost was the incident at Darcy House. To have her objections so forcefully rebuffed, and then that chit had the nerve not to kowtow to her. Instead the little nobody gave more consequence to her uncle, refusing to keep him waiting despite Lady Catherine wishing to speak to her. The fact that Lady Catherine had been prevented from abusing the new Mrs Darcy, and venting her spleen, made the young lady's offence even greater.

And Darcy backed up his wife. Not only that, but he had Lady Catherine effectively thrown out of the house and barred her from returning.

Then her brother had not only brushed off her objections to this abominable marriage, but he had refused to offer his hospitality. She had been forced to remove to the de Bourgh townhouse, which was only maintained by a skeleton staff.

How she had suffered with insufficient servants to cater to her just demands.

Finally, she was publicly humiliated by the Earl refusing to admit her into the house, and those articles in the newspaper…

She had gone to see the editor to retract the first story, but he told her that since they had only reported the truth, they would not only not retract the story but print a second one.

Lady Catherine nearly suffered an apoplexy at the man's insolence.

~~~ooO0Ooo~~~

At last Rosings was in sight. Lady Catherine breathed a sigh of relief. At least in her home she was the undisputed ruler. Here, everyone obeyed her, and no one dared to contradict her.

As soon as she exited the carriage, she swept up the steps to the front door, which she expected to be thrown wide for her entrance.

Instead they remained persistently closed.

When she ran out of patience, she knocked on the door, which was opened by… a strange man, who asked, 'how may I help you?' while blocking her from entering.

'You, stand aside so that I can enter my house,' demanded Lady Catherine. 'And then you can tell me who you are and what business you have opening the door.'

'I am sorry, Madam, you must be confused. I know my employer, the Mistress of this house, and you are not she.'

'What do you mean? I am Lady Catherine de Bourgh and I am the Mistress of Rosings Park.'

'Ah, you must be a relation of Miss de Bourgh. Please wait here, and I will enquire if she is available to see you.' He promptly closed the door in her face.

Lady Catherine stood there dumbfounded. Had the whole world gone mad? After everything that happened in London, and now she was denied entrance to her own home? To her own property?

It was too much.

~~~ooO0Ooo~~~

Eventually, after what seemed to be an eternity, but was only a few minutes, the door opened again.

But instead of being admitted, the door was blocked yet again. This time not only by the strange man, but also by her daughter and Mr Thompson, the family solicitor.

An outraged Lady Catherine demanded, 'what is the meaning of this? Stand aside and let me enter my home.'

To her astonishment and disgust, her daughter replied politely but firmly. 'Good afternoon, Lady Catherine. You are not welcome in *my* house. If you wish, you may repair to the Dower House, which is *your* home. All your possessions have been moved there.'

'WHAT? How dare you! You have no right to prevent me from entering my home.'

'No one is preventing you from entering your home. Which is the Dower House,' Anne replied coolly.

'I must send for a physician. You have obviously lost your senses.'

'Lady Catherine, Miss de Bourgh is perfectly sane. And she is also correct. According to the will of your late husband, Miss de Bourgh was to inherit Rosings Park on her twenty-fifth birthday or the occasion of her wedding, whichever came first. Since Miss de Bourgh celebrated her twenty-fifth birthday three weeks ago, Rosings Park now belongs to her.'

'I have replaced *your* servants, and all of the new staff are loyal to me,' Anne informed Lady Catherine. 'Your servants are awaiting you at your new home. What you do with them is up to you.'

Lady Catherine gaped at Anne and the solicitor. Since she had hoped to marry Anne off to Darcy, she had not paid attention to Anne's birthdays.

Now she was confronted by her worst nightmare. Her daughter was unmarried, of age and fully aware of her rights. How could this have happened? Her shoulder slumped as she conceded defeat. Could her day get any worse?

As she wordlessly turned to walk down the steps to her carriage, the heavens opened. At least the freezing rain washed away her tears of frustration.

~~~oo0Ooo~~~

</div>
~~~

6   Rosings Park

Earlier that year

Lady Catherine was seriously displeased. When she had granted the living at Hunsford to Mr Collins, she had thought him eminently suitable for the position.

During the interview he had been diffident and appreciative of her wisdom. It had been most agreeable to her that he espoused the correct ideas about the importance of everyone knowing their place in the world.

But in retrospect, she realised that he had worded his replies excessively subtly. Due to his servile manner during his audience with her, his words seemed to have indicated his full agreement with her views, but on reflection she realised that he had not actually agreed with her.

Now it was too late. The living had been granted. The Bishop had approved and she was stuck for life with a parson who favoured his parishioners over his patroness.

Within weeks she found out that the people of Hunsford liked and respected Mr Collins. Not only did he not spy on her tenants on her behalf, his sermons actively encouraged the parishioners to defy her.

<p align="center">~~~oo0Ooo~~~</p>

William Collins was pleased with his latest sermon. His theme had been "the first will be last and the last, first". While the words had been well received by most of his parishioners, Lady Catherine had turned bright red in anger and glared at him.

But since he was quoting directly from the bible, using Jesus' exact words, she had no recourse but to endure. Although, as soon as the service concluded, she had stormed out of the church without a backward glance, muttering about heresy.

Collins considered that today was possibly the first time that Lady Catherine's beliefs had been publicly contradicted.

He had been pleased at the reaction of the rest of his congregation. While most had tried to keep a serious and attentive demeanour, he had noticed many gleeful sideways glances at Lady Catherine. The less restrained members of the community had smiled and nodded.

After the service, once Lady Catherine had taken her leave so precipitously, the people of Hunsford had all taken the time to thank him for his wonderful sermon. Old Mrs Chatters had even gone so far as to pat his arm and say, 'well done, boy. It was good to hear you tell the old battle-ax that she is not as high and mighty as she thought.'

Collins returned to his home, and after a light nuncheon, he changed into some older clothing to tend his garden. He had discovered that nurturing the plants gave him a sense of quiet contentment, which he found relaxing.

He was weeding a flowerbed in his front garden, when Miss de Bourgh, accompanied by Mrs Jenkinson, her companion, stopped at the gate of the parsonage.

He rose to his feet and greeted the lady politely, while wondering as to her reaction to his sermon.

Miss de Bourgh did not keep him long in suspense. 'Mr Collins, I wanted to congratulate you on your sermon. It has been a long time since I heard someone speak so from the heart. What prompted you to do so?'

'Miss de Bourgh, I thank you for your kind words. I chose that sermon because I care about all of my parishioners, and I believe it is incumbent on me to open their hearts to the truth.'

'I believe you have achieved a partial measure of success, although I happen to know that at least one person will take a long time to convince.'

'I did not expect to succeed all at once, but since I will be here for the rest of my life, I have plenty of time.' Collins smiled almost mischievously.

Miss de Bourgh's eyes widened in surprise at his response. 'You are determined to continue on this path?'

'Yes, Miss de Bourgh. That is why I took orders. I am hoping to encourage all my parishioners to a greater understanding and respect for each other.'

A hesitant smile graced the features of Miss de Bourgh. 'In that case I wish you well, Mr Collins. You have chosen a difficult endeavour. I hope your resolve will remain strong in the face of opposition.'

With those words, Anne de Bourgh took her leave.

Collins remained, watching the phaeton until it was out of sight. He wondered how a woman like Lady Catherine could be the mother to such a thoughtful and lovely daughter.

~~~oo0Ooo~~~

The following day Lady Catherine demanded the presence of Mr Collins.

She barely gave him a chance to utter a polite greeting, when she chastised him. 'Mr Collins, I was most displeased with your sermon yesterday. I did not award you the living to have you undermine me.'

'I am sorry, Lady Catherine, if you feel that presenting the words of the Bible to my parishioners constitutes undermining you.'

'You ought to choose your words more carefully. *The last will be first and the first will be last* indeed. I will not have you preaching such heresy.'

'Heresy against whom, My Lady?'

'Against me, your patroness, of course.'

'Lady Catherine, surely you do not mean that. You are my patroness, and I respect you for that. And I will do all in my power to assist you. But heresy? I am sorry, My Lady, but you are not god.'

'I am as far as you are concerned. I gave you the living, and I can take it away.'

'As a matter of fact, you cannot. A living is for life. The only one who can oust me from this position is my Bishop. And only if I do not perform my duties.'

'How dare you contradict me. I will not be spoken to in such a way.' Lady Catherine huffed. 'In the future you will present your sermons for my approval. I will not be insulted like this again.'
~~~

'Lady Catherine, I will be happy to present you with a copy of my sermon ahead of time, but I will preach as my conscience dictates and what I think is best for my whole congregation.'

'How dare you have an opinion of your own. I will not stand for it.'

'I am afraid that you must. If you have an issue with my sermons, you are welcome to inform my Bishop. If he agrees that my performance is unsatisfactory, I am certain he will take the appropriate measures.'

Lady Catherine cried, 'you may depend upon it. I will write to your Bishop at once to inform him of your impertinence. We will see how long you remain in Hunsford after that. Leave me.'

'Very well, Lady Catherine. Good day to you.' Collins bowed politely and exited the drawing room.

In the hall he encountered Miss de Bourgh, who whispered in passing, 'well done.'

While the confrontation with Lady Catherine had upset Collins since her attitude reminded him of his father, Miss de Bourgh's comment cheered him immeasurably.

He wondered how she tolerated her mother's overbearing and controlling nature.

~~~ooo0Ooo~~~

A few days later Collins received a note from Bishop Parkhurst, asking him to forward the sermon which had put Lady Catherine into such a lather.

Collins complied, and the following Sunday he noticed the bishop sitting quietly in the back of the church, observing intently.

After the service the bishop approached Mr Collins and stated loud enough for all, and in particular Lady Catherine, to hear. 'Excellent sermon Mr Collins. I was also most impressed with the sermon about the first and the last which you sent to me. Your congregation is lucky to have a man of your ability serving them.'

He turned and addressed Lady Catherine. 'Do you not agree, My Lady?'
~~~

'I certainly do not. I will never approve of his revolutionary ideas. You must remove him,' demanded Lady Catherine, who had recognised Bishop Parkhurst.

'I see no reason to do so.' The bishop smiled politely and hoped that Collins could maintain his attitude, since he had an issue with the lady interfering in people's lives for her own aggrandisement. 'The Church approves of him. I believe that given time, he will grow on you. Now, if you will excuse me, I must leave. Goodbye, Lady Catherine.'

Lady Catherine gritted her teeth, and thinking of barnacles, stalked off to her own carriage. Everyone else smiled and quietly thanked Mr Collins for another inspiring sermon.

~~~oo0Ooo~~~

Over the next several months, William Collins and Anne de Bourgh became very well acquainted.

She stopped ever more frequently at the parsonage during her outings in the phaeton.

Miss de Bourgh confided in him that her mother was determined for her to marry her cousin, Fitzwilliam Darcy. While that was not news to Mr Collins, the fact that Miss de Bourgh had not the slightest interest or intention of doing so, came as a surprise.

'Would that not be an excellent match for you? I have heard of Mr Darcy, and he is reputed to be a gentleman of great wealth.'

'He is also a pleasant man, as well as young and handsome. But we would not suit. He seems more like a brother to me.'

'Have you not told your mother that you have no interest in your cousin?' he asked.

'Of course, I have. But you know my mother. Once she has conceived of an idea, she will let no one nay say her.'

'Is there any risk that your cousin would offer for you, putting you in a difficult position?'

'Fortunately, there is no such risk. He and I discussed this many years ago, and he is equally disinterested in marriage with me.' Anne sighed and looked uncomfortable. 'Perhaps I should not say so, but I suspect
~~~

that my mother wishes for me to marry Darcy, so that I would go and live at Pemberley, leaving her in control of Rosings.'

'Pardon me if I have misunderstood, but why would that make a difference?'

'Because, according to my father's will, on the occasion of my marriage or my twenty-fifth birthday, Rosings Park will be mine.'

Suddenly all the pieces came together for Collins. 'That is monstrous,' he exclaimed. 'Your mother has kept you mewed up at Rosings and away from society, to ensure you could not meet anyone whom you would want to marry. If you did, you and your husband might want to settle at Rosings, and she would have to give way to your husband.'

'Exactly so, Mr Collins.' Anne smiled a little sadly. 'I admit, once I reached my majority, I was tempted to marry my other cousin, Colonel Fitzwilliam, who is the second son of the Earl of Matlock, just to spite her. But the Colonel and I are an even worse match than Darcy and I.'

Anne was curious about Collins' attitude. 'But I am surprised that you would object to my mother ordering my life. Is that not the right of all parents?'

'It depends on their motives and the manner of the control...' Collins fell silent, remembering his own father and the fear the man had inspired in him while he was alive.

Anne noticed the pensive look on the parson's countenance. 'Mr Collins, pardon me if this is an uncomfortable topic, but you look like you might know something of excessively controlling parents.'

Collins came out of his reverie and nodded. 'I do indeed, Miss de Bourgh...'

Encouraged by Anne de Bourgh, Collins related to her the circumstances of his early life. Anne was horrified to learn of the beatings, both physical and emotional, which Collins had endured. She was sympathetic. 'I thought that my mother was controlling, but at least she does not harm me physically.'

'I think you are wrong on two counts. Physical wounds heal relatively quickly, and, since they are visible to all, you can garner sympathy and help from others. On the other hand, I believe that emotional abuse is much harder to deal with. I also think that Lady Catherine has harmed you physically by not allowing you to learn anything, or do anything. It has kept you physically weak and sickly.'

'But I became sick as a child and have never fully recovered.'

'Has it ever occurred to you that it is much harder to stand up to someone, who has a domineering personality and is strong physically, when you are physically weak?'

'You think that after I recovered from my illness, I could have recovered completely, if I had been allowed to learn things and be physically active?'

'Exactly so. The more you exercise your mental and physical muscles, the stronger they become. By not allowing you to do so, Lady Catherine kept you weak and compliant. And the worst part is that she claimed to do so out of consideration for you.'

Now it was Anne's turn to consider the past. The more she thought about it, the angrier she became.

Eventually she asked, 'Mr Collins, will you help me to become strong?'

Collins gave her a brilliant smile. 'It will be my pleasure, Miss de Bourgh.'

~~~ooo0Ooo~~~

The summer and autumn of 1811 became the best time Anne de Bourgh had ever known since her father died. She was determined to exercise her mental and physical muscles with the assistance of Mrs Jenkinson and Mr Collins.

Mrs Jenkinson had been hired by Lady Catherine to look after Anne's comfort, and had been given strict instructions how to do so. Over the years Mrs Jenkinson had become fond of her charge, and tried to help her as much as she could without overtly going against Lady Catherine's orders.

Since she had never understood the ramifications of those orders, she never had an incentive to disregard them. Now that Mrs Jenkinson had been informed of the consequences of Anne's enforced inactivity, she was eager to help.
~~~

Since Mrs Jenkinson's rooms were in an out of the way part of the house, no one was disturbed when she practised playing the pianoforte. Not even when she started to teach Anne how to play.

She also procured the library catalogue for Miss de Bourgh, and then fetched whichever volumes the lady wanted to study.

At last Anne de Bourgh discovered a zest for life.

~~~ooO0Ooo~~~

During her outings in the phaeton, Miss de Bourgh often stopped at the parsonage, where she would go for a gentle stroll through the gardens with Mr Collins and Mrs Jenkinson.

At those times, Mr Collins would often regale the ladies with stories of his cousins and Mrs Mortimer. Anne, although a little envious, was pleased for the clergyman, that after his horrendous childhood, he had found a supportive family.

When she commented on both her pleasure and her envy, Collins asked, 'Did you ever ask your family for help?'

Anne was startled at the concept and had to admit, 'no, it never occurred to me.'

Now that Collins had raised the subject, Anne started to consider the possibilities, especially since her twenty-fifth birthday was to occur in November.

~~~ooO0Ooo~~~

Quite a number of people of Hunsford had noticed the frequent visits by Miss de Bourgh to the parsonage. They had also seen the phaeton stopped in various places away from Rosings, while Anne went on ever more brisk walks with Mrs Jenkinson.

No one ever bothered to mention either the visits or the walks to Lady Catherine, since the Mistress of Rosings was almost universally despised in the area.

Although the senior staff at Rosings was fiercely loyal to Lady Catherine, only some of the junior staff felt that way. Many served at Rosings simply because they needed the job, and they could not afford to lose that position. But they neither liked nor respected Lady Catherine.

On the other hand, most of the junior staff at Rosings liked Miss de Bourgh and felt sorry for her, and looked the other way when they saw the young lady doing something which they knew that Lady Catherine disapproved of.

<p style="text-align:center">~~~oo0Ooo~~~</p>

7   Coup d'état

At the end of October William Collins received a gleeful letter from his youngest cousin. They still corresponded sporadically, since they had formed a bond during his first stay at Brook Hall.

Amongst other news, she informed him that Elizabeth seemed to be head over heels in love with none other than Mr Fitzwilliam Darcy, the nephew of his patroness. And if Lydia judged correctly, the gentleman reciprocated her feelings.

After he read the letter a plan began to form in his mind.

The next time Miss de Bourgh stopped by the parsonage he asked, 'what would happen if Lady Catherine found out that Mr Darcy was about to get married... to someone else?'

'She would immediately go to see him and drag me along,' Anne replied. 'While it is an amusing thought, I know that Darcy has avoided all the traps set for him for years. I cannot imagine him getting married any time soon.'

'It seems your imagination needs improving,' Collins grinned when he replied. 'I have it on good authority that *your* cousin may be in love with one of *mine*.'

Anne looked surprised, and then started to consider the personalities of Collins' cousins as he had described them. 'If what you have told me of your cousins is accurate, I suspect it must be Miss Elizabeth. Am I correct?'

'You know your cousin well, since you picked the correct lady. But you think it would be counterproductive to inform Lady Catherine of his intention of getting married?'

'What do you have in mind?'

'I thought that if Lady Catherine was out of the house on, or soon after your birthday, you could ask your solicitor to come and confirm you as Mistress of Rosings. Then you could replace your mother's most loyal staff with your own choices, and move her into the Dower House, leaving you in charge.'

'The only way that it would be possible for Mother to leave here without me, would be if she learned that Darcy was already married.'

'In that case we have to ensure that she does not learn of the attachment prematurely.'

~~~oo0Ooo~~~

Mr Collins paid a brief visit to Brook Hall. His timing was propitious, since, shortly after his arrival, Darcy proposed to Elizabeth.

The following afternoon he had a chance at a private conversation with Mr Darcy.

'Mr Darcy, please forgive me, but I must speak to you about matters pertaining to your family.'

Darcy was intrigued and prepared to listen, as Collins explained Miss de Bourgh's problem and their tentative plan. He was pensive as he considered Anne's options.

After a few minutes' cogitation, during which Collins sat quietly waiting, Darcy sighed. 'I had not considered Anne's plight to be so great. I must admit that in recent years I have avoided her as much as possible, so as not to raise any expectations with my aunt. Unsuccessfully obviously.'

He straightened as he said, 'very well. I will ensure that news of my engagement is kept quiet. But you said that Anne will need to replace key staff. Anne may not have mentioned that at Pemberley we are in the habit of training staff to move up the ranks, if a position becomes vacant. If no position is likely to become available, we are happy to recommend them to suitable employers.'

Darcy's smile turned to a wolfish grin. 'As it happens, we currently have three exceedingly competent junior staff, who are ready to move into senior positions. A butler, a housekeeper and a steward. I can probably lend Anne some footmen and maids as well.'

'That is indeed a fortuitous happenstance. Although I had thought of hiring some stevedores from Mr Gardiner for a short period, to take
~~~

care of the heavy lifting and provide some protection to Miss de Bourgh during the changeover.'

'That is an excellent idea. In the meantime, I think I will send for anyone who can be spared from Pemberley. Anne can decide who suits her, and she can send the others back when she is ready. Send word to Darcy House when she needs her new staff.'

~~~oo0Ooo~~~

Mr Collins returned to Hunsford on Friday in greater comfort than usual. Darcy, in a fit of generosity, had sent his own carriage to take Collins as far as Bromley. Since it was inadvisable for the Darcy carriage to be seen in Hunsford, Collins had taken the post from Bromley for the final stage, which only took an hour.

He arrived at Hunsford in excellent spirits. Since Lady Catherine was once again in a snit about the sermon of the previous Sunday, he did not expect a summons from that quarter.

Instead at midmorning on Saturday, a phaeton pulled up in front of the parsonage. As was only proper, he went out to pay his respects to Miss de Bourgh.

'How was your visit with your family, Mr Collins?' she enquired politely.

'Most enlightening and profitable. You can expect an explosion at Rosings on about the eleventh or twelfth of December. And it appears that your cousin has excess staff in Derbyshire, who will temporarily relocate to London.'

'You, Mr Collins, have proven yourself to be a godsend. Most appropriate for a man of your calling.' Anne de Bourgh nodded at him and smiled happily.

~~~oo0Ooo~~~

It appeared that Mr Darcy wanted at least a few uninterrupted days with his new bride. The expected explosion did not occur till the twelfth.

Late that morning, while Mr Collins was taking some fresh air in his garden, the large de Bourgh coach drove past the parsonage at the best speed possible for an extended journey.

Soon afterwards, Miss de Bourgh's phaeton pulled up at his gate.

After pleasant greetings, Anne de Bourgh told Collins, 'I have sent for reinforcements.'

The reinforcements, including Mr Thompson, the family solicitor, arrived the same evening. While Mr Thompson was invited to stay at Rosings, everyone else stayed at the inn, to be well rested for the next day.

~~~ooO0Ooo~~~

Anne de Bourgh woke up feeling in excellent spirits. The last few months had been a revelation for her.

Anne wanted to be free of her mother's influence and control, but she knew that she could not achieve her ambition on her own.

Her conversations with Mr Collins had given her the impetus to change her life. Due to his own background he understood the difficulties she faced. He did not expect her to suddenly stand up to her mother.

Instead he had helped her to regain her health. He supported and encouraged her when she faltered in her resolve.

And by some strange coincidence their cousins had fallen in love and had married, giving her the freedom to act at last.

~~~ooO0Ooo~~~

The takeover of Rosing went smoother than Anne had anticipated.

The new staff arrived immediately after breakfast. As soon as she had greeted them, she ordered the butler to assemble all current staff in the large foyer.

Once everyone who could be spared was assembled, Miss de Bourgh took up a position on the stairs, to ensure everyone could see her. She was flanked by Mr Thompson and Mr Collins, with her new senior staff arrayed behind her, while Mrs Jenkinson hovered nearby.

Anne de Bourgh addressed the staff. 'I have called you together to inform you of the new situation at Rosings. As of three weeks ago, on my birthday, I became the legal owner of Rosings. Mr Thompson, our family solicitor is here to confirm this.'

'Sir Lewis' will provided that Miss de Bourgh is his sole heir and would inherit his whole estate on her twenty-fifth birthday. That day has come and gone. Since Lady Catherine has not seen fit to hand the estate over to the legal heir, I am here to confirm that Miss Anne de Bourgh is now the legal Mistress of Rosings and in full control of the estate.' Mr Thompson nodded politely to Miss de Bourgh.

'Thank you, Mr Thompson. That should be clear enough for all of you. Now, I realise that some of you have been here for many years and have a personal loyalty to Lady Catherine.' Anne called out a list of names and asked them to step forward. 'Your services are no longer required by myself. You may await Lady Catherine's return at the Dower House. She may want you to take up your positions with her in her new residence, or not. That is her decision.'

The housekeeper, a sour faced woman of Lady Catherine's generation, objected. 'I do not rightly think you know what you are doing. I think I will just stay here until the Mistress returns.'

The butler concurred. 'Yes, Miss, I think we will all wait until Lady Catherine returns and see what the Mistress says.'

'That is not your choice to make. There is a Mistress at Rosings right now, and I am that Mistress. I have no need of your services, since I have a butler and a housekeeper of my own.' She indicated the relevant people behind her. 'I also have a steward who will look after the welfare of the estate, rather than lining Lady Catherine's pockets.'

The former steward spluttered, 'I have always served Lady Catherine well.'

'Too well to my mind. I have need of a steward who will serve the estate. I have no need for a sycophant. You are not the man for the job of steward for Rosings Park.'

'You cannot make us leave,' protested the butler.

'You are correct. I personally cannot. But all those delightfully large gentlemen at all the exits can do so on my behalf. And they will do so now.'

Once the old guard had been removed, protesting all the way, Anne turned towards the remaining staff. 'I wish to thank you for your loyal service. You will find that while I expect good service, I will be fair. You may now return to work.'

The rest of the day, the footmen and all those delightfully large gentlemen removed Lady Catherine's possessions to the Dower House. Mr Thompson, who supervised the packing of Lady Catherine's personal possessions, ensured that items belonging to the estate rather than the lady remained behind.

The stevedores also ensured the peaceful removal of the former staff, and coincidentally prevented them from sending messages to the former Mistress of Rosings.

The new Mistress of Rosings was well pleased.

~~~ooo0Ooo~~~

At Rosings Park, Anne de Bourgh was settling into her role as Mistress of the estate.

The first few days had been hectic. Touring the house to familiarise her new housekeeper and butler with her home, and discussing the changes she wished to make.

The only rooms Anne liked, were the library, which her mother had never used, and her father's suite, which had remained untouched since his death. Although the furniture was too dark and heavy for her taste, she found the greens of the rest of the décor soothing.

'Once Lady Catherine's possessions have been moved to the Dower House, switch the furniture from my rooms with the ones in the Master's suite,' she instructed, since she had no intentions of using her mother's rooms.

The rest of the house was another matter. When Mr Collins called on her on Saturday afternoon, Anne thought to ask his advice.

'I do not know what to do. I hate the overdone furniture and décor in this house, but my mother has spent so much money on her follies, that there is barely enough to meet all necessary expenses, particularly the repairs to the tenant's houses. She has shamefully neglected them.'

Collins looked around the room and reluctantly agreed with Anne. The furniture, although expensive, was ostentatious and in bad taste.
~~~

That thought gave him an idea. 'From what I can tell, while I abhor the taste, the furniture is expensive…'

'It is. Lady Catherine almost bankrupted the estate to furnish this house.'

'There must be other people with similar taste. Why not sell the furniture and use the profits to make the changes you wish?'

Anne suddenly brightened. 'Do you suppose that your cousin, who provided us with my large gentlemen, would know someone in the market to purchase a houseful of furniture?'

'I can enquire,' Collins replied cheerfully.

Mr Thompson, who had remained at Rosings to support Miss de Bourgh against her mother, when Lady Catherine returned at last, watched his client with approval, concealed behind a polite façade. Against all odds, the young lady was growing into the competent Mistress, Sir Lewis de Bourgh had hoped for, in his heir.

<p style="text-align:center">~~~ooO0Ooo~~~</p>

At last, on Monday, Anne de Bourgh received word that Lady Catherine's carriage was approaching.

The messenger had also alerted Mr Collins, who arrived to lend his own quiet encouragement from the background.

When the butler informed them that Lady Catherine was at the door demanding admittance, Anne rose, brushed non-existent wrinkles from her dress, and taking a deep breath, steeled herself to face down the woman who had intimidated her all her life.

Mr Thompson courteously offered his arm to escort her to the front door, and when Anne placed her hand on his arm, he gently patted her hand. 'All will be well. You have the law on your side.'

'You can do this… for yourself and the people of Rosings. You are not a weak child anymore,' Mr Collins added with an encouraging smile.

Anne raised her head and squared her shoulders. 'Yes. You are correct. The people of Rosings need me.'

She led the way to the front door with Mr Thompson by her side. Mr Collins and Mrs Jenkinson, who had remained quietly in the background, followed behind and stayed out of sight, when the butler opened the door.

~~~ooO0oo~~~

As soon as Lady Catherine had left, and the door was closed again, Anne's shoulders slumped and she started to tremble.

Mr Collins solicitously rushed to her side to offer his support.

'That was more difficult than I anticipated,' Anne said quietly.

The gentlemen led her back into the small parlour, and Mrs Jenkinson ordered tea and brandy to be brought.

Once she had had a few sips of both fortifying beverages, colour came back into Anne's cheeks, and the stress left her body.

'That was well done, Miss de Bourgh,' complimented Mrs Jenkinson. 'Polite and firm.'

'Indeed, I concur. I believe that you will now be able to deal with everything else without me. If it is agreeable to you, I will return to London in the morning,' Mr Thompson suggested.

'I believe that you are correct. I thank you for your invaluable assistance, Mr Thompson.' Anne was recovering swiftly.

Now that the dreaded confrontation was over, and she had emerged the victor, her mood lightened considerably. She suddenly felt free.

'Thank you. All of you. For everything that you have done for me. I have not the words to express the true extent of my gratitude.' She beamed at the people who had helped her to come into her own, in so many ways.

For the first time in her life, she was truly in control of her life. It was a heady feeling.

~~~ooO0oo~~~

While she waited to hear about the contents of the house, Anne toured the estate with her new steward, accompanied by several of the large gentlemen.

The servants' grapevine had already spread the news that a change in management had occurred at Rosings. When Anne met with the tenants, they were friendly and cautiously optimistic, particularly when the lady admitted, 'I am new at this. I will do the best I can for the estate and everyone in it, but I expect I will make some mistakes. I can only hope that those mistakes can be easily fixed.'

Mr Potter, whose grandson now managed the farm that had been his, fondly remembered Sir Lewis de Bourgh. He was pleased to discover that the daughter was a chip of the old block. 'With that attitude you will do well enough,' he said contentedly. At last he did not have to worry about his family any more.

~~~oo0Ooo~~~
~~~

8   Netherfield Park

Ever since the attack on the Mortimer ladies, Mr Bingley had become a little withdrawn. He was still pleasant and amiable when in company, but he was more thoughtful and a little quieter than before.

He had been tempted to return to London, but he remembered that he had taken on the responsibility for Netherfield. Even though he might not be the owner, he was now responsible for the running of the estate; and after all, that was what he had come here for, to learn how to be an estate-owner.

Of course, he also could not deprive his friend of a place to stay, while he prepared for his wedding. Darcy had been a good friend to him and it was only right that he reciprocated.

To Bingley it had been a pleasure to see Darcy so happy and excited. His friend had previously been exceedingly uncomfortable in company. Now he was relaxed and sociable. Bingley guessed that not being prey for the matchmaking mothers and ladies of the *ton* anymore allowed Darcy's true personality to come to the fore.

In the weeks they had been in Hertfordshire, Darcy had given Bingley enough advice that he felt sanguine about coping on his own for a while, after the newlywed couple went to London.

Once he was in sole charge, Bingley realised that Netherfield had become his home. Having his sister Louisa, who was now officially expecting her first child, and her husband staying with him, furthered that feeling.

And then there was Colonel Fitzwilliam. Once the wedding was over, that gentleman offered to move to an inn, since he felt awkward about imposing on Bingley, while he was courting the lady his host had previously been interested in.

Bingley would have none of that. 'I may be oblivious to many things, but even I can see that you are much better suited to Miss Mortimer than I would have ever been.'

He shrugged in a deprecating manner. 'I am ashamed to admit that I was bedazzled by her beauty and did not look much deeper. Yes, I found her conversation and company enjoyable, and combined with her looks, I had thought myself in love. It might have worked if there were not aspects to the lady that I had not considered, even though she made no secret of them. But they make it impossible for us to suit.'

Bingley now smiled. 'I am glad that we found out early enough, and that it turns out that you two appear much more compatible. I may not be in love with Miss Mortimer, but I do love her and want what is best for her. And I believe that is you. So, feel free to stay here as long as you want.'

Bingley was so sincere in his speech that Richard was happy to accept the invitation.

~~~oo0Ooo~~~

Corporal Bennings was even happier. The food and beds at Netherfield were much superior to what he was accustomed. But he had become curious about the ladies at Brook Hall.

'You know, now that I have recovered, I could use a workout and get back into training,' he suggested to Fitzwilliam. 'I wonder if the arms-master at Brook Hall would be willing to help me out?'

Richard looked suspiciously at the bland expression of his batman. 'You know perfectly well that the arms-master is a woman and therefore, technically, an arms-mistress...'

Benning grinned impudently. 'I am hoping that as a woman she will be soft-hearted enough to go easy on me, while I get back into shape.'

'I would not bet on that. But I am happy to enquire,' replied Richard. He thought of Bennings more as a friend than a subordinate, and had therefore no issues requesting permission to introduce him to the ladies.
~~~

Permission was granted, since with Elizabeth gone, Miss Martin had much more time on her hands, and was happy to train with the Corporal.

Bennings found out that although Miss Martin had a soft heart, she was also a hard task-mistress. But he was able to get back into shape. She even helped him improve his technique. He figured the outcome was worth the bruises.

~~~ooO0Ooo~~~

Once it was settled that Richard would stay, Bingley threw himself into the care of the estate. He visited tenants to ensure they were properly prepared for the winter and had everything that they needed. He met with the steward to make plans for the new year.

He also socialised with his neighbours with whom he was very popular due to his amiable nature, and the fact that he was no longer focused on Jane Mortimer.

This all came to an end a few days before Christmas.

Bingley found Richard, just before the Colonel was going out to visit Brook Hall with Bennings. 'I received an express this morning, which makes it imperative for me to leave. There is a family emergency which I need to take care of. I do not know how long it will take. I could be away for a few days, or possibly weeks. It depends on what I find when I get there,' he explained.

'I have already informed Mrs Nicholls to take her orders from you. Feel free to invite anyone you wish,' Bingley added.

Richard was surprised that Bingley would want to leave him in charge. 'Surely, Mrs Nicholls should be taking her orders from your sister and her husband, not a guest.'

'I am afraid that I need my sister to come with me. As I said, it is a family matter, and I suspect I will need her assistance. I know that leaves you without a hostess, but I imagine that you will spend much of your time at Brook Hall.'

'But if you will be gone for weeks, why not close up the house?'

'Close the house just before Christmas? That would be very bad for the servants. And if all goes well, I will only be gone for a few days. It is
~~~

much better to leave things as they are. I am only sorry that I have to be a bad host…'

'If you have a family emergency, that should be the least of your worries. As you said, I will be spending much of my time at Brook Hall, and when I am here, Bennings is amusing company. Also, I suppose that if I wish to hold a dinner party, I could always borrow Georgiana and Mrs Annesley.'

'See, you have things under control already.' Bingley smiled in relief. 'But now I must see the steward before I leave. I expect we will be gone within the hour. I want to wish you a merry Christmas, if I do not see you before then. Goodbye, Fitzwilliam.'

Bingley rushed off, leaving behind a bemused Colonel Fitzwilliam.

~~~ooO0Ooo~~~

Richard arrived at Brook Hall and relayed the news about Mr Bingley's sudden departure and the living arrangements at Netherfield to the ladies.

Mrs Mortimer explained thoughtfully, 'while I would normally invite you to stay with us in Mr Bingley's absence; but, considering that you are courting Jane, I think it is best for you to stay at Netherfield. Although I trust both you and Jane implicitly, I would not want to start tongues wagging.'

'I believe that was Bingley's reasoning for having me remain at Netherfield. Or possibly to give the servants something to do.'

'It could be both. The previous tenants at Netherfield left suddenly, which was hard on the servants. It would be especially bad to close the house up just before Christmas.'

'I guess Bingley has learned more than I gave him credit for. That was his exact argument.'

'In that case, I expect he will become a good Master for whichever estate he buys.'

~~~ooO0Ooo~~~

Soon afterwards, Jane suggested that they should go for a ride. 'I promised Lizzy that I would exercise Phoenix while she is in London.'

They were accompanied by Miss Martin to act as chaperone, as well as the Corporal, who enjoyed the outing in her company.

While they rode at a moderate pace, Jane and Richard chatted comfortably. Since each was curious about the other's life, they exchanged stories about their experiences.

Although Richard realised, and appreciated, that Jane was no delicate damsel, who had to be sheltered from the realities of life, he censored his description of life in the army.

When Jane realised that he edited the stories and complained, he explained, 'Jane, there are some things I truly do not wish to talk about. This is for my benefit, not yours. I do not wish to be reminded of the more horrendous aspects of war, since I still have nightmares about some of the things I have seen.'

'My apologies, I had not considered that aspect,' Jane was immediately contrite when she heard his explanation. 'It is unfortunate that war stories always sound so much more exciting once they have been sanitised. It gives young men a false impression. They talk of honour and glory, since they are unaware of the realities.'

Richard grinned with a touch of chagrin. 'If young men were told about the realities, how would a monarch entice them into joining the army and going to war? Although, most young men think they are immortal, and would still think it a glorious adventure. I must admit I was one of those young men.'

'Now you have learned better.'

'I am also not as young as I used to be.'

Jane thought to lighten the mood. 'I think you are the perfect age,' she said with a flirtatious smile.

She succeeded in distracting Colonel Fitzwilliam from the war and bringing him back to more immediate interests. He smiled back at her. 'I am excessively pleased that you should think so.' He hoped that the comment was also an indication that Jane was developing feelings for himself, since he found himself becoming more enamoured with her, the more he came to know her.

Jane blushed at the smile directed at her and noticed a fluttery feeling which she had never experienced before. Not even when dancing or conversing with Mr Bingley.

Fortunately for her peace of mind, she was distracted as they arrived at the long field. 'Please forgive me, I need to leave you for a few minutes, Phoenix really wants his run.' She indicated the alert attitude of the now prancing and restless stallion, who was more than ready for his all-out gallop.

Before Richard could respond, she let Phoenix have his way and took off.

Miss Martin who had caught up with Fitzwilliam, laughed. 'There is no point trying to catch them, Colonel. I know of no other horse that can keep up with Phoenix on that run. Especially since Miss Mortimer is much lighter than you.'

Richard was distracted from the rider and instead watched the horse in admiration, and mused, *I wonder if Elizabeth is prepared to lend me that stallion as a stud?*

<p style="text-align:center">~~~oo0Ooo~~~</p>

9   Arrivals & Departures

Late morning on Christmas Eve, Elizabeth and Darcy returned to Brook Hall, to spend Christmas with the family.

They were greeted by Mrs Mortimer, who, after one look at Elizabeth, commented, 'married life certainly agrees with you. You are positively glowing.'

'Since I have a very considerate husband, I am indeed delighted with the married state,' Elizabeth replied with a beaming smile.

Georgiana too observed the couple. She was pleased by the body-language between them, as well as by the contented and relaxed smile on her brother's countenance.

She had just finished greeting Darcy, when the other sisters could not restrain themselves any longer. They swept Elizabeth off to their rooms to regale her with questions about the last two weeks. Georgiana, refusing to miss out, joined the group.

Elizabeth was amused to find that during her absence her former room had acquired a new occupant. Georgiana seemed to have become a fully-fledged Mortimer sister, who was just as curious as the others.

While Elizabeth was happy to describe most of the events since her wedding, she was not about to satisfy anyone's prurient curiosity.

In the meantime, Darcy related those same events to Mr Mortimer and the ever-present Richard.

The one unexpected event for Richard, was the news that Anne, with the help of Collins, had successfully ousted Lady Catherine from Rosings.

Anne had sent a letter with the staff she returned to Darcy, relating her successful assumption of her new role as Mistress of Rosings. She also explained that while the butler, the housekeeper and the steward were just what she needed, she had enough maids and footmen, since

Lady Catherine had hired an overabundance of them to cater to her whims.

Since those servants had travelled in winter from Pemberley to London, to Kent, and back again to London without complaint, Darcy allowed them to remain in London over the Christmas period, before sending them back to Pemberley.

Richard laughed when he heard the news. 'What is it about the Mortimer ladies and their relations? I used to have three taciturn, shy and reserved cousins. But since they have had contact with this family, they have all come out of their shells. I never expected Darcy to enjoy dancing or Georgiana to speak up in company. But all that pales in comparison to Anne standing up to her mother.' He shook his head in amazement.

~~~ooO0Ooo~~~

Christmas Day at Brook Hall was a fun extended family affair. Richard and Bennings had of course been invited to spend Christmas and Boxing Day with the family, to save them traipsing around the countryside in the dark.

With Darcy and Elizabeth occupying the Mistress' suite, Mrs Mortimer felt that propriety was well enough served.

After church services in the morning, the whole extended family returned to Brook Hall for a light breakfast.

The girls took turns entertaining the family with music. the highlight of those performances was a duet by Mary and Georgiana, which they had practised for the occasion.

In the afternoon, a sumptuous Christmas dinner was served. There was something for every taste, and everyone ate more than was probably good for them.

Afterwards they exchanged presents. Even the servants were not forgotten.

While they were in London, Elizabeth and Darcy had enjoyed shopping for gifts. New music for Mary and Georgiana, some particularly lovely pastels for Kitty, an enticing citrusy perfume for Jane
~~~

and a Lexicon Balatronicum for Lydia, to ensure she knew what *not* to say in polite society.

Mrs Mortimer was touched to receive a simple but very elegant ruby necklace which had once belonged to Mrs Darcy. Elizabeth too was the recipient of some of Mrs Darcy's jewellery.

Richard was pleased to receive a handkerchief from Jane which she had embroidered with his initials, which had been formed depicting various riding implements. 'I am pleased you did not depict weapons,' he commented gratefully to Jane.

'Since you were planning a new career in horse-breeding, this seemed more appropriate,' replied Jane with a blush. She hoped that he would understand the message implied with the gift.

It seemed the Colonel was as quick on the uptake as she had hoped, although the blush gave an extra hint. 'Am I planning a new career?' he asked with a delighted smile.

'I certainly hope so...' Jane replied, looking him in the eye, and blushing even more.

'In that case, I had better resign my commission first thing in the new year.' Richard smiled at Jane and kissed her hands.

'Thank you. I would like that very much.'

Later that evening they did manage to find a kissing bough, and take full advantage of the opportunity it presented.

<center>~~~ooo0Ooo~~~</center>

Anne de Bourgh was surprised when she received a letter from her Aunt and Uncle Matlock, inviting themselves to Rosings for Christmas.

Although she had not had much contact with the couple in recent years, since everyone avoided Lady Catherine if they could, she had always liked them. The visit seemed the perfect way to reconnect with the rest of her family. She was not disappointed.

When the couple arrived at Rosings, Lady Fitzwilliam explained, 'since your uncle needs to be in town for the season, we decided not to travel all the way to Derbyshire just for a few days. And we thought you might not want to spend Christmas on your own. But because you are too new in your position to leave the estate just yet, we thought we would come to you, rather than inviting you to stay with us in town.'

'Thank you. I appreciate the company… I think. How do you feel about what I did…'

Lord Matlock sighed. 'It was necessary. I wish you could have done things differently, but my sister made that impossible. You did what you had to do. I for one am happy for the people of Rosings. Although I am not happy with Darcy. He must have known something of what you were planning, but he never said a word until after the event.'

'It all depended on the element of surprise. I suppose that my cousin thought you might let something slip to your sister, after all, you are rather blunt.'

'It is called being forthright, my dear, never blunt. I would be drummed out of the first circles if anyone suggested that I was so inurbane as to be blunt.'

'Whatever you call it, Uncle, I know that you and your sister have been trying to get the better of each other on many occasions. Could you have resisted tweaking her nose about it, if you had known?'

'Hoist by my own petard,' laughed Lord Fitzwilliam. 'Now I am curious. Will we be able to meet this miracle worker who has turned the little grey mouse into a lioness?'

'You can meet him after services tomorrow, and he will come to Christmas dinner.'

'You are inviting an unrelated single man to dinner? What will your neighbours think?' her aunt asked in mock horror.

'That I am in need of spiritual guidance perhaps? But you forget that he is family.'

'Family?'

'Indeed. He is cousin to Elizabeth, who is married to my cousin, Darcy. Therefore, he is family, and all is proper.'

'That is yet another thing Darcy forgot to mention. I really must have words with that young man.'

<p style="text-align:center">~~~oo0Ooo~~~</p>

The whole Mortimer family was excited that Jane and Richard had come to an understanding, which added to the festive mood that Christmas.

Unfortunately, that mood was shattered three days later, when a letter arrived for Colonel Fitzwilliam, ordering him to return to duty on the second day of January.

'You can still resign,' pleaded Jane. It was too cruel to have her happy future snatched away when she had barely had a chance to enjoy it.

'I know. Technically I can resign at any time, except in the middle of a battle. But I am still a serving officer, and I have received orders. To send out orders at this time, they must really need me. I have been ordered to serve with General Wellesley. I am sorry, but it is a matter of honour...'

'Ah yes, honour and glory.' Jane said, hurt that the man she had just promised to marry, would choose glory in battle over her.

His shoulders slumped and he sighed. 'No glory, just honour and duty. But... I will return,' vowed Richard. 'Now that I have found you, nothing will prevent me from coming back.

'You had better see that you do, or I shall never forgive you.' Jane was mollified, and although still hurt, now the pain was due to fear of losing the man she loved.

~~~ooO0oo~~~

New Year's Eve and New Year's Day were subdued for the family.

The only saving grace for Jane was the superstition that the person you started the year with, would be the one with whom you would end it. She prayed that it was not just superstitious nonsense.

When it was time for Richard to leave, Mrs Mortimer allowed them some time in private.

Jane clung to him fiercely while she kissed him goodbye with a passion that she had not known that she possessed.

When they eventually broke apart, she put on a brave smile and said simply, 'come back soon, my love.'

'I will, dear heart,' Richard promised, hoping that fate would not make a liar of him.
~~~

~~~ooOOoo~~~

A few days later, Darcy and Elizabeth took their leave to travel to Pemberley for a few weeks.

Georgiana pleaded with Darcy to let her remain at Brook Hall, to give him more time alone with his new bride. She even promised to keep up her studies, arguing that Mrs Mortimer was a much sterner task-master than he had ever been.

Considering that Darcy relished the idea that, for a few weeks at least, he could focus on his own happiness with Elizabeth, he agreed to let her stay.

~~~ooOOoo~~~

At the end of February, Mary accepted an invitation by the Darcy's, who felt they needed to be seen, even if briefly, during the season, to spend a few weeks in London, giving her the opportunity to visit the opera and the theatre.

Since Georgiana's bond with Kitty and Lydia had grown stronger still, she was allowed to remain in Meryton.

In her completely honest moments, Mary also admitted to herself that she was desperate to get away from Brook Hall at present.

Even though Jane presented her usual serene exterior, Mary knew that her sister was worried sick about her fiancé. It had been over six weeks since Richard left, and in the whole time, there had not been even one letter from him. Every time the post arrived, Jane was eager for news, only to be disappointed yet again.

Mary, who was sensitive to emotions, could not tolerate the tension any longer. When Elizabeth offered an escape, she jumped at the chance.

~~~ooOOoo~~~
~~~

10 New Ideas

Mary's visit coincided with a brief visit in town by Patrick Mortimer, who had come to London for business reasons. Since his business left him free in the evenings, he was pleased to escort his cousin, who still refused to be called aunt, to the opera. He enjoyed music and the Darcy Box was much better positioned than his own.

Mr and Mrs Darcy, accompanied by Miss Mary Mortimer and Mr Patrick Mortimer were politely chatting with acquaintances in the lobby of the opera house before the first performance of Mozart's *The Marriage of Figaro*.

Patrick turned to Mary to comment on the program, when he exclaimed, 'watch out,' but it was too late. A gentleman, wearing thick spectacles, had been too engrossed in reading the program, and walked straight into Mary.

The collision brought him out of his abstraction, and he looked up and cried, 'my most humble apologies, Madam. I did not see you.'

'You mean that you still do not watch where you are going, eh, Harrison?' Patrick laughed as he recognised the gentleman.

The man peered through his thick glasses at Patrick and exclaimed, 'Mortimer, is that you? A thousand apologies. I am afraid I was engrossed in reading tonight's program...'

'And in the process walked straight into my cousin.'

Mr Harrison turned back to Mary and said worriedly, 'I hope I did not injure you with my carelessness? I would never forgive myself. I may be absent-minded and easily distracted, but I am not insensitive...'

Mary, who, after her initial surprise at the collision, was inclined not to make a fuss over something so negligible. When she noted the serious concern and embarrassment on the gentleman's countenance, she was quick to reassure him. 'Sir, do not discompose yourself. There was no harm done as I barely felt a thing.'

Patrick decided to intervene. 'If you two are going to converse, I suppose I had better perform the introduction. Cousin Mary, may I introduce my good friend from Cambridge, Mr Reginald Harrison. Harrison this is my cousin, Miss Mortimer.' He gave Darcy and Elizabeth a quick look, and at their nods, added, 'and this lovely lady is Miss Mortimer's sister, Mrs Darcy and her husband, Mr Darcy.'

'It is my great pleasure to meet you, Miss Mortimer, Mrs Darcy, Mr Darcy. I hope I have not spoiled your evening with my carelessness.'

'Not at all, Mr Harrison. As my sister said, she is perfectly well and accidents will happen.' Elizabeth assured the man.

'Are you looking forward to the opera, Mr Harrison?' asked Mary, trying to change the subject.

'Indeed, I am. It is the main reason I came to London. Although Cambridge has much to recommend it, opera is not on the list of entertainments available there.'

'Are you still at Cambridge? I thought you had finished your studies years ago.'

Mr Harrison beamed. 'I now hold a position at the University as a Professor of Philosophy. While I have to spend part of my time teaching, it affords me the opportunity to conduct further research.'

'Philosophy you say? Which particular aspect are you researching? I admit that I am fascinated by Epistemology as propounded by Mr René Descartes,' Mary exclaimed.

'You too are interested in Descartes? What a delightful coincidence. What do you think of his view on...'

'Stop, Harrison. You cannot start one of your philosophical discussions in the lobby of the opera. Especially as the performance is about to begin.'

'Why did you not say so before? I must go and find my seat. I would hate to miss the performance by Giuseppe Naldi.' He looked around distractedly.

Darcy had noticed the sudden interest in Mary, and looking at his wife for confirmation, saw that she seemed to approve that her sister was for once happy to speak to a new gentleman.

Before Harrison could rush off, an amused Darcy offered, 'why not join us in our box, Mr Harrison. There is more than enough space.'

'You are all kindness and generosity, Mr Darcy. If you are certain that I will not be in the way...'

'Not at all, Mr Harrison. We would be delighted to have you join us.'

Harrison let himself be persuaded and accompanied the party to the Darcy box.

When Darcy offered Harrison a seat at the front, the gentleman demurred, stating, 'even with these spectacles I can barely see the stage. I will be quite content to sit at the back.'

Since Darcy preferred to sit next to his wife, he did not argue the arrangement, leaving Patrick to sit at the back with his old friend.

Mr Harrison seemed to be so engrossed in the music, he even took off his glasses. When the interval came, Mary commented on the fact.

'Miss Mortimer, I find wearing my spectacles is a distraction when I am trying to appreciate the music.' He smiled in a deprecating manner which Mary found quite charming.

Darcy and Patrick Mortimer offered to fetch refreshments for the ladies, which they gratefully accepted.

'If it is all the same to you, I will remain behind and keep the ladies company. I find the crush for the refreshments rather too much,' suggested Mr Harrison. While that statement was perfectly true, Harrison had an ulterior motive.

Mary mentioning Descartes had caught his attention. He wanted to find out if she had only heard the name in relation to philosophy and was using it simply to make conversation, or if she was truly interested in the subject.

When the other gentlemen left the box, he chatted pleasantly with Mary and Elizabeth about the music they had enjoyed, but eventually he could not resist any longer. 'Miss Mortimer, you mentioned Descartes earlier. Have you read any of his books?'

'The first of his books which I read was actually on music theory. But then I became interested in his other works, such as his Meditations on First Philosophy and the Principles of Philosophy, which I found easier to read, since my French is better than my Latin.'

'Vos can lego latine? (*You can read Latin?*)' asked Harrison in astonishment.

'Sic possum. sed modo tardius. (*Yes, I can. But only slowly.*)' Mary replied carefully.

'Φοβάμαι, είναι όλα ελληνικά για μένα. (*Fovámai, eínai óla elliniká gia ména. I am afraid it is all Greek to me.*)' Elizabeth could not resist to tease.

'Ladies, I am all astonishment. You are both a wonder. I have never before encountered such educated ladies.'

'How would you know, Mr Harrison? Most gentlemen are not interested in women who are better educated than they are. Therefore, ladies will hide it,' Mary pointed out.

'I have heard many of my colleagues claim that education is wasted on women.'

Mary, for whom this attitude had been a bone of contention for years, replied heatedly. 'I suppose it has never occurred to those gentlemen that education is only wasted on women because we are generally not allowed to use it. Gentlewomen loose status if they hold a paid position. Therefore, unless they are independently wealthy, the only option they have is to get married. And if a woman wants to have a chance at finding a husband, she had better pretend to be brainless.'

'But your sister, Mrs Darcy, is obviously an educated woman, since her Greek accent is better than mine. Yet she is married...'

'My husband is an exceptional man. He is not intimidated by my accomplishments,' Elizabeth stated proudly.

While Harrison considered their statements, Darcy and Patrick returned with drinks.

Patrick noticed his friend's preoccupation and teased, 'Harrison, you look like you have been hit with a plank.'

Startled out of his reverie, Mr Harrison responded, 'I feel like I have been hit with a verbal plank. The ladies have given me much to think about.'

He turned to Darcy. 'Mr Darcy, may I presume on our short acquaintance and call on the ladies at their convenience. I would dearly love to continue the fascinating discussion we had in your absence. They have raised points which I have never previously considered. It would be immensely helpful for my studies to further explore their point of view.'

'And which point of view is that, Mr Harrison?'

'That women can benefit from education.'

Darcy and Patrick looked at each other and barely contained their laughter. 'In that case you have come to the right place. If the ladies are agreeable, I have no objection.'

'I would be delighted to continue our discussion, Mr Harrison, since you appear to have opened your mind,' Mary agreed, mollified by the gentleman's attitude.

~~~ooO0Ooo~~~

The next morning Darcy called on Patrick Mortimer.

After their greetings, once they settled comfortably in the study, Patrick grinned at Darcy. 'Let me guess. You have come to find out about Harrison.'

'Elizabeth thinks that Mary has taken a fancy to the man. I thought it prudent to ensure that he is...'

'Suitable?' supplied Patrick.

'Indeed. Mary is now my sister and currently under my protection. So... what can you tell me about him?'

'Harrison is the second son of a gentleman with an estate in Cheshire. When I met him at Cambridge, he was a brilliant student. I believe he took the position as a professor because he wants to do research, not because he has to earn a living. I heard on the grapevine that some years ago he inherited a considerable sum of money from a distant uncle, whose favourite he was.'

'What about his character...'
~~~

'Darcy, you met him last night. Most people would consider him dull. It is difficult to get him to focus on anything other than philosophy and music. He is brilliant when discussing his interests, but socially he is moderately inept.'

Patrick considered his words. 'He is aware of his shortcomings, which makes him seem a little diffident at times. Although when he does take notice of his surroundings and in the right company, he exhibits a rather dry sense of humour.'

Patrick's grin became wider. 'To the best of my knowledge he has never noticed a woman before. But then again, I do not know many women who would be interested in Descartes and openly say so.'

Darcy looked dubious. 'Since Mary is Elizabeth's sister, I want her to find someone with whom she can be happy. If he is socially inept, he may never manage to get his interest across... if he is interested in the first place.'

'I can think of another socially inept man who did very well once he met the right woman.'

'Who?'

'You.'

'Oh...'

'Darcy, if I did not like and respect Harrison, I would not have introduced him last night. Look, we both know that most men in our circle are terrified of intelligent women, unless they are highly intelligent themselves. Mary is an intelligent woman. She will need an intelligent man to make her happy. I think Harrison would be delighted with an intelligent woman, particularly one who shares his interests. Why do you not let them work it out themselves?'

'He is coming this afternoon to find out more about educated women. It will be interesting to see how he handles the situation.'

<center>~~~oo0Ooo~~~</center>

When Darcy returned home, his uncle was once again waiting for him. After they exchanged greetings, Darcy asked his uncle suspiciously, 'I hope your presence does not indicate that Aunt Catherine is in town again.'

'No, she is not, but maybe I should have brought her along as punishment for you not telling me that Anne was planning a coup d'état.'

'I did not know any details either. Collins simply asked me to keep my engagement quiet. Since I had no desire for Aunt Catherine to spoil my wedding, I was happy to comply.'

'I suppose I can understand that. But speaking of Collins. You also did not mention that the rector at Hunsford was your wife's cousin.'

'I cannot see that it is in any way relevant.'

'If we had known, your aunt and I would have been better prepared to see the changes in Anne.'

'Has she changed much? You seem to forget that I have not seen her since last Easter and only had one letter from her recently.'

'You have seen the change in Georgiana. Her improvement pales in comparison to Anne. I spoke to my sister when we were at Rosings over Christmas, and Cathy is furious that Anne faced her down, completely cool, calm and collected, and completely in control of the situation.'

'I gather that Aunt Catherine is unhappy about the situation?'

'That is an understatement if I have ever heard one. Anne is taking precautions to ensure that my sister cannot burn down Rosings in revenge for being evicted.'

Now Lord Matlock chuckled. 'You should have seen Catherine nearly foaming at the mouth the day that Mr Gardiner, another one of our new relations, arrived with several carts to remove some of the furniture. I was so proud of Anne when she cut across Cathy's tirade, saying, *I am selling that tasteless junk to pay for the repairs to my estate which you so shamefully neglected.* Then some large gentlemen escorted my sister back to the Dower House.'

It was Darcy's turn to chuckle. 'I wish I could have seen that.'

'The most amazing part was, that Anne was on her own when she faced her mother. I was inside the house when I heard Cathy rant, and had only opened a window to call out, when Anne ended the confrontation.'

Lord Matlock shook his head. 'I do not know what it is about that new family of ours, but they seem to bring out the best in people.'

'Collins did not succeed with Aunt Catherine though.'

'Some people are incorrigible.'

<center>~~~ooO0Ooo~~~</center>

11 Quite Contrary

Mr Harrison arrived punctually at the appointed hour. He was welcomed by the sisters and Darcy.

'I hope you do not mind my presence, but I always find it fascinating when my wife and sisters discuss their ideas.'

'Of course, I do not mind, after all this is your home and I am only a guest. As a matter of fact, it might be helpful to hear the male perspective to the ladies' ideas. I have spent much of the night contemplating the attitudes you discussed, and to my shame I must admit that I had accepted my colleagues' attitude as correct, since I had never before encountered a lady who was educated and prepared to admit it. While I now...'

'Please, Mr Harrison,' Elizabeth interrupted the enthusiastic flow of words. 'Will you not sit and have some tea, or coffee if you prefer, since this will probably be a lengthy discussion, and we will be more comfortable while seated.'

'I beg your pardon. I am afraid I become excessively focused when I become fascinated with a subject. I would appreciate a cup of tea, thank you.'

They sat down and Elizabeth served tea to everyone.

'Mr Harrison, based on your comments, am I right to presume that you have not had much contact with ladies?' asked Mary.

'You are correct, Miss Mortimer. I grew up in an all-male household with only my father and an older brother. My mother died when I was very young and Father never remarried. We do not have any close female relations. And at school women are, of course, not admitted.'

'Because men like to feel superior to women. Or even other men who are not born into wealth and privilege, and must earn a living.' Mary countered.

Harrison looked startled. 'You raise yet another issue. But I would prefer to stay with the original topic. You contend that more women are educated than we are led to believe, but they hide that fact due to society's attitude.'

'Correct. Consider the attitude towards Bluestockings. Many sneer at them for their desire to be recognised as the intellectual equal of men. Few men are prepared to marry a bluestocking. The question is, why do men feel that way. I have my opinions, but no scientific proof for them.'

'It would be a fascinating subject to study,' agreed Mr Harrison. 'Once we knew the cause of the attitude, measures could be taken to change it, although I suspect it would take decades at least, to achieve any noticeable results.'

They settled down into a detailed discussion about women's abilities. Harrison became curious enough to enquire about the extent of Mary's education.

'By Jove, at least half the men at Cambridge are not half as knowledgeable as you, yet they would deny even the possibility that you could learn half as much as they.'

During the discussion, Darcy had remained quietly in the background. He was proud of Mary, the way she conducted herself. Certain and firm in her knowledge and beliefs, but polite and courteous in expressing such controversial opinions. Elizabeth too, remained on the periphery of the discussion, unless specifically asked a question.

To Darcy's mind, Patrick had been correct. Harrison was brilliant, but also openminded enough to ignore customary perceptions, and willing to listen to opposing opinions and give them serious consideration.

It would be interesting to see if Harrison would notice Mary as a woman, not just a mind.

'How do you tolerate such injustice?' Harrison blurted out.

'With great patience and fortitude for the limitations of mere males...' Mary replied with a bland expression, but a suspicious little twitch about her lips.

Harrison's stunned expression was all she could have hoped for, before he burst out in delighted laughter. 'Well said, Miss Mortimer. Exceedingly well said, indeed.'

Darcy looked at the clock, and entered the conversation. 'While this is a fascinating subject and deserves to be debated, I am afraid it will have to continue at another time.'

Harrison looked at the clock and exclaimed, 'my profound apologies. I had not realised what the time was. I am afraid that I lose track of time when engaged in such a delightful intellectual discourse. Ah... might I impose... I mean... would it be acceptable...'

Elizabeth and Darcy exchanged looks, and she offered, 'Mr Harrison, would you be free to come to dinner the day after tomorrow? We will have greater opportunity for discussion then.'

'Yes, I am free, and I would be honoured as long as you are certain it is not an intrusion. You are kindness itself, Mrs Darcy.'

'Not at all, Mr Harrison. It is a pleasure to have an intelligent conversation with someone outside our family.'

<div align="center">~~~ooo0Ooo~~~</div>

Mr Harrison became a frequent visitor at Darcy House. Sometimes he arrived during visiting hours when the ladies were receiving other callers.

Mrs Darcy was still a novelty in town, and everyone was curious to meet her. Between Mrs Mortimer, the Viscount and the Viscountess Middlebrook, and the Countess of Matlock, Elizabeth had been coached well enough to deal with all the different personalities. With her charm she managed to win the approval of most of the ladies, particularly the friends of her coaches.

On the occasions of those visits, Mr Harrison generally quietly listened to the others, only giving his opinion if specifically asked. It was amusing to Elizabeth and Mary to watch the reaction of some people to the gentleman. It appeared that those people equated his use of spectacles with deafness or feeblemindedness, in that they spoke to him more loudly or carefully.

Yet he took it in good humour and never seemed to mind. Instead he delighted in starting a discussion about music with Mary, discussing the finer points of the various pieces of music they favoured.

On days when there were no other visitors, he happily discussed more esoteric subjects, although he was still endlessly fascinated by the education Mary had received. Which led them to discuss their respective families, as well as ideas of what they hoped for in their lives.

Mary caught herself looking forward to his visits with ever greater pleasure. Once he had overcome the surprise that she could understand and converse on his favourite subjects, he always treated her as his intellectual equal.

Mary had always been quieter and more given to introspection than Elizabeth. She preferred more intellectual rather than physical pursuits. Mr Harrison's limitations due to his poor eyesight were not an issue for her, although she would have liked the opportunity to dance with him.

Mary felt herself drawn to the gentleman. She felt that she could discuss anything with him, and be understood and not judged. Although when she pictured Mr Harrison, the way his light brown hair refused to be tamed, the surprisingly broad shoulders on a man given to mental pursuits, the lips that smiled so easily… she felt something stir in her that she found impossible to describe.

Based on what Elizabeth had told her about her courtship with William, Mary suspected that she was falling in love with this rather eccentric professor.

~~~ooO0Ooo~~~

The eccentric professor had once again been invited to dinner at Darcy House.

Conversation during dinner had been wide-ranging, as always between these four people. Due to the lack of feminine gossip, the gentlemen did not feel the need for the traditional separation of the sexes after dinner. Instead they joined the ladies in the music room to enjoy their brandy with their coffee.

When Elizabeth requested that Mary should perform for them, Mary declared herself quite willing, since she loved to play the pianoforte.

But then there was some awkwardness when Elizabeth suggested that Mr Harrison should turn the pages for Mary.

'I am sorry, but I cannot.'
~~~

'But you know music. I know that we have discussed musical notation...' Mary looked upset. Was he refusing because he did not wish to sit next to her?

Harrison suddenly looked resigned. He removed his glasses and addressed Mary and his hosts. 'I must apologise for deceiving you. I am fully aware that I lack in social graces. To cover that fact, when I was at school, I took to wearing glasses, because most people assume that someone who wears glasses is deficient in more than eyesight, and they do not expect scintillating conversation, or my joining them in the entertainments popular amongst students.'

He sighed and lowered his gaze. 'My eyesight is perfect without glasses. With the glasses I have trouble seeing because everything looks blurred. Which is why I often run into things, and have difficulty reading. And I struggle to maintain my balance while dancing.'

He looked up again, expecting to see derision or anger at his deception. Instead he saw... vast amusement, barely held in check.

Elizabeth recovered her equilibrium first. 'Please forgive us, Mr Harrison. I was reminded of my husband's method of dealing with social discomfort... He used to scowl at everyone. Your method is considerably more subtle.'

'You are not angry at me for my deception?'

'Not at all. It has been most amusing watching other people speak to you. Speaking too loud or carefully enunciating every word, as if your *supposedly* poor eyesight affected you hearing or your mind.'

'I admit, that appeals to my sense of humour as well.' Now he smiled shyly at Mary. 'If you are still inclined to play for us, I would be happy to turn the pages for you.'

'I would be glad to have your assistance.' Mary took her position at the pianoforte selecting the longest piece of music she owned and had practiced enough to play well.

Harrison took his place beside her on the bench. 'I am ready when you are, Miss Mortimer.'

Mary started to play, deliberately focusing on the music, because the warmth radiating from his body could easily distract her. Somewhere in the back of her mind she realised that she never had this reaction when one of her sisters turned the pages for her, before she lost herself in the music.

~~~oo0Ooo~~~

Lady Axingham, an old friend of Lady Matlock, had taken a great liking to Elizabeth Darcy. Naturally, when she invited Mrs Darcy to her Easter ball, and the lady requested that she might bring her sister and a gentleman friend of the family, she was happy to extent the invitation. Especially as she was curious who the gentleman might be.

The Darcys, together with Mary and Mr Harrison, arrived punctually, and were greeted by Lord and Lady Axingham. While Darcy introduced his party to Lord Axingham, Lady Axingham looked suspiciously at Mr Harrison, whom she had met during a visit at Darcy House.

When Harrison greeted his hostess, she smiled mischievously. 'I am glad to see that your eyesight has improved since last we met, Mr Harrison.'

'You could even say that my eyes have been opened recently,' he replied with equal levity.

The Lady glanced curiously at Mary, who blushed under the scrutiny. 'Indeed. I am excessively happy for your improvement. I hope you enjoy the dancing tonight.'

'I expect I will, since Miss Mortimer has granted me the first and supper sets.'

Lady Axingham decided that since the gentleman was standing up straight, and without his glasses, he now presented a very pleasing image. She thought it would be amusing to watch the young ladies vie for his attention this evening. Although, if she was as good a judge as she thought, they would be wasting their time.

~~~oo0Ooo~~~

Their hostess was correct on two counts.

Now that he could see where he was going, and without the blurred vision throwing him off balance, Mr Harrison turned out to be an excellent dancer as well as being pleasing to look at. Many a young lady gave him second and third glances, and tried to catch his attention.

Although he was polite and danced with several ladies, Mr Harrison had eyes only for Mary.

Since Mary had arrived with the Darcys, several gentlemen asked to be introduced to her and requested dances. Mary too was polite and accepted the invitations to dance.

But she also used the opportunity to test her theory. During the dances, when the opportunity to converse presented itself, she introduced subjects dear to her heart and mind, and was amused to see the gentlemen recoil.

Apart from Mr Harrison, with whom she enjoyed a pleasant discourse during supper, only one other gentleman enjoyed her conversation.

Lord Axingham found the conversation stimulating, and joined in Mary's and Harrison's mirth when he discovered that he was a part of Mary's study, and that he was the only man, other than Mr Harrison, who was not put off by her choice of topics.

'This is of course only a small sample, but I conversed with ten gentlemen tonight about subjects more esoteric than the weather, and only two were prepared to engage in these discussions,' Mary explained to her two listeners. 'And both of you are here to hear of the results of my study.'

Lord Axingham laughed and noted, 'you may find that men who have been happily married for a number of years, are more inclined to be receptive to the idea of intelligent women. They have had time to discover that an intelligent wife is a greater asset than a wife who is merely beautiful.'

'I concur,' said Darcy, who had just joined their group with Elizabeth on his arm. 'Although I have been exceedingly lucky to find a woman who is both.'

Harrison smiled and said, 'I hope to be equally as lucky.' He turned to Mary and asked with a questioning smile, 'if you are available, might I be so bold as to request your hand... for the last set?'

Mary's breath caught for a moment. Looking at Mr Harrison she wondered whether he was asking what she thought he was, by requesting a third set and using that particular phrasing. Seeing that smile and a slight nod, she replied with a beaming smile, 'yes... I should be delighted.'

The following day, they formalised their engagement, subject to Mrs Mortimer's approval.

~~~oo0Ooo~~~
~~~

12 Interlude

On Easter Saturday, Mary returned to Brook Hall in high spirits. She was accompanied by her sister and Darcy, as well as Mr Harrison.

After the introductions were made to all but Jane, who was reportedly indisposed, and they had settled in the parlour for refreshments, Darcy said to Mrs Mortimer, 'Since Mary was under my protection when Harrison proposed, I have given conditional approval to his suit, subject to your agreement.'

Mrs Mortimer was aware of the proposal, since she had received a letter from Mary extolling the many virtues of the gentleman. But she wanted to hear from Mr Harrison his reasons for proposing.

'Mr Harrison, why do you wish to marry Mary?'

Harrison had expected questions from Mrs Mortimer, because Mary had described her as very protective.

'Miss Mary is everything I could have hoped for but did not expect to find. She is talented in many ways, she is lovely and kind, but most importantly to me, she is intelligent and she challenges my mind.'

He directed a fond smile at Mary.

'I had not expected to ever marry, since I had no liking for the insipid ladies whom I had met in the past. Miss Mary is strong enough to stand up to me and speak her mind. I find that combination of attributes irresistible. Mrs Mortimer, I wish to thank you for allowing Miss Mary to become the wonderful lady that she is.'

'There is no need to thank me, Mr Harrison. It was by her own efforts that Mary became who she is.'

'But you not only allowed her to follow her own interests, but she told me that you actively encouraged her to expand her education.'

'She was an intelligent child; how could I do ought but encourage her to learn.'

'I have learnt that it is a rare parent who sees their children as individuals, not just smaller copies of themselves.'

'I suppose that it was easier for me in that respect, since I adopted my daughters. But I am pleased that she has found someone who appreciates her for who she is.'

'I certainly appreciate her. When we discussed the future, Miss Mary has agreed to collaborate with me in my research.'

'Collaborate rather than assist?'

'I have too much respect for Miss Mary's abilities to consider her merely an assistant.'

At that comment, Mary proudly declared, 'I hope that you can now understand why I wish to marry Mr Harrison, even though we have known each other for only a short time. I have never before met a man with whom I have so much in common, and who accepts me for who I am.'

'Not to mention, easy on the eye...' Lydia could not resist her contribution to the conversation, making both Mary and Harrison blush.

He gave Mary a significant look. 'Yes, I know, you warned me...' he said, eliciting laughter from the rest of the company.

<center>~~~ooO0Ooo~~~</center>

After tea, Mary went to look in on Jane. She was shocked by Jane's appearance. Her sister looked drawn and even ill.

Mary rushed to Jane and hugged her sister. 'I gather you still have had no word?'

'No, and it has been more than three months. I do not know what to think. Richard could be dead, for all I know. Or he could have had second thoughts of our engagement, and is trying to distance himself.'

'Or he could be in the army, living in difficult circumstances, such as not having ink and paper. Perhaps he has written, but the messenger was waylaid, or the ship carrying the message was sunk.'

Jane smiled faintly. 'Perhaps any or all these things. Not knowing what is going on is driving me to imagine all the worst-case scenarios. I have been having nightmares again, but I do not wish to impose constantly on Lydia and disturb her sleep as well as my own.'

'But why did you not ask Kitty and Georgiana to help?'

'Kitty still feels guilty about not protecting herself and putting that burden on Lizzy and myself. And Georgiana is still full young for me to feel comfortable to confide in her.'

'Lydia is younger still.'

Jane managed a weak chuckle. 'Lydia was never that young, and she is my sister...'

'Very well. Until July, when I get married, I will be happy to share your room, if that will help. I am certain that we will have heard something by then.'

Jane sighed, but looked a little more hopeful. 'I pray that you are correct.'

'I hope that you will feel well enough to join us for dinner. Although I have no wish to rub salt into your wounds, I would dearly like you to meet Mr Harrison.'

Jane smiled faintly and agreed. 'Very well. Meeting your gentleman will distract me from my own thoughts.'

~~~ooO0Ooo~~~

They had barely sat down to dinner, when Mr Kirby entered and presented a letter to Darcy. 'This has just arrived by express from London.'

Darcy broke the seal and quickly scanned the brief note. His countenance had taken on a grim cast when he looked up at all the ladies, waiting for him to speak.

'I am sorry, there is no easy way to tell this. The note is from Lord Matlock, who just missed us in London, and says that this morning he had received word that Richard has gone missing in action. When he was last seen, it was in battle at Badajoz. He had been wounded,
~~~

seemed to be almost unconscious and his horse was bolting. No one has seen him since.'

'But he was not dead?' Jane asked anxiously.

'No. But his horse was headed for the enemy lines. I am sorry. It is difficult to tell this, but you deserve the truth. I hope he still lives and will return to us.'

'Thank you for being honest, William. My imagination would paint much worse pictures than almost anything that you can tell me.' Tears were streaming unheeded down Jane's cheeks. 'At least we have had some news. He is alive.' *He must be*, she thought fervently.

Dinner was a little subdued, although everyone tried to distract Jane, walking a fine line between being supportive without being insultingly cheerful. They were partly successful.

<p style="text-align:center">~~~ooO0Ooo~~~</p>

During church services the next day, Jane at last managed to find some comfort in Mr Stewarts sermon about hope and resurrection.

At the end of the service, Mr Stewart surprised the congregation by reading the banns for Miss Mary Mortimer and Mr Reginald Harrison. He finished by saying, 'I understand that the couple plan to marry at the beginning of July at Pemberley.'

The date and location had been agreed to the previous day, since Darcy had invited the whole family to Pemberley for the summer. Derbyshire was also more convenient for Mr Harrison's family who lived in Cheshire.

When they left the church, the family was delayed by a bevy of well-wishers, amongst them Charlotte Lucas. Although they did not have a chance to converse much in the hubbub, Elizabeth did manage to ask Charlotte to visit her that afternoon.

After they returned from the service Kitty, Lydia and Georgiana sat talking to Jane, to give Mary a chance to spend as much time as possible with Mr Harrison, who was due to leave for Cambridge the following day.

Elizabeth and Darcy discussed with Mrs Mortimer their plans for the whole family to visit Pemberley over the summer.

This discussion was interrupted by the arrival of Charlotte Lucas.

'Charlotte, it is so very good to see you. I am exceedingly happy that you were able to get away and visit,' Elizabeth said to her friend.

The two old friends excused themselves and went to sit away from the others to catch up on each other's news.

They chatted for a while until Elizabeth was a little surprised when Charlotte enquired for news of Mr Bingley.

Elizabeth looked searchingly at her friend. 'Charlotte, do you have a tendre for Mr Bingley?'

Although Charlotte did not answer the question directly, her blush was answer enough.

'But why did you never say anything?'

'Elizabeth, you know full well that Mr Bingley had eyes only for Jane. At least until the attack. There was never any hope that he would even give me a second look. But... I did enjoy some conversations with him when Jane was not around. I find him a most amiable man. And just because he would never have any romantic interest in me, there is no reason why we should not have a friendship.'

'There is no reason at all why you should not be friends. You are my dearest friend, and Mr Bingley is William's best friend. It is only logical that the two of you should also be friends.'

'But as to your question. Mr Bingley is still in London. The immediate problems of that emergency which made him leave is now taken care of. Unfortunately, the repercussions will take a few more weeks to straighten out.'

'Do you know what is happening?'

Elizabeth sighed. 'I do know, but it is not my story to tell.'

'But Mr Bingley is well?'

'Yes, Charlotte. He is well. But what about you? Have there been any interesting visitors to Meryton?'

'No one since Mr Bingley and the Colonel left. But there is some news I have not yet shared. I have decided to look for a position as a companion, since my skills are not adequate to be a governess.'

'A paid position? Oh no, Charlotte. Things cannot be that desperate.'

'Elizabeth, I am eight and twenty years of age, not exceptionally pretty or accomplished, and I have a small dowry. While I would welcome any respectable man who is not vicious, and who could provide me with a home, even widowers and older gentlemen prefer to marry young and pretty girls. There is simply no one who wants to marry me, and I am getting tired of being a burden to my family.'

Elizabeth was shocked to hear her friend speak in such a downhearted manner. 'Charlotte, please promise me not to do anything precipitate. We are having the whole family at Pemberley for the summer. You must come and join us as well. William tells me that there are more gentlemen than ladies in Derbyshire. Please say that you will come.'

'Very well, Eliza. I shall have a last holiday before I join the working class.'

'Excellent. We shall have a wonderful time.' Elizabeth did not mention that William had also invited Charles Bingley to Pemberley for the summer. On the other hand, it was true that there were a number of eligible gentlemen in Derbyshire. At least her friend would have a better chance to find a match than in Meryton.

<div align="center">~~~ooo0Ooo~~~</div>

The following morning, Elizabeth, Darcy and Georgiana left for Pemberley.

They offered to convey Mr Harrison as far as Cambridge. He had gratefully accepted, since travelling in good company was much more pleasant than travelling alone.

After they dropped him off, they planned to collect Mrs Annesley, who was currently visiting her own family since Georgiana had shared all her lessons with her sisters.

<div align="center">~~~ooo0Ooo~~~</div>

Mrs Bennet had received the latest news with stunned disbelief.

Mary, her plainest and quietest daughter was getting married.

When she heard that Mr Harrison was a professor at Cambridge, she was mollified. Obviously, Mary had to settle for an inferior husband, because teachers, while necessary, were not held in any great esteem, since they had to work to earn a living.

Her world fell apart again when she learned that Mr Harrison was the son of a wealthy gentleman, had significant wealth of his own, and only held the position at Cambridge because he enjoyed it.

Now her two least favourite daughters were married, or almost married, to wealthy men no less, while Jane, her oldest and most beautiful daughter, although engaged, was still unmarried due to the continued absence of her fiancé.

The world was definitely determined to vex her.

~~~oo0Ooo~~~
~~~

13 Journey

Wedding preparations for Mary's wedding were relatively painless for the family, since Mary and Harrison had agreed that they only wanted a simple ceremony with family and one or two friends.

Elizabeth and Darcy arranged for the ceremony and the wedding breakfast at Pemberley, while Mrs Mortimer took Mary shopping.

Harrison had visited Brook Hall twice in the three months of their engagement. The first time he had brought the settlement papers, the second time he brought brochures for houses available for purchase in Cambridge.

Mrs Mortimer was impressed with the settlement which Harrison intended for Mary, to which his response was simply, 'I have no one else to benefit from my death. I want my wife and potential children to be well taken care of.'

Harrison had offered to buy an estate outside Cambridge, but Mary declined on the grounds that the care of the estate would take away from the time they would have for research. 'A house with a large garden in town will be much more suitable,' she argued, and Harrison was pleased to concur. Eventually they agreed that they would spend part of their honey-month looking for a house to buy.

Meanwhile Jane still fretted over the continued absence of Richard. Mary made good on her promise to sleep with Jane, which helped to lessen her nightmares. This in turn improved Jane's health.

Kitty and Lydia bemoaned the absence of Georgiana, complaining that correspondence was simply not enough. They could hardly wait for the visit.

~~~oo0Ooo~~~

At last it was time to leave. Because of the number of people travelling, the ladies required two coaches. The first carriage carried Mrs
~~~

Mortimer, Jane, Kitty, Lydia, Miss Martin and Tilly, the second, smaller carriage was assigned to Mary, Charlotte, Mrs Taylor, as well as Mr Harrison, whom they would pick up on the way through Cambridge.

Because Kitty and Lydia were anxious to get to Pemberley, while Mr Harrison could not leave until the end of the school term, it was decided that since they were travelling in two carriages, the first would leave a few days earlier, and only be accompanied by one outrider, leaving the other three for the second carriage. Mrs Mortimer expected that, since Miss Martin and most of her pupils travelled in the first carriage, they should provide adequate protection.

Mrs Mortimer decided to take the journey to Pemberley in easy stages. Instead of spending two days on the road, she opted for three days, which allowed them to spend the second night at Bridgewater, Patrick's estate. He had become Master of the estate two years earlier, when both his parents perished in a freak carriage accident.

Kitty was pleased by those travel plans, since Patrick's younger brother was in residence as well.

On the second day of travel, Mrs Mortimer was both excited and a little sad. Bridgewater used to be her husband's main estate and had been her home for twenty years. She had not been back since her husband's death.

At noon they stopped for a leisurely lunch at an inn which served rather good food, and appeared popular. Mrs Mortimer noticed one patron paying particular attention to her daughters, but given their beauty, particularly Jane's, that was not surprising.

As they were leaving, Mrs Mortimer sent their outrider ahead to alert Patrick of their impending arrival, while they set off at an easy pace to spare the horses.

Apart from the dust it was quite a pleasant drive, until they heard a shot. A moment later, the carriage stopped at the shouted command of a gruff male voice.

Mrs Mortimer had just enough time to extract a knife from its hiding place in the carriage before both doors were wrenched open, and on each side one man was leaning through the door.

'Well, well, well. Bert has outdone himself this time. Six women and all their goods, and no men to make a fuss. We are going to have some fun today.'

'I dunno. A couple are a bit long in the tooth, and that one is not so pretty,' the second man replied, indicating Miss Martin's scarred face.

'Stop complaining. When was the last time you had a chance at any woman?'

'Do we not get a say in this, gentlemen?' Mrs Mortimer asked politely.

'No, you don'. All you have to do is *entertain* us.'

'And how many of you shall we have to entertain?'

'As it happens, there are six of you and six of us.'

'Indeed. We had better get started then.'

Mrs Mortimer smiled and held out one hand as if expecting to be helped out of the carriage. When the unsuspecting man leaned forward to take her hand, with a grin at her apparent compliance, Mrs Mortimer lashed out with the other hand which held the concealed knife.

As the man collapsed into the carriage, Miss Martin casually leaned forward and used her own knife on the man on her side of the carriage.

'Ladies, we have four more to deal with.'

'I think I had better distract them,' offered Lydia, pulling at her decolletage. Ever since hearing of her sister's adventure the previous year, she had felt envious that she had not had a chance to prove that she could do as well, if not better, as they. She had trained just as hard as they, and felt that she was better equipped to deal with such excitement.

'Are you certain?' asked Mrs Mortimer. She was concerned for the young girl, but she was also fully aware that Lydia could provide an excellent distraction, giving them a better chance of success.

'They are not interested in killing me. At least not yet.' She grabbed her reticule and jumped out of the carriage, avoiding the body of the dead man.

Kitty, whose first reaction had been to freeze in fear, shook herself out of her stupor, and followed suit on the other side. Miss Martin reached out a hand as if to stop her, but Jane prevented her by saying quietly, 'she needs to do this.'

Miss Martin nodded briefly in acknowledgment and followed her charge, while Mrs Mortimer followed Lydia.

Lydia glanced back over her shoulder and saw that while she could still see the legs of the dead man, the door shielded the view of his body. Satisfied with the ruse, she called out gaily, 'I hear there are some bucks looking for a frolic, maybe even a brush with a woman.'

Two men were holding the two lead horses to ensure that the driver could not whip up the horses and take off, while the one man held the driver and apparently injured footman at gunpoint. She could not see the last man, and assumed that he was on the other side of the carriage.

Lydia sauntered past the gunman on her side of the coach. As she came close to the second man she reached into her reticule as if she were searching for something. 'Drat, where did I put that...'

She looked behind and saw Mrs Mortimer approaching the first man. Mrs Mortimer also had her hand in her reticule, although in her case it was to hide the blood which coated her hand.

Lydia turned back to the man who was holding the horse with one hand, while he held a gun in the other. 'I hear that you are gentlemen of the road.'

The man grinned at her and said, 'it's what we do to make a living.'

As he started to raise the gun in her direction, Lydia said, 'Not anymore.' She raised her reticule and fired the concealed gun.

Within seconds she heard three more shots, and then Miss Martin's voice. 'Excellent shot, Miss Kitty. Well done.'

~~~oo0Ooo~~~

The driver helped the injured footman from the driver's seat, and, after removing the bodies from the doorways of the carriage, into the seat previously occupied by Miss Martin.
~~~

Jane checked out the man's injured shoulder, and declared that while the injury was painful, it was not life-threatening. She bandaged it as well as her limited supplies allowed.

Meanwhile the driver and Miss Martin dragged the bodies of the highwaymen to the side of the road, and Mrs Mortimer left a note which simply said "Highwaymen". While she did so, she recognised the patron from the inn who had appeared inquisitive. She supposed that this man must be Bert.

Miss Martin joined the driver on top of the carriage, while the other ladies boarded the carriage, and they took off for Bridgewater.

Once they were on their way, the footman apologised, 'I am sorry, ma'am, that I could not help. They shot me before I even saw them. And afterwards, while they had us covered, I hoped that those lads would underestimate you, since you all look like proper defenceless ladies.'

'Like all those story book damsels in distress?'

'Just like that... only I knew better.'

'You were right. I only wish that you had not been hurt. But now I need you to rest.'

Now that the excitement had worn off, the footman was happy to comply.

Mrs Mortimer turned to her daughters. 'How do you feel?'

Lydia shrugged. 'At the moment I feel fine. Based on how Lizzy reacted, later on I might not be, but for now I have no problem. I am simply glad that they are dead and we are alive. And that we did not have to *entertain* them. Those men stank.'

'What about you Kitty?'

'I am well enough, although I feel conflicted. Part of me is elated that this time I was not a victim. I did not have to rely on someone else to stop those men violating me. Another part of me knows that killing is wrong, and because of that I feel guilty for feeling elated. It is very confusing.'

Tilly, the maid, who had stayed as quiet during the whole episode as she had been during most of the journey, spoke up for the first time. 'Focus on the part that feels good, Miss Catherine. Those men do not deserve your sympathy or regret. They would have used you and killed you without hesitation. If you had captured them alive, they would be hanged. A clean death from being shot is better than they deserved.' She shrugged and added phlegmatically, 'life is cheap.'

Kitty was startled at the woman's speech, but after giving it some thought thanked her for her words. They did indeed make her feel at least a little better.

She then remembered a question she had wanted to ask Mrs Mortimer. 'Mama, why did you stab those men? Would it not have been easier to shoot them? After all we have enough guns.'

'It would have been easier and probably less messy, but it would have been louder and alerted their friends that there was a problem. They would have been on their guard, and we could not have dispatched them as easily. One or more of us might have gotten hurt,' explained Mrs Mortimer.

'Oh...'

'But now I am truly looking forward to a bath.'

Just before arriving at their destination, Mrs Mortimer donned clean gloves and removed her blood-spattered travelling coat, to appear less gruesome.

~~~oo0Ooo~~~

An hour after the incident, they arrived at Bridgewater. Patrick and James were waiting to greet them when they exited the carriage.

After they exchanged greetings, Mrs Mortimer asked, 'Patrick, do you have a problem with highwaymen in this district?'

'As a matter of fact, in the last few days I have heard some rumours that a new and rather vicious band has moved in. They seem to be becoming quite a problem.'

'Not anymore,' claimed Lydia, holding up her reticule.

When the cousins looked perplexed, she pointed out the bullet hole.

Patrick asked, 'was that hole made on the way in or out?'

'Out, of course.'
~~~

'About an hour down the road there are six corpses of gentlemen of the road. Or at least there were an hour ago,' Mrs Mortimer clarified.

'Are any of you hurt?' Patrick asked in concern.

'Peter Landis, our footman was shot. Could you please send for a doctor?'

'Of course.' Patrick arranged for the footman to be taken care of, and then escorted his visitors inside.

'Is there anything you need right now?'

'I desperately need a bath to wash off the blood.'

'Of course, Grandmama,' he said facetiously, but bowed with the greatest respect.

Mrs Mortimer resisted rolling her eyes at the appellation. While it was an amusing family joke for the boys to call her grandmama, since she was younger than their parents, it sometimes grated on her to be addressed as such by her late husband's step-grandson.

~~~oo0Ooo~~~

Since they were expected, and her habits were known, water had been heated in preparation for her arrival. Therefore, it did not take long until the ladies could clean up from the rigours of journey.

Even though it was tempting, they did not linger in their baths, and soon joined their host in the parlour.

Patrick had sent word of the incident to the local magistrate. That worthy was now in attendance, after having sent men to collect the bodies and search the rest of the area for the highwaymen's horses and equipment, as well as any remaining loot they might have.

After Patrick made the introductions, Mrs Mortimer described the incident to the magistrate. While her account was essentially accurate, she implied that Lydia and Kitty had simply been decoys. The gentleman was having enough problems crediting the women with having successfully defended themselves against six highwaymen. Having a pretty seventeen-year-old girl and an even prettier sixteen-year-old girl shoot one of the men each would have stretched his credulity.
~~~

Since Miss Martin had changed into her favoured outfit of jacket, breeches and boots, and explained that she had been hired as a guard to the ladies, he grudgingly accepted their account, assuming that Miss Martin had done most of the killing.

As they were finishing their discussion, one of the magistrate's men, who was introduced as Mr Black, was ushered into the room. He reported that they had found the bodies, their horse, since only the leader appeared to have owned a mount, as well as some items which they knew were stolen.

He added significantly, 'one of the men was Bert Randall.'

Based on the reaction the name caused, Mrs Mortimer asked, 'I gather that man is familiar to you?'

The Magistrate sighed, 'yes, he is a local hothead and has been giving us problems for years, but never enough to hang him. His brother will not be pleased to hear that Bert is dead.'

'What is he likely to do?' asked Patrick in concern.

'He may decide to come after the ladies in revenge.'

'But only if you tell him who killed his brother. Why not say it was a party of gentlemen who accounted for the band?'

'Because he would never believe that Bert would attack anyone who could fight back.'

'Who knows the identity of the men we killed?' asked Miss Martin.

'Only the people in this room,' explained Constable Black, looking confused.

'In that case, keep the information to yourself, pretend that they were six unknown men, and have them buried. No one need to be the wiser. Mr Randall will probably assume that his brother moved on to greener pastures.'

The Magistrate laughed, 'and so he has.'

<div align="center">~~~ooO0Ooo~~~</div>

The rest of the quick visit passed more pleasantly. When they exchanged the latest news, Patrick and James had the most exciting intelligence to impart.

'Gerald has done it at last. He has proposed to Miss Emily Grantham and they will be married in September.'

'It is about time, one of you considered the future,' laughed Mrs Mortimer. 'When will the rest of you grow up?'

'When we are ready and in our own good time,' James said with great dignity, which caused laughter amongst all his relations.

'But speaking of marriage reminds me, I have been meaning to give Elizabeth and Darcy a belated wedding present. James, would you be available to paint Pemberley? I have seen your landscapes, and Elizabeth still treasures your picture of the view from Oakham Mount. I believe they would be thrilled to have a picture of their home painted by you.'

'Yes, I would be happy to paint Pemberley. It cannot be worse than many of the houses I have seen.'

'Many years ago, I saw their home, and I believe you will be pleasantly surprised.'

'Very well, but it will probably mean that I will have to stay longer than we had originally planned.'

'I am sure that Elizabeth will not mind,' replied Mrs Mortimer, while thinking that another daughter would be pleased by the situation.

It was arranged that James would bring his supplies when he visited for Mary's wedding.

Mrs Mortimer was correct. Kitty was thrilled to have the company of her cousin.

<p style="text-align:center">~~~oo0Ooo~~~</p>

14 Pemberley

Everyone had congregated at Pemberley for Mary's wedding. When Mary and her fiancé arrived, they were accompanied not only by Patrick and James Mortimer as expected, but also by their cousin Charles, Gerald's younger brother.

Charles explained his presence by simply mentioning his mother and wedding preparations, while rolling his eyes. James offered to share a room with his younger cousin.

Darcy, although he was not going to admit it to the ladies, was pleased by the presence of not only Harrison, but also the three cousins. While he liked and respected all the ladies, it was a relief for him to have some male company for a change. Especially since most where close to his own age. He was even more pleased when Harrison's father and brother arrived a day later. They promptly went fishing.

All the sisters, including Georgiana and also Charlotte, enjoyed their reunion.

Once the first excitement was over and they had caught up on each other's news, Mrs Mortimer, Elizabeth, Mary and Kitty, who was to be the bridesmaid, went over the final details of the wedding.

Mary, although blushing furiously, was pleased to discover that Elizabeth had the Dower house cleaned and prepared as a honeymoon cottage for the couple. 'To give you some privacy, but you will be close enough to join our company when you need a break from each other,' Lizzy explained cheekily.

The whole party got along famously, although they had to overcome one issue. The younger men had to call each other by their given names, since having three Mortimers and three Harrisons, made the customary use of surnames confusing. Although out of respect for his age, the groom's father remained Harrison.

Of course, when the final guest arrived, he too was called by his surname, so as not to confuse Charles Mortimer with Charles Bingley. In the excitement of the wedding, no one seemed to notice that while he was still his amiable self, Bingley was quieter and more thoughtful than he used to be.

~~~ooO0Ooo~~~

Mary was excited. Her big day had arrived at last and she was looking forward to being Mrs Harrison. Despite Darcy's fishing expeditions, she had managed to spend some more time with her fiancé, and was even more convinced that she had found her perfect match.

Mrs Mortimer and Elizabeth helped her prepare and dress for the occasion, while the other girls helped Kitty.

The two ladies were well pleased with Mary. Not only did she look beautiful in her new dress, she positively glowed in anticipation.

When everyone was ready, they travelled the five miles to the church in Lambton, where the wedding was to be held. As with Elizabeth, even though both Darcy and Patrick offered to do so, Mrs Mortimer insisted on walking her beloved daughter down the aisle to meet her groom at the altar.

There, Harrison waited, attended by his brother. Since he had stopped wearing his glasses, Harrison could appreciate how beautiful his bride looked. He was now pleased that when he met her, he had not been able to see her properly, since it allowed him to become attracted to her mind and personality. He suspected that her beauty might have deterred him from speaking to her, and he would never have known such happiness as was his today.

When Mrs Mortimer placed Mary's hand in his, he gave her a grateful look and said, 'thank you' before focusing entirely on his bride.

Mary too was oblivious to all but her groom, although they both managed the correct responses when required, albeit with the occasional prompting, to the amusement of the families.

~~~ooO0Ooo~~~

After the ceremony, the couple returned to Pemberley in their own carriage, a wedding present from Mr Harrison, who said, 'it is well and good for you to ride everywhere, but you cannot expect your wife to be as unconcerned with discomfort.'

'And there are no blinds on a horse,' quipped Harrison's brother, making both bride and groom blush, but caused an appreciative chuckle from Lydia.

The wedding breakfast was all that anyone could expect at Pemberley. Mrs Reynolds, who had missed out on seeing her employer married, had spared no effort to ensure everything was perfect for Mrs Darcy's sister.

As expected, Mr and Mrs Harrison left the party as soon as they possibly could. Over the following week they only made occasional brief appearances amongst the family.

~~~oo0Ooo~~~

Mr Bingley had attended yet another wedding. While he was happy for the couples, he was also a little envious. Mary and Harrison had looked ecstatic. Bingley had hoped for such bliss for himself, but so far it had always eluded him.

It was late in the evening and the rest of the party had gone to bed. He too had pretended to go to bed, so as not to force Darcy to be a good host and stay up to keep him company. Tonight, Bingley only wanted the company of his own thoughts.

He had returned to the library, an unusual place for a man who hardly ever opened a book, but he liked the atmosphere in the room. It felt that he was surrounded by wisdom, and he hoped a little would rub off on him.

While he slowly sipped a brandy, he reminisced about the happenings since he left Netherfield.

~~~oo0Ooo~~~

Bingley had left Netherfield after receiving an express from a Mr Sanders, who informed him that his sister Caroline, had been in a serious accident, and was recuperating under the care of his sister.

When he and Louisa had arrived at the address supplied by Mr Sanders, they were immediately taken to see their sister.

When they entered the room, they could barely recognise her, so swathed in bandages was she. The small portions of exposed skin were all bruised.

Caroline was awake and greeted them weakly.

Bingley was shocked and blurted out, 'Caroline, oh my Lord, what happened to you.'

Instead of treating it as a rhetorical question, Caroline answered.

'Do you remember Miss Smythe-Brown?'

'The one who wore even more feathers than you did?' asked Louisa.

'The very same.' Caroline sighed. 'It seems I insulted her when I commented on her lack of looks, accomplishments and suitors.'

'Tact was never your strong suit.'

'As you say. When I returned to town, she invited me to dinner, pretending it was supposed to be a large party. Since I was smarting from what happened at Netherfield, I agreed to attend, thinking I could snare another man, hopefully of even greater status and wealth than Mr Darcy. But there was no party. Only she and Mr Thornton were present. I believe she even gave the staff the night off. And I found out that I was to be the entertainment.'

'Mr Thornton, was he not one of your suitors last year? The one who proposed and you turned him down, rather nastily as I recall,' asked her brother.

Caroline sighed. 'The same. When Mr Thornton let me in, the foyer was badly lit and I mistook him for the butler. He escorted me into the parlour, where I recognised him at last. That was when I found out that no one else was in the house. He lashed out at me and beat me while Miss Smythe-Brown sat and watched, sipping wine. I do not know how long this went on for, but it seemed to be an eternity. Eventually I passed out, and did not awaken until two days later.'

She sighed. 'I was being taken care of by Miss Sanders, whose brother had found me unconscious in an alley. Being a good Samaritan, he had brought me to this house. When I could tell them who I was, he sent for you.'

'Has something been done to bring them to justice?'

'Mr Sanders went to see Miss Smythe-Brown, but she claimed I had arrived at her place severely in my cups and left again immediately because she had company. Mr Thornton backs up her story. It is their word against mine. They hypothesised that I was attacked on the streets, but threatened to imply that I was offering myself to strangers.'

'And you are disliked enough, that not only nobody wants to believe you, but is happy to think the worst of you. After all, many of the *ton* love malicious gossip.'

'Just so,' she sighed again.

'Caroline, I hate to tell you this, but you brought it on yourself. I tried to tell you for years to moderate your manners. But you thought it so very fashionable to be disdainful of everyone. This might be acceptable for members of the nobility, but from the daughter of a tradesman it is deplorable, not to say obnoxious.'

'But I have no wish to toady up to people who look down on me.'

'There is a big difference between toadying and being polite and gracious. Remember how Mrs Mortimer put you in your place? You tried to sneer at her, and because of that, she told you that you had made a laughing stock of yourself at her brother's ball.'

'She did not know it was me…'

'Yes, she did. You were so eager for malicious gossip that you encouraged her to tell you that it was you who had made a fool of yourself.'

'How would you know? Did you discuss this with her when I was not around?'

'I know because Darcy told me.'

When he mentioned that name, she changed the subject. 'You know that I wanted to marry him. He is wealthy, well connected and has a large estate. Even without a title, his family is part of the first circle. We could have made such a fine couple in town…'

'But do you still not understand that Darcy hates being in town? He prefers to be in the country. And you hate the country. On top of that, he wanted a wife who was interested in him for himself, not his wealth, connections and all the rest of it. You never saw him as a man, only a bottomless purse. He despises women like you.'

'I know... but it does not matter anymore. With the damage done to my face, no man will ever look at me again. After all, men are always looking for a pretty face.'

That last comment gave him pause. He too had fallen in love with one pretty face after another. But in each case, there had been something lacking, and so, he had moved on.

Was he so very different from his sister? She wanted wealth and status while he wanted a pretty face and a fun companion. Neither of them had looked for substance in a partner, they had only ever looked at the surface.

Neither of their inclinations were a good foundation for a successful marriage, of at least mutual respect.

He started to wonder how many wonderful women he might have missed the chance of knowing, since he was so focused on physical beauty that he ignored the person belonging to the appearance.

But that was a subject for later contemplation, one which he returned to many times over the next few months.

In the meantime, he had his sister to take care of.

After his initial conversation with Caroline, Bingley went in search of her hosts.

Mr Sanders received Bingley in his study. He very quickly stemmed Bingley's flow of thanks. 'It was the least I could do. I came across your sister purely by chance, since I was taking a shortcut from a friend's house, who lives in a street difficult to access in a carriage. She was a pitiful sight, but I could tell by her clothing that she was not someone from the streets. Since it was not far to the street where my carriage was waiting for me, I was able to convey her thither and brought her to my sister to care for her.'

'You may not think much of your actions, but I am most grateful to you. Is there anything I can do for you...' he left the question hanging, since he did not know anything of the man's circumstances. The house was in a good, but not fashionable neighbourhood. He might be well off, or he might not.

'You could answer some questions for me, if I might be so bold.'

'What would you like to know?'

'Tell me about your sister. What kind of person is she?'

Bingley thought that under the circumstances, the man deserved to know the truth about Caroline, so he proceeded to tell their story.

'I thought as much. There seemed to be something familiar in the situation,' commented Mr Sanders.

When Bingley looked confused, he explained. 'I once was much like your sister. I too gave myself airs, and reached too high above my station. As a reward I was set upon by a bunch of ruffians, who told me they were the message from a certain Lord whom I had mocked. They left me alive to consider my shortcomings. But not all my bones mended cleanly.' He shrugged in self-deprecation. 'I now use a cane.'

'And yet you still managed to carry Caroline? She is not a small woman.'

'When needs must, one can do whatever is necessary.'

'What happened to this Lord?'

'What usually happens in such situations... Nothing.'

~~~oo0Ooo~~~

After this conversation, Bingley and Louisa, at the invitation of Mr Sanders, became daily visitors, until Caroline was well enough to be moved to his own house, to finish recuperating from her injuries. At that point, Louisa and Hurst removed to the country for her confinement.

Bingley was horrified the first time he saw his sister after the bandages had been removed from her face. Her broken nose had been well set, but nothing could disguise the scars on her face.

'I told you that no man will ever want to look at me again. Not even you can bear it,' Caroline said angrily, when she saw her brother's reaction.

'You are wrong. Mr Sanders has asked to see you when you are recovered enough to receive him.'
~~~

'Since I probably owe him my life, I suppose I can tolerate being gawked at once. You can invite him to tea next week,' she replied ungraciously.

Bingley relayed the message during Sanders' next visit. The two men had struck up a friendship over recent weeks, and were often in each other's company.

When Sanders came to tea with Caroline, she was initially rather abrasive. But he ignored her abrasiveness as he ignored her scars. Gradually Caroline thawed towards the man.

Now that she was not part of society anymore, and had no salacious gossip to share, she fell back on her native intelligence and education, and found Mr Sanders remarkably easy to talk to.

Bingley watched in amazement as a friendship grew between these two broken people, until, in June when they married.

<center>~~~ooo0Ooo~~~</center>

Now he sat in the library at Pemberley and thought about all those conversations he observed, and sometimes participated in, between Caroline and Sanders. The ease of their conversation about anything or nothing in particular.

Bingley tried to remember if there had ever been an instance when he felt that relaxed in a conversation with a lady, any lady. When he was not trying to impress her with his charm and amiability. A time when they just talked... like friends.

Eventually, it came to him that there had been exactly three occasions in recent years. And they had all occurred while he was at Netherfield. And they were all with the same lady.

He had enjoyed their conversation, because at the time it meant nothing to him. It was simply a pleasant way to pass the time. The lady did not meet his ideal in looks, and he had been enamoured with Miss Mortimer's beauty during that period. He had thought of the lady fondly, as a friend even, but did not then consider her in a romantic light.

With the experience of watching his sister go from dislike, to friendship, to, dare he say it, even love with Sanders, the friendship he had struck up with that lady took on new meaning.

Instead of starting with an infatuation which withered within weeks, would it not be a better foundation for a marriage to start with friendship? Someone he liked and respected. Would it then not be easy to proceed to love? He had already discovered that beauty was no guarantee for compatibility.

As it happened, the lady whom he had enjoyed talking to, was also a guest at Pemberley. Tomorrow he would try to find out if his new theory was correct.

Bingley finished his drink and went to bed with new hope.

~~~ooo0ooo~~~
~~~

15 Engagements

The following day, Elizabeth and Georgiana had arranged a picnic at the far side of the lake for the whole party, except for the newly married couple, whom they did not expect to see for a few days.

Since the servants had taken the food and blankets to the site, the party could all enjoy an unencumbered stroll. Some took the direct route, while others, including Elizabeth and Darcy opted for a longer walk.

By chance they had an even number of gentlemen and ladies; it was therefore only natural that they paired off.

To give Elizabeth and Darcy a chance for a longer walk, Georgiana decided that she would proceed directly to the picnic site, to ensure one hostess was present. Charles Mortimer offered to accompany her.

Mr Robert Harrison offered his arm to Mrs Mortimer, as she was the only lady close to his own age and he found her to be pleasant company.

Jane and Kitty also were not in the mood for a long walk on a day that promised to get hot, and were accompanied by Patrick and James respectively.

Mr Bingley offered his arm to Charlotte and asked hopefully whether she would enjoy a longer, although leisurely, ramble through the extensive gardens, to which the lady was happy to agree.

Lydia turned to the last gentleman and asked, 'I hope that you are in favour of the longer walk, if you are planning to accompany me?'

Randalph Harrison declared himself pleased with the longer walk and they set off with Elizabeth and Darcy.

<p style="text-align: center">~~~oo0Ooo~~~</p>

Bingley started his conversation with Charlotte by asking, 'are you enjoying your visit with your friend?'

'Indeed, I am. We only saw each other briefly at Easter, and it has been good to spend a little more time with her. Although I am hoping that now that Mary's wedding is over, we will not be quite so rushed.'

'I did not have a chance to get to know Mr Harrison. Do you think he and Miss Mary are a good match?'

'I think they are exceedingly well suited. According to Mary, he is the most brilliant man she has ever met, and he is not frightened off by the fact that Mary is also highly intelligent. Apparently, he is prepared to discuss things with her and listen to what she has to say.'

'I am pleased to hear that. Lately I have come to realise that common interests and respect are an important aspect of a marriage.'

He sighed. 'In the past I thought myself in love with one pretty face after another. But it was only infatuation and it never lasted. I admit I was a shallow and callow youth.'

'And now you are a wise and venerable greybeard?' Charlotte teased, trying not to show how his words affected her.

'I claim neither wisdom nor a grey beard, but watching my sister, Caroline undergo a marked change in recent months, has opened my eyes to my own folly.'

When Charlotte asked about his family, Bingley told her of the happenings in London. While most of her was horrified at the lady's experience, a small part of Charlotte was secretly pleased about the comeuppance Miss Bingley had received, although she felt guilty about such an uncharitable thought. When Bingley explained the friendship and love which had grown between these two unlikely people, she was pleased that the story had a happy ending.

'As you can see, my sister's situation has made me re-evaluate my own perceptions. I realised that I want that kind of friendship and love.'

'I am certain that you will find it someday,' Charlotte assured him, while sadly wondering who the lucky lady would be.

'I may already have found the lady. When I thought about all the ladies I have known, I remembered that I particularly enjoyed conversation with one special lady, whom I already consider a friend.'

Before Charlotte could reply with some platitude to disguise her breaking heart, Bingley shocked her by saying, 'Miss Lucas, you are that very special lady. Would you allow me to court you? I am not as rich and sophisticated as Darcy, or a mental giant like Harrison, but I greatly like and respect you, and I would do everything in my power to make you happy.'

Charlotte stared at him in disbelief for a moment, until a brilliant smile overtook her features. 'Yes, Mr Bingley, I would be pleased and honoured.' Bingley absently noted that the smile made Charlotte look radiant.

Now that they had come to an understanding, their conversation flowed easily while they continued their stroll towards the picnic site.

When they reached the others, who had all arrived before they did, Bingley asked, 'may I tell them?'

As Charlotte blushed, but nodded, Bingley turned to the group and announced, 'Miss Lucas has done me the signal honour to consent to a courtship.'

At the announcement, everyone crowded around to congratulate the couple.

~~~oo0Ooo~~~

After a week, Mr and Mrs Harrison set off for Cambridge to find their perfect home.

Mrs Mortimer insisted that they take all the outriders with them until they reached Cambridge. After which the guards could return to Pemberley.

The Harrisons and Patrick also took their leave, after all, they also had estates to manage.

~~~oo0Ooo~~~

While Mary and Harrison, as well as Bingley and Charlotte were busy with their own concerns, James started his painting of Pemberley.

As Mrs Mortimer had promised, the house was beautiful and perfectly situated in its surroundings. While the gardens near the house had been tamed, there did not seem to be anything artificial about them.

For the first few days after his arrival, when Darcy did not insist on fishing, he had explored the area to find not only the best vantage point to capture the image, but also the right time of day to show the house in its best light, both literally and figuratively.

He opted for the largest canvas he had brought to do the house justice. He spent most of the day at his labours, and when he returned each day, he would not allow anyone to see the picture.

The only exception was Kitty, since as a painter of great skill herself, they could discuss his work.

During one such discussion Kitty asked, 'you are a brilliant painter, but why do you only paint landscapes? Why do you never paint portraits?'

James shrugged. 'When I paint people, the pictures never come out right. Yes, they are quite good technically, but they are flat. There is no life to them. I simply do not have the knack for portraits.'

He gave Kitty an admiring look. 'Unlike you, who excel at them. I have seen the picture you painted of your family, which Patrick has hanging in his study, and every time I look at it, I have the feeling that at any moment Grandmama and the cousins are going to rise from their seats and step out of the picture.'

He shook his head. 'I do not know how you can invest so much life into a portrait.'

Kitty listened carefully and thoughtfully before she asked, 'when you paint a portrait, do you have your subject sit still for hours while you paint them?'

'Yes, of course. How else can I get a proper likeness?'

'That explains why there is no life in your portraits. Your models are effectively lifeless while they sit still. If you want your picture to show animation, your models must be animated. Try chatting with them, make them laugh. If they enjoy the experience of being painted, it will show in the painting.'

James stared at her dumbfounded. 'It cannot be that simple. But if they move about, the folds and drape of their clothing will constantly change…'

'It is their expressions which need to be animated. When you paint their clothing and the background, they can hold still, because then their expressions do not matter.'

'Your explanation may be the answer to my problem.' He searched her expression. 'When I have finished the portrait of Pemberley, would you allow me to paint you, to test your theory?'

Kitty's breath hitched before she answered, 'I would be delighted to prove my point.'

~~~ooo0Ooo~~~

The painting of Pemberley was finished at last, and James presented it to Elizabeth and Darcy on Mrs Mortimer's behalf.

Darcy became quite emotional when he saw his beloved home so lovingly detailed. James had risen very early on several morning to capture the morning light, adding a slightly rosy hue to the white-washed building.

Elizabeth interpreted her husband's speechless expression. 'Thank you, James, the painting is magnificent. I happen to know that morning is William's favourite time of the day to view our home, and you have captured the light perfectly.'

Darcy found his voice again. 'Yes, I agree. Thank you, James. And thank you, Aunt Stephanie, for thinking of this. Once it is framed, this picture will have pride of place in my favourite room.'

'It will be perfect for the library,' agreed his wife.

~~~ooo0Ooo~~~

Since his commission was complete, James asked permission from Mrs Mortimer to paint Kitty.

She gladly granted his request. 'Kitty has provided me with portraits of all members of my family, but I do not have one of herself. I would be delighted to add her likeness to my collection.'

'As it happens, portraits are not my speciality, but Kitty has described her method and she has agreed to let me try it out on her.'

'In that case, I will be pleased to see the result of your experiment.'

James spent the next several days painting Kitty's portrait. He had a few false starts, but eventually seemed to get the knack. It may have helped that they had chosen to conduct the experiment in the conservatory, since the natural background played to his strengths.

The room was also large enough that while he worked at one end, it was not obtrusive or distracting that Mrs Taylor sat quietly reading at the other end of the room.

He chatted with Kitty while he painted, watching expressions chase each other across her features.

James suddenly looked distraught and threw down the brush. 'I cannot do this.'

'Why? What is wrong?' Kitty rushed to his side. 'Tell me, what is the problem?'

James shook his head helplessly, reluctant to explain.

Kitty glanced at the picture for the first time and gasped. She had never in her life looked as beautiful as all that, even though the painting was unfinished.

The main thing missing was, that James had not yet painted her mouth. There was a faint outline, but he had not yet finished it.

'James, this painting is simply beautiful,' she exclaimed. 'Although you have exaggerated. I am not that beautiful...'

'I have painted you as I see you.'

'But why have you not painted my lips? They are not that difficult, and the outline seems accurate.'

James hesitated before answering. 'Because they distract me... since I keep wanting to kiss them,' he grated out at last.

Kitty beamed. 'You want to kiss me?'

'Yes, I do. But it is not right since you are not even out yet,' he replied gruffly.

Kitty laughed. 'James, it is true that I am not out in London society, and have not yet been presented at Court. But I am not a child. I am nearly eighteen years of age. I was merely waiting for Georgiana and Lydia to be ready to be presented. We thought it would be fun to have a season together.' She did not mention that part of her reluctance with society had been that she had no interest in being courted by anyone other than James.

James' expression changed from worried to thoughtful as he listened to her explanation, to mischievous when he slowly leaned forward, and gently brushed his lips against hers. Kitty did not pull back despite having enough notice of his intentions.

'I have wanted to do that for the last two years,' he admitted.

'I did not think you even noticed me.'

'I most certainly noticed you… too much. Which was why I tried to keep my distance.'

Kitty laughed happily in surprise. 'I have been in love with you for years…' She suddenly stopped and blushed at her unintended confession.

'You were?' James asked with a delighted grin. 'I wish I had known that. But I was waiting for your coming out, before saying anything. I wanted you to be old enough to know your mind, and not feel like you were being rushed into anything which you might later regret.'

He lightly brushed her cheek with his fingertips, sending a delicious shiver down her spine.

Kitty laughed softly at the explanation. 'And here I was, delaying my coming out because I did not want to be importuned by other gentlemen….'

'To think, how much time we have wasted…' James said with chagrin.

'Nearly a year.'

'Kitty, I love you too. If I were to ask you to marry me, would you say yes?'

'Yes.'

'Even though I have very little to offer you in the way of material things.'

'Yes.'

'Even though I have to paint to make a living?'

'Yes.'

'Even…'

James got no further. Kitty took his face between her hands and kissed him, albeit briefly. 'Yes, James, I will marry you.'

'I was just going to ask if you would marry me tomorrow.'

'No.'

'No?'

'No. I suppose you want Patrick to stand up with you?'

'Yes, I would like that.'

'In that case we have to give Patrick time to return. I would also like to wait until my eighteenth birthday. We can get married in three weeks.'

Now that Kitty had agreed, James did not hesitate any longer. He pulled his fiancée into his arms and sealed their engagement with a passionate kiss, which Kitty returned in kind.

They might have continued for some time, but were interrupted by Mrs Taylor, whom they had forgotten. 'While I offer my congratulations on your engagement, I think it is time you stopped.'

Mrs Taylor was still in her seat, and she smiled at the couple, but there was no doubt they had reached the limit of her tolerance.

'Yes, ma'am,' James said dutifully, and picked up his discarded brush again.

'Are you not going to speak to Mama?' asked Kitty in confusion.

'I will, as soon as I have finished this picture…'

At last he managed to paint those luscious smiling lips perfectly.

<div align="center">~~~ooO0Ooo~~~</div>

As far as Charlotte Lucas was concerned, as long as Mr Bingley did not change his mind, the outcome of this courtship was never in question.

The pragmatic part of her wanted a home of her own. To be Mistress in her own house and not be a burden on her family any longer.

But there was also a romantic side to her character which she had rigorously repressed for years. The fact that she had developed feelings for Mr Bingley, and had them reciprocated, was a heady sensation.

During the month they spent much of their, chaperoned, time together, conversing and strengthening their friendship, until the right moment came along and Bingley proposed. Charlotte was delighted to accept.

They announced their engagement at dinner that night. While everyone was pleased for them, no one was surprised. Although there was a sotto voce comment, 'what is it about the air at Pemberley? This is the second engagement in as many weeks.'

The assembled family exclaimed in various degrees of consternation, 'Lydia!'

The young lady grinned unrepentantly, 'it is true.'

~~~ooo0Ooo~~~

Three weeks after James proposed, and the day after Kitty's eighteenth birthday, the couple married. Mrs Mortimer again walked down the aisle with yet another daughter, and handed her over to James, while Patrick watched with a pleased, but also slightly wistful smile.

Later that evening the newlywed couple found time to talk.

'Could you not have told me that you loved me earlier?' James asked.

'Why should I make it that easy for you? And you forget, in our society ladies are not supposed to be so forward. At least not unless they had significant encouragement.'

'Even ladies who have been raised in such an unconventional fashion as you and your sisters?'

'Especially us. Otherwise people will think we are hoydens.'

'I thought you *are* hoydens?'
~~~

'We are, of course. But it simply would not do for people to *think* so.'

'Well, I think that you are perfect as you are,' James declared, and proceeded to prove it.

<div align="center">~~~oo0Ooo~~~</div>

16 Returns

Charlotte Lucas and Charles Bingley had stayed a few more days after their engagement at Pemberley, to attend the wedding of Kitty and James, before the two returned to Meryton the day after. They were accompanied by Mrs Taylor to ensure the appearance of propriety.

As soon as they arrived back in Meryton, Bingley immediately approached Charlotte's father to inform him of their attachment. Naturally, Sir William was happy to give his blessing to their union.

Lady Lucas, although initially stunned that her daughter had caught the eye, and even better, the hand of Mr Bingley, was pleased and excited for her daughter.

Once she calmed down from the news, she asked about Charlotte's time at Pemberley and Mary's wedding. She was pleased to hear that Kitty too had made a match and was already married.

Now that Charlotte's own wedding was on the horizon, she could not begrudge the Mortimer girls their good fortune. Especially the three middle girls.

But so much good news simply had to be shared.

When she visited Mrs Phillips to impart all the news which Charlotte had passed on to her, Mrs Bennet too was present.

Since the Mortimer girls, as she thought of them, had been living with Mrs Mortimer for so many years, Lady Lucas had forgotten their origin.

Not so Mrs Bennet. When she heard of Charlotte's engagement, she accused, 'how dare you snatch away Jane's suitor. Have you no shame?'

Lady Lucas defended her daughter. 'Mrs Bennet, you know full well that Jane has been engaged to Colonel Fitzwilliam since Christmas. Although Mr Bingley was showing marked attention to Jane for a while, he then left for town. Charlotte only met him again this summer, and he declared himself for her.'

Mrs Phillips decided to head off the incipient argument and asked about Mary's wedding. Charlotte was happy to speak about her friend's wedding, which of course led to the revelation that Kitty had also married just before Charlotte returned to Meryton.

This news was too much for Mrs Bennet. First, Elizabeth had married the exceedingly eligible Mr Darcy, then Mary had snatched up a very rich husband while in London as a guest of Elizabeth, and now even Kitty, that sickly little girl and also as a guest of Elizabeth, had married a man, whose family had a house in town.

Now even plain old Charlotte Lucas was getting married... to the wealthy Mr Bingley.

And MY beautiful Jane is still unmarried!

It was enough to make even the angels weep, and Mrs Bennet was no angel.

<p style="text-align:center">~~~ooO0Ooo~~~</p>

At Pemberley, the family and guests, which had reduced in number due to the departure of Charlotte, Bingley and Patrick, who had estate business to attend, had just sat down to dinner, when the butler announced, 'The Honourable Mr Richard Fitzwilliam.'

The announcement was immediately followed by the entrance of the gentleman, who looked a little worn but seemed to be in good spirits.

There was a clatter of cutlery being dropped on a plate and the crash of an overturned chair. Richard had only a moment to brace himself before a human-sized projectile collided with him.

Jane without the slightest care for propriety clung to her fiancé and kissed him with the abandoned relief of seeing him alive and apparently well. Richard, who underneath his genial demeanour, had been worried about the reception by the woman he loved, after such an extended separation, was relieved and responded enthusiastically.

The rest of the family and friends looked on with varying degrees of relief, while they gave Jane a chance to greet Richard properly... or rather improperly.

When they broke apart from their kiss, Jane recalled the months of agonised waiting and demanded angrily, 'could you not at least have written, even once?'

'When I was able to get my hands on pen and paper, I did write a letter and dispatched it to you by the fastest possible means.' He pulled a letter from his pocket and handed it to Jane. 'Me.'

Jane looked in consternation from the letter to the sender several times. Relieved anger warred with the preposterousness of the situation, and at last humour won the day. She burst into an exasperated chuckle. 'Only you, Colonel Fitzwilliam, could have the audacity…'

'That appellation is no longer mine,' he interrupted. 'Did you not hear Mr Cavendish? I am now simply Mister Fitzwilliam.'

The family decided that they had been patient long enough and now came forward to greet Richard.

While they were distracted, Mr Cavendish arranged for another place to be set at the table, next to Jane.

Once they sat down again for their meal, Richard told them a little of what had happened to him, to keep him from returning for so long.

'At Bajadoz a bullet grazed my head and almost knocked me out. Another one grazed my horse's rump and he bolted while I was in no shape to control him. Bennings chased after me, but he only caught up with me when we were well behind enemy lines. By the time we stopped, Bennings thought we were halfway to Salamanca.

I do not know much about what happened the first few days. Bennings found a place for us to hole up in, and looked after me until I was well enough to ride again. That took quite a while as I suffered from headaches and dizziness for weeks. For a while I could not even remember how we came to be in that situation.

Once I was well enough to sit a horse, we spent time trying to sneak back to our own lines. Fortunately, we were able to observe the French troop movements, and when we returned to our regiment, I could report on them. It saved me from looking like a deserter.'

'I think that scar had something to do with it as well,' Jane commented on the scar just above his temple.

'Perhaps.' Richard shrugged off his injury. 'When we reached Lisbon, I had something of a relapse. I was lucky that Bennings was still with me to look after me, since the doctors wanted to stick me into a hospital with others who had suffered similar injuries. Eventually I was well enough to get transport back to England. As soon as I arrived, I resigned my commission and came here.'

'I am glad that you are back and still in one piece,' commented Darcy, 'but could you not have sent an occasional note. We have all been worried.'

'I did write twice, but I gather those letters never made it here.'

'They did not.'

Richard sighed. 'That is the problem about trying to send letters from a war-zone. But enough of me. I would like to hear what has happened while I have been away.'

His wish was granted, and during the rest of the meal, Darcy and the others brought him up-to-date.

When Harrison was mentioned Richard asked, 'tall, excessively bright and wears glasses?' Darcy confirmed the identification. 'I met him at Cambridge, we were in some of the same classes.'

Richard received the news of Bingley's engagement with great pleasure. 'I am glad he has grown up and realised that there is more to women than just a pretty face.'

'Says the man who is engaged to the most beautiful woman of our acquaintance.'

Richard's reply 'but I love her more for her spirit than her physical beauty,' made Jane blush with pleasure.

Finally, they came to Kitty's and James' wedding, for which Richard heartily congratulated them.

'It sounds like it has been an eventful year. I am glad that I will be sticking around, since I like weddings.'

At that point, he could not repress a huge yawn. 'But I am done for. I am afraid it has been a long day for me. If you will excuse me, I will seek my bed. It has been a while since I had the pleasure of a soft bed with clean sheets.'

~~~ooO0Ooo~~~

The following day several conversations were taking place.

Richard and Jane went for a stroll in the garden after breakfast, to allow them to speak privately.

'I think we should wait with the wedding,' Richard said cautiously.

Jane was taken aback. 'Why, Richard? At Christmas you seemed to be eager to be married as soon as possible. What has changed? Do you wish to break our engagement?'

'NO! That is the last thing I want,' he exclaimed in consternation. 'Thoughts of you were at times the only thing that kept me going. Wanting to return to you.'

He shook his head, calming down a little. He looked uncomfortable and rather embarrassed. 'It is just that I was hoping that once we were married, we would sleep in the same bed.' He valiantly ignored Jane's furious blush at the mention of their marriage bed. He sighed. 'But Bennings tells me that I am not good company at night at the moment. Apparently, I thrash around a lot just before I wake up from a nightmare. And I am not quiet when I do so.'

'I gather Corporal Bennings does not hold and comfort you on those occasions.'

'Of course not. What do you take me for?'

'A man who has nightmares because he has seen and done too much for a sane mind to bear, and who needs comforting.' Jane gave him a sad little smile. 'The same way that last year I needed comforting when I woke up with nightmares. Lydia and Mary spent many a night with me, to be on hand when I woke up from a ghastly dream, where I relived my actions to save Kitty.'

Richard looked at her in astonishment. 'Having Mary and Lydia with you helped? They did not mind?'

'Yes, they helped and no, they did not mind. We are sisters, and sisters help each other. And so, incidentally, do husbands and wives. At least in a marriage built on love and respect.'

'I had not wanted to impose my... restlessness on you...' Richard now looked rather sheepish.
~~~

'It is no imposition. I found that, when I had one of my sisters holding me, I was able to go back to sleep, and I usually slept soundly after that. I do not know if that would work for you, and there is only one way for you to find out… After we are married,' Jane concluded firmly.

'Yes, ma'am.' Richard saluted facetiously, covering his embarrassed gratitude with humour. 'How soon would you like to get married?'

'If we get a common licence, we could be married in a few days.'

'Would the day after tomorrow suit you?'

'Can your parents get here in time?'

'Yes, otherwise I would have suggested today. But mother would never forgive me if I were to exclude her.'

~~~ooO0Ooo~~~

'Not again,' cried Elizabeth. She was uncertain if she felt consternation or elation. 'Poor Mrs Reynolds. Mary's wedding had been planned for months, and was therefore not a problem. Kitty and James gave us three weeks to prepare. But two days…'

Elizabeth sighed theatrically. 'Jane, if you were not such a dear sister, I would be tempted to be vexed with you.'

'Think of it as a rescue mission for your new brother.' When Lizzy looked confused, Jane added, 'you remember the nightmares I used to have because of that incident last year? How much worse do you think it might be for someone who has seen as much as a soldier.'

'Was that battle at Badajoz so very bad?'

'Thousands of men killed or wounded.'

'Why do men do such stupid things, like make war. The leaders argue, and the average man or woman, who generally just wants to live in peace and get on with their lives, is made to suffer for their stupidity and arrogance.' Elizabeth shook her head sadly.

She recovered herself. 'Very well, we will mount a rescue mission to save your brave, retired soldier from his spectres.' She rang the bell for the housekeeper.
~~~

'Mrs Reynolds, you have had significant practice arranging wedding breakfasts in recent times. I am afraid we need you to cater yet another one.'

'I thought so, when I heard the Colonel had returned. How much time do we have to prepare?'

'Until Lord and Lady Matlock arrive.'

'Oh dear. I had better hurry up then. If I am not mistaken, the Lady will be here no later than tomorrow afternoon, even if she has to carry the horses.'

'You know our family so well, Mrs Reynolds. What would we do without you?'

'Drive another housekeeper to distraction,' replied the lady with a fond grin. 'Is there anything else I can do for you in the meantime? Arrange a ball, prepare a banquet to host the King?'

'No, Mrs Reynolds. We are keeping it simple. One wedding breakfast and one Earl with his Countess. No balls and no royalty. At least in the foreseeable future. I will let you know if our plans change.'

'Thank you, Mrs Darcy. I would appreciate a day's notice...' Despite her words, Mrs Reynolds returned to her duties in high spirits.

<p style="text-align:center">~~~ooO0Ooo~~~</p>

After Richard sent an express to Matlock, informing them of the prodigal son's return and his desire to wed as soon as possible, Darcy had taken the men off on secret men's business, also known as fishing.

Mrs Mortimer was busy writing letters to Mr Phillips and Mr Gardiner, informing them of Jane's upcoming wedding, and the need for her dowry to be released. She expected Jane and Richard would get a pleasant surprise. As her guardian, Mr Phillips had kept her informed about the state of the girls' dowries, but since at Christmas there had not been enough time to obtain accurate figures, the couple only knew that her dowry was 'generous'.

Mr Gardiner had employed the same strategy of investments for all the girls. He had invested half the contributions in his everyday business, at a good rate of return, and the other half in high-risk ventures, which brought a correspondingly high profit.

While Jane's and Lydia's dowries, did not quite match up to her adopted daughters' dowries of thirty thousand pounds each, they would still receive twenty-five thousand pounds each. An amount which was exceedingly respectable for the daughters of a minor gentleman.

While everyone else was busy, the sisters had a chance to chat.

Under the circumstances they understandably discussed marriage.

'Three weddings in one summer, that is almost unheard of in one family.'

'Can you imagine the fuss Mrs Bennet would have made if this were happening in Meryton?'

'Ugh, that does not bear thinking about. The nerves and vexations...'

'Not to mention the bragging.'

Lydia, uncomfortable with the turn the discussion had taken, decided to change the subject, and could not resist to tease Georgiana. 'When are you going to get married? You are the next oldest, and you have had a most attentive swain for several months now.'

Georgiana blushed. She did not think anyone had noticed the attention she had received from the youngest Mortimer 'cousin'.

'I may be the next oldest, but I am not even out yet,' she defended herself.

'But it is never too early to look, and Charles is rather handsome. It seems to run in the family.'

'And who have you been looking at? Patrick is very pleasing to look at, and I have noticed you flirting with him.'

'Good heavens, no. I like him well enough, and he is fun to tease, but he is too old and stuffy for me.'

Jane mused, 'Gerald is engaged, James is now married, and Charles seems to be interested in Georgiana. But I have never seen Patrick show a preference for any girl. I wonder who he is looking for.'

Elizabeth reminded Jane, 'remember the year we had our coming out in London? He was there looking for a wife. It seemed that he had found someone, but it never went anywhere since she was only interested in his estate.'

'Kitty, has James said anything about Patrick's interest?'

'No. He is just as much in the dark as everyone else, although he suspects there is someone.'

~~~ooO0Ooo~~~

Mrs Reynolds knew the family well indeed. The following afternoon Lord and Lady Matlock arrived, having left their estate early in the morning.

Lady Susan greeted her son enthusiastically, even if only briefly, before she demanded a conference with Jane, Elizabeth, Mrs Mortimer and Mrs Reynolds.

She was a little shocked when she was casually informed that everything was under control.

'How can everything be under control when my irresponsible son has only given you two days' notice?' she demanded.

'Because we have had practice this summer,' was the phlegmatic reply from her hostess.

Mrs Mortimer took pity on her friend and explained. 'This is the third wedding since July, and we also had an engagement. You know what they say, practice makes perfect. And if not perfect, we can do a creditable job in the time available.'

'Richard and I do not wish a big, elaborate wedding. We simply want to get married in the company of our families,' explained Jane. 'And the food Mrs Reynolds and her staff serve us on a regular basis is wonderful. We do not need anything else.'

'Wedding dress?' asked Lady Susan succinctly.

'That has been ready for months,' said Jane.

'And I made sure we brought it along. Just in case.' Mrs Mortimer cut in before Lady Susan could ask.

'Decorations for the church?'

'I sent several footmen and a carriage full of flowers from the garden to the church.' Mrs Reynolds explained her part.
~~~

'And I am doing my best to keep the bride calm,' Elizabeth added cheekily.

'Did anyone think of a ring?'

'Yes, but we expected that you would bring one.' Mrs Mortimer smirked when Lady Susan produced the object from her reticule.

'Then why did I rush to get here as quickly as I did?'

'Why did you?'

~~~oo0Ooo~~~

As expected, the latest wedding went off without any problems whatsoever. The church was again beautifully decorated.

Mrs Mortimer yet again walked another ecstatic daughter, even though not formally adopted, down the aisle and handed her over to yet another loving man.

The couple managed to say their vows without prompting, and Darcy, as the best man handed a ring to the groom.

The wedding breakfast was more elaborate than the guests expected. It seemed Mrs Reynolds was trying to make a point.

Kitty and James had vacated the Dower House to give the newly married couple some privacy.

During the night, Richard roused briefly from an unpleasant dream, but quickly went back to sleep in the loving and comforting arms of his wife.

~~~oo0Ooo~~~

17 New Beginnings

September arrived, and with it the date when the guest had to leave Pemberley.

A convoy made its way south. Mrs Mortimer had presented her smaller carriage to Kitty and James, while Darcy had gifted his cousin with one of his own smaller carriages.

To give the two couples more privacy, Mrs Mortimer conveyed the rest of her party, plus Corporal Bennings who had come with Richard.

Charles, who had no longer an excuse to remain at Pemberley rode with them to their first stop at Bridgewater.

Richard carried with him a letter of introduction from his mother to the steward at Meadowbrook, his new estate. Since the estate was only ten miles past Cambridge, Mrs Mortimer chose to return to Meryton via that city, keeping the whole party together until then.

It gave her the opportunity to see Mary, who had written to say that she and Harrison had found the perfect house. It was large enough for a family, with a substantial garden and conveniently located to the university. She had also asked for the family to stop by on their way home.

~~~oo0Ooo~~~

Mary was pleased to welcome her now extended family to her new home, although she explained that she had barely started with the redecorating.

'How are you enjoying the society in Cambridge?' asked her mother.

'Well enough. I have not yet met many ladies, although I have met several of Reginald's students, who have come to tea. It was most amusing to watch their reactions, when I was able to converse about topics which they used to consider too esoteric for simple female minds.'
~~~

'Used to… I gather you have enlightened them?'

'Reginald encouraged me to do so. Although one of the students brought a friend from the Analytical Society, whose ideas had me struggling to follow. A fellow by the name of Charles Babbage. He propounded an idea of building a mechanical calculating machine, which he calls a difference engine. Although I found the concept fascinating, I admit I floundered trying to understand him.'

'I would not worry about it,' interjected her husband, 'hardly anyone understands him.'

'I do not worry. Everyone has limitations. But I am looking forward to meeting some of the professors and their wives.' She gave Harrison a playful look. 'While I have learnt to enjoy male company, I miss having female companionship.'

'Mary, you know that Richard and I will be only ten miles away. I am certain that we will be able to visit regularly,' offered Jane.

'That would be wonderful,' agreed Mary.

Mrs Mortimer was pleased that the sisters would have support nearby.

~~~oo0Ooo~~~

Richard Fitzwilliam had thoroughly enjoyed the journey from Pemberley to Cambridge with his new wife. He was grateful to Mrs Mortimer for providing transport for Corporal, now Mr Bennings, which allowed him to be more openly affectionate with his new and delightful wife.

He was happy that Jane had insisted on marrying immediately, rather than waiting for his nightmares to go away on their own. While they still woke him up most nights, they were not as bad as they had been, and generally he was able to go back to sleep as soon as he realised that Jane was with him. Although there had been occasions when they had both been in the mood to stay awake.

They had spent a day with Mary and Harrison, before setting off on the last leg of the journey to Meadowbrook, this time accompanied by Mr Robert Bennings, who would be taking on the duties of assistant studmaster.
~~~

They covered the ten miles at a leisurely pace, and after two hours turned into the gates of the estate. They were greeted by a sight of lush paddocks populated by mares with foals at their sides.

Jane, who looked eagerly at her new home, through the window at her side of the carriage, suddenly checked the view on the opposite side, and discovered an almost identical sight.

'How many mares did your mother say the estate had?' she asked her husband.

'There were forty mares in foal, according to the last report she received from her studmaster.'

'I wonder how good that man is with numbers. I counted at least that many on my left, and there appear to be a similar number on our right.'

Richard looked at her in consternation. 'Mother had been complaining that the stud was not doing as well as she had expected, but she had been too busy to investigate.'

'Some men count on the gentry being absentee landlords to line their own pockets,' opined Bennings. 'You might want to tread carefully so as not to spook your manager.'

'It seems that your first job is to count noses, and talk to the stable lads. Find out who might be in on it.'

'Yes, Sir,' Bennings grinned. He had been afraid that things would get boring when he retired from the army. It seemed he might get some excitement after all.

They warned the footmen, and when they arrived at the house one of the footmen opened the carriage door while the other remained hidden at the back. Jane too was requested to remain concealed in the carriage.

As Richard and Bennings exited the coach, they saw a man approach them from the house.

'I am Mr Rousten, the manager of this estate, and who might you be?'

'I am the Honourable Mr Fitzwilliam, the new owner of this estate. Here is my letter of introduction from Lady Matlock,' replied Richard, and handed the man the letter.

Rousten did not invite him into the house. Instead he opened and read the letter while he kept Richard and his party waiting,

When he finished reading, Rousten looked up and let out a peculiar whistle. Within moments, five men carrying cudgels came running.

'It seems we have here some very brazen horse thieves,' Rousten told his men, while scrunching up the letter and dropping it on the ground.

'It appears that you will get your wish. You will not be bored in retirement after all,' Richard commented to Bennings and sighed. 'Unlike me who only wanted peace and quiet.'

'You are going to have lots of peace and quiet soon enough,' growled the largest of the men, as he advanced on Richard, while he raised his cudgel.

'Do you mean to kill us all?'

'That is what we do to trespassers who try to steal our horses,' the large man replied.

'I am not a trespasser, I am the Honourable Richard Fitzwilliam, son of the Earl of Matlock, and the new owner of Meadowbrook.'

'You would say anything to avoid what is coming to you.' The man hesitated a moment, lowering his weapon.

'So said the letter your master threw on the ground.'

'Too bad that Mr Fitzwilliam never arrived...' the large man grinned nastily. 'If you had arrived after the October sales, it might have worked out differently. Too bad... for you.'

He raised his cudgel again, this time with serious intent, when a shot from the rear of the carriage felled him.

Rousten and his thugs looked up and saw the second footman pointing another gun at them.

While they were distracted, the footman who had remained at Richard's side drew two pistols from his pockets, as did Bennings, while Richard pulled the sword from his walking stick.

'You may wish to reconsider your options,' Richard said to Rousten. 'Call your men off, or you will all die.'

'Maybe, maybe not,' Rousten said with a smirk as he glanced past the carriage.

Jane had remained in the carriage as requested, but she had pulled her own guns to support the men, and watched the interaction with a sense of sadness. Here was another group of men willing to kill for gain. She hoped that they would see reason and surrender. Her musing was interrupted by the squeaking of the right-hand carriage door.

When she looked, she saw yet another man with a cudgel trying to enter the carriage. His intention was clear enough. She was to be a hostage to subdue her husband. They expected her to be weak and defenceless. The thought made her angry. She raised one of her guns and pointed it at the man's face, while giving him a viciously pleased smile.

It was the smile almost more than the gun which stopped him in his tracks. He lowered his weapon, and put it on the floor before raising his hands in surrender.

Jane called out over her shoulder, 'Mr Rousten, you had better surrender, since your man in the carriage does not want to die.'

She took careful aim and fired, nicking the ear of her potential assailant. He screamed.

Rousten looked horrified, while Richard grinned. 'That's my wife.'

<center>~~~ooO0Ooo~~~</center>

After that, the situation was brought swiftly under control. The men were tied up, and Richard retrieved his letter. He sent Benning and a footman to discover who else might be in charge or who could shed light on the situation

Benning shortly returned with a middle-aged woman, who was the housekeeper. When she saw the restrained men, she walked up to Rousten and slapped him.

'I told you that your bullying ways would end badly for you, and I am glad that I was proven right. You will never have a chance to lay another hand on my daughter.'

She turned to Richard, 'I am sorry, Sir. I could not inform Lady Matlock of the situation here. He threatened to kill my daughter if I did.'

'I do not blame you, Mrs Jennings. But tell me, are there any more of his supporters?'

Since the seven men were the only ones who had been in league, Richard and his party were soon established in the house.

The magistrate and constable were sent for, and after explaining the situation which had prevailed for the last year at Meadowbrook, the miscreants were taken away to be charged.

It turned out that Rousten had reported that the stud had made just enough money to break even, and pocketed the excess profits for years. Over the last year the rest of the staff had become suspicious, and he had brought in the bullies to ensure no word of his deception came to light.

It appeared that he had planned to decamp after pocketing all the profits of the October sales.

Instead Richard would do very well out of those sales. While Rousten may have been dishonest, he did know his business of breeding horses. At least now, the right people would profit.

The only fly in the ointment was that for the first week at Meadowbrook, Richard's nightmares flared up again. Fortunately, due to her own experiences, Jane was prepared and helped him calm down again. Although, considering the methods she had to employ at times, it made her wonder how long it would be before they were presented with the consequences.

That thought made both of them smile.

<center>~~~ooo0Ooo~~~</center>

On leaving Cambridge, the party had split up. Mr and Mrs Fitzwilliam, accompanied by Bennings, had headed for Meadowbrook, while the others returned to Meryton. Kitty and James planned to spend a few days at Brook Hall, to allow Kitty to pack her belongings, before moving on to London.

The day after they arrived, they received a visit from Charlotte Lucas and Charles Bingley, who came to deliver an invitation to their wedding, which was to be held the following week.

Charlotte admitted, 'I will be well pleased to be married at last, because then, Charles and I can leave the area.'

'You are giving up the lease for Netherfield? I thought you liked it here?'

'I liked it well enough until our banns were read for the first time,' he sighed and looked at his fiancée.

Charlotte explained. 'Would you believe Mrs Bennet objected to the marriage on the grounds that Charles had to marry Jane? She was very shrill and vocal about it. Mr and Mrs Phillips had to forcibly remove her from the church. Although Mr Phillips returned within minutes and explained to the congregation quite firmly that Jane was engaged to Colonel Fitzwilliam, and papers had been signed to that effect. He also pointed out that Jane had no interest in marrying Mr Bingley. But speaking of Jane, where is she? I was hoping to speak to her.'

'She is at an estate called Meadowbrook, near Newmarket, with her husband, The Honourable Mr Richard Fitzwilliam,' Mrs Mortimer said with a smile.

'Jane is married? And the Colonel has returned? That is wonderful news.'

'It will also help to calm down Mrs Bennet. Hmmm?'

'I too am glad that Richard is back. I was worried that we had not heard from him,' Bingley agreed.

'You are welcome to spread the news through your mother,' Mrs Mortimer suggested to Charlotte. 'Although I suggest you avoid mentioning the name and the location of the estate. Mrs Bennet might get it into her head to visit...'

'Jane would hate that, but she would be too polite to say so, I think.'

'I think she would not admit the lady into her home, but there is no need to force the issue, since it can be avoided.'

'Now that the dragon has been laid to rest, do you still wish to leave the area?'

Bingley and Charlotte looked at each other. 'Yes, we do,' he said. 'While the bone of contention has been removed, I would rather not have Charlotte be the target of snide remarks. I thought to look for an estate somewhere in Derbyshire. We both would like to have friends close at hand.'

'Somewhere near Pemberley then,' surmised Mrs Mortimer.

'Precisely.'

~~~oo0Ooo~~~

Kitty and James stayed long enough to attend Charlotte's wedding.

Charlotte had asked her younger sister Maria to be her bridesmaid. While Maria was pleased to be the bridesmaid at her sister's wedding, the looks she was giving the couple were poorly veiled incredulity that Mr Bingley had chosen her sister, as well as envy.

Mrs Bennet, who was also amongst the guests, congratulated the happy couple, but also made a snide comment that she was happy that Charlotte had married Mr Bingley, thereby saving her Jane for the son of an Earl.

The Mortimer ladies who observed all this, felt it was for the best that Mr and Mrs Bingley were leaving Meryton.

~~~oo0Ooo~~~

Kitty had packed all her belongings at Brook Hall, and the day after Charlotte's and Mr Bingley's wedding, she and James departed for London.

On the way James told her about the family's townhouse where he planned for them to live, at least in the short term, until he could find a house to buy for the two of them. It had been bequeathed by Mrs Mortimer's husband to his oldest son, who in turn had left it to Patrick.

While Kitty had been to London on many occasions, they had always stayed at Mrs Mortimer's house. Since her cousins had all been single men, they had come to visit, rather than invite them to their house.

Now that he was married, James planned to be somewhat more sociable.

When they arrived at Patrick's townhouse, they were greeted by the butler, who appeared to have a problem maintaining his professional stoic demeanour. 'I am sorry, Sir. I have had instructions from the Master that you are not to live in this house. He enclosed this letter to you to explain.'

James accepted the letter in astonishment. There was no reason for his brother to deny them accommodation in this house. The brothers, despite their differences in interest had always been close. Still standing in the foyer, he ripped open the envelope and read with amazement.

Dear James

Your wedding present awaits you next door at number 10.

I hope that you and your bride enjoy it.

Your affectionate brother

Patrick

James handed the missive to Kitty, who was equally as baffled.

The butler cleared his throat, 'If I may be so bold and to escort you?' he offered as he ushered the confused couple out the door.

They went down the front steps and walked to the next house and up to its front door. The butler knocked on the door, which was immediately opened... by the housekeeper of Patrick's house.

She beamed at the couple as she curtsied. 'Welcome to your new home, Mr Mortimer, Mrs Mortimer.' She opened the door wide and ushered them inside.

'I have tried to get the house ready for you, since I received your brother's message, and I have hired some staff, subject to your approval, of course. I am to tell you that the house will need decorating to your taste, but it is sound structurally, and even though the décor is a little dated at present, the house is perfectly liveable.'

James started to recover during her speech. 'Thank you, Mrs Brown. Could you show us around, after we have had some tea and refreshed ourselves?'

'Certainly, Sir. If you would like to step into the parlour,' she indicated the room, 'I will have tea brought to you in a minute.'

Kitty and James entered the parlour, and while the décor was rather too ornate and not quite to their taste, it was clean and in good condition.

While they were still looking around, Mrs Brown returned, accompanied by a maid carrying a tea tray, which she set on a table and exited the room after a quick curtsy.

Mrs Brown handed him another letter, before leaving them to enjoy their tea.

While Kitty poured the tea, James opened the letter.

Dear brother

I hope you will forgive me my little joke. When you announced your wedding, I immediately thought that you should have your own home for your bride.

I knew this house was on the market, but was uncertain if I could arrange the purchase before you arrived in London. Therefore, I did not say anything to raise your expectations.

Since you are now reading this letter, I guess my surprise worked. This house is my wedding present to you and Kitty.

May you live in it for many happy years.

Your affectionate brother

Patrick

James read the letter to his wife, who smiled happily. 'I guess, I will start decorating sooner than I thought.' She suddenly turned impish. 'At least we will not have to be satisfied with second rate paintings.'

~~~oo0Ooo~~~
~~~

18 Relations

Lydia simply had to get out of the house. Without her sisters to distract her, her restlessness would no longer be contained. She changed into her riding habit and asked for a horse to be saddled. 'Whichever needs the exercise,' she instructed.

When she arrived at the stables, she was handed the reins for a sturdy gelding. He was not the fastest horse available, but he had strength and endurance. Lydia was content with the choice, since she was in no hurry to get anywhere, but needed time by herself.

She took off, criss-crossing the estate and finally deciding to enjoy the view and the serenity from the top of Oakham Mount.

~~~ooO0Ooo~~~

Lydia smiled and took a relieved breath. As her sister Elizabeth had so often found, Oakham Mount was a place where the stress of the day held no sway.

She dismounted and tethered the gelding to a shrub. Lydia was about to sit down on a convenient rock, when she heard an unexpected sound. Someone whimpered in the bushes behind her.

When she investigated, she found a boy of about six years of age lying on the ground. To her astonishment she recognised Joshua Bennet, whom she had seen a few times in Meryton with his mother.

She knelt next to the boy just as he opened his eyes.

'Are you an angel, come to take me to heaven?' he whispered, then grimaced because his movement caused him pain.

'Not at all. I am your sister, and I will take you home.'

'Mama will be so very vexed with me, and never let me out of her sight again,' he said mournfully. 'She is so worried that I might get hurt.'
~~~

'It seems that she was right to be worried, young man. Now, very carefully, move your arms and then your legs. Let me know if anything hurts.'

Joshua followed her instructions. 'My left ankle hurts abominably, my left shoulder a little, and my head hurts.'

'Can you sit up if I help you?' When he was sitting up, she told him, 'Excellent. You are very brave. I will get my horse.'

When Lydia returned with the gelding, Joshua took one look at the big horse and exclaimed, 'I cannot get up on him, he is as big as a house.'

'I will lift you, but I will need you to grab the pommel and throw your leg over.'

'But you cannot lift me. You are a lady. You cannot be strong enough,' the boy protested.

Lydia grinned at him. 'I am stronger than I look.'

She helped him to his feet and had him facing the horse. She crouched behind him and grasped his waist firmly. 'Get ready. Now.'

Lydia straightened up and lifted her brother high enough that he could pull himself onto the horse. 'See, that was easy.'

'I cannot reach the stirrups,' Joshua complained.

'I know, but I can. Scoot forward a bit.'

Joshua complied and Lydia mounted behind him. With one hand she pulled the boy close, while she took the reins with the other. Lydia nudged the horse into a gentle walk down Oakham Mount in the direction of Longbourn.

~~~ooo0Ooo~~~

Despite the horse's surefootedness in his gentle walk, Joshua was jostled enough that he frequently hissed in pain.

To distract him, Lydia asked, 'how did you come to be injured?'

'Jasper, our horse, was spooked when we accidentally flushed a covey of quails. I did not expect him to rear and I fell off, while he ran away.'
~~~

'Did you not have someone with you to help you? I am surprised that your mother would let you go riding on your own.'

Lydia noticed a slight flush on Joshua's face as he answered. 'Mama does not know I went out by myself.'

'Let me guess. She does not want you to go out at all…'

'No, she does not. She will not even allow me to go out on the old mare with our stablemaster. She never lets me do anything that is fun.' Joshua now pouted. 'She does not want me to climb trees, or play with other boys or do anything.'

'That must indeed be boring for you,' mused Lydia.

Now that he seemed to have a sympathetic ear, the floodgates opened and Joshua poured out a litany of woes.

Even though it had been many years since Lydia had lived at Longbourn, she could see many similarities in their upbringing.

Joshua was given every material thing that he could possibly want, but he did not receive what he craved. An opportunity to learn, to experience new things, and to be himself.

Lydia felt sorry for her brother, but, given the personality of Mrs Bennet, she did not think there was anything she could do to help.

<p style="text-align:center">~~~ooO0Ooo~~~</p>

They had nearly reached Longbourn when they encountered Mr Smith, the stablemaster of the estate. 'Ah, Miss Lydia, you have found our runaway,' he exclaimed in relief when he saw the pair.

'I did not run away. I just went for a ride. It was the horse who ran away,' protested Joshua.

'That is why you should never ride out alone. You have had us all worried, because your mount returned without you.'

'I am sorry, Mr Smith. Do not blame Jasper, he was startled by a covey of quails.'

'Very well, Master Bennet. I will keep that in mind. Now I have to signal that you have been found.' He addressed Lydia. 'The agreed signal is two shots. I hope your horse does not startle easily.'

'No, Mr Smith. Our horses are all used to the noise,' Lydia replied, but as a precaution grasped the reins more firmly and tightened her grip with her legs.

When Mr Smith fired his two shots, Lydia's mount tossed his head but did not react otherwise.

'Shall I relieve you of your passenger?' Smith offered, but Lydia declined, explaining about the injuries.

Soon they rode into the forecourt of Longbourn.

Alerted by the shots, several of the servants were already returning to the house. Mrs Hill, who had stayed to look after a frantic Mrs Bennet, followed her Mistress out the front door.

'Joshua, where have you been? Have you no consideration for my nerves, disappearing the way you did. How you vex me.'

Mr Smith had dismounted and passed the reins of his horse to a nearby servant. He carefully lifted Joshua of Lydia's mount, and held the boy in his arms, explaining, 'Master Bennet has had a slight mishap and sprained his ankle. I shall carry him to his room, if you will allow.'

'Injured? How did that happen? Lydia did you take your hatred for me out on my son?'

Lydia gave the agitated woman a disgusted look, but before she could say anything, Joshua exclaimed, 'Mama, how can you say such a horrid thing. Miss Lydia rescued me. My horse spooked and threw me, and then she found me and brought me home.'

Lydia straightened up to her full height and added, 'Mrs Bennet, you labour under a misapprehension. What I feel for you is so much worse than hatred... I am completely indifferent to your fate.'

Mrs Bennet had the grace to blush. Her own guilt for her actions towards her daughters, when Joshua was born, made her assume the worst about the girls she had rejected.

'You do not hate me? You have forgiven me for my poor actions?'

'No, Mrs Bennet. I have simply accepted that you are a poor excuse for a human being, and you are not worth wasting a moment's thought or unease.'

Mr Smith, who thought that it would be to everyone's benefit if he took Joshua away from this confrontation, carried the boy to his room and asked for a servant to be sent for Mr Jones, the apothecary.

Mrs Hill also stepped into the house to be out of sight and ensured that Mrs Bennet was not being embarrassed in front of her servants. Although she stayed close enough to listen, in case she was needed.

'You feel nothing for me…'

'Be grateful that my sisters and I have had an excellent role-model in Mrs Mortimer. She taught us not to waste feelings on someone unworthy, otherwise you would have been reviled in all of Meryton as an unfit mother.'

It occurred to her that she had spoken the literal truth. She truly did not care about this grasping woman. For the last seven years, even though Lydia called her Aunt, Mrs Mortimer had been a better mother to her than Mrs Bennet ever was.

Mrs Mortimer had loved her for herself, and respected her enough to let her make her own choices, provided those choices did not hurt anyone else. Lydia had been encouraged to learn and grow.

Mrs Bennet on the other hand, was trying to stifle the natural inclinations of her son out of fear and a desperate craving for security.

Lydia sighed, remembering Joshua's words. 'Give Joshua a chance to live and be himself,' she advised.

'I must keep him safe. If anything should happen to him, I will lose my home…'

Lydia glared. 'I changed my mind. You disgust me. You do not care about Joshua as your son, but merely as a means of keeping your home. You are prepared to make his life miserable, just to ensure that you can live in comfort. Heed my warning. If you continue in this way, by the time he grows up and comes into his own, he will not want to know you. You will lose what you are so desperately clutching.'

Mrs Bennet was horrified. Although what Lydia was saying made a ghastly sort of sense, it could not be true. Joshua would never reject her for looking after him. No Lydia was wrong. She must be wrong. There was only one explanation. 'How can you be so cruel to your mother. You are just like Jane, who not even invited me to her wedding. I should have been there as the mother of the bride, when my beautiful Jane married the son of an Earl.'

'You abdicated the role of being our mother the day after Joshua was born. This is of your own making. You made that choice,' Lydia replied calmly. But I think you should go and see to your son.'

Mrs Bennet was glad of the excuse to get away from this most uncomfortable conversation.

Before Lydia could leave, Mr and Mrs Phillips arrived.

'Joshua has been found?' Mr Phillips asked, while acknowledging Lydia with a nod.

'Yes, Uncle, I found him on Oakham Mount. It appears he wanted an opportunity to breathe freely.'

'How did he get that far?' Mrs Phillips was perturbed.

'It seems he borrowed a horse and rode there. Unfortunately, he had a small accident and could not return.'

Lydia thought that her uncle might be able to influence Mrs Bennet. 'Please make your sister understand that she is smothering her son. Considering he is the product of two excessively selfish people he may take after them if he is opposed at every turn.'

'You know...' gasped Mrs Phillips.

'How could I not. She was not quiet.'

'If you know that, you must also know that it was not her choice.'

'I know that too. But please keep in mind that Joshua is innocent. Love him and let him be his own person. If she continues to try and wrap him in lambswool, he will become rebellious.' Lydia sighed, 'you might consider getting Joshua away from her from time to time.'

'I will try,' agreed Mr Phillips.

<div align="center">~~~ooo0ooo~~~</div>

The following week two unexpected visitors called at Brook Hall. Mr Phillips accompanied by Master Joshua Bennet asked to speak to Miss Lydia.

Joshua performed his best bow. 'Miss Lydia, I wanted to come and thank you for your assistance last week.' He bowed again and held out a slightly bedraggled bunch of wildflowers to her.

'Thank you, Joshua. These are lovely. It was very thoughtful of you to take the trouble.' Lydia was touched that he had gone to the effort.

'I picked them myself.' Joshua said proudly. 'Uncle Phillips says that ladies like flowers. I thought these were much nicer than the ones in our garden.'

'They are indeed.' She grinned at him. 'It is also more fun to pick flowers in a field than in a garden.'

'I just knew you would understand.' Joshua beamed. He then looked up at his uncle, who, after a brief greeting to the ladies, had remained quiet. 'Uncle…' Joshua prompted.

'Lydia, due to your assistance and your partisanship of Joshua the other day, he was hoping that you would allow him to come and visit with you. Possibly on a regular basis… say, once a week?' Mr Phillips asked. He had thought much about his nephew since Lydia's rescue of him, and her words about Joshua's circumstances. The more he observed Mrs Bennet and her son, the more he realised that Joshua was being stifled.

While there was little that he could do at Longbourn, Mrs Bennet trusted him just enough to allow her son to accompany him on an outing. Although Mr Phillips had to promise not do anything with the boy that could possibly allow him to be hurt. Mr Phillips could not break his word, but Lydia had not made any promises. He admitted to himself that this was the sophistry of a solicitor, but that was his profession after all.

Lydia looked at the eager and pleading face of her brother, and could not resist. 'Very well, but you must understand that I will not always be in residence. We are already committed to a season in town after Christmas.'

'Whenever you have time will be wonderful,' exclaimed Joshua.

'In that case, Joshua, I would like to show you a game my sisters and I used to play.'

<p align="center">~~~ooO0Ooo~~~</p>

19 Master of Rosings

It had been nearly a year since Anne de Bourgh took over as Mistress of Rosings Park.

She had done well by the estate and the tenants. With the help of her new steward, she had identified and implemented all the repairs which were needed.

With the cooperation of the ecstatic tenants, they had improved on farming practises. Although it would be another year or two before they would reap the full rewards of the improvements, even this year the harvest was already better.

There had been one fly in the ointment. A few weeks ago, her mother had set fire to the Dower House, in order to make it unliveable.

Fortunately, a footman who could not sleep, (he was sneaking back to his quarters from a tryst,) smelled the smoke and discovered Lady Catherine trying to set the small parlour on fire. He alerted the household. The drawing room was already well on its way to being gutted by the fire by the time the servants managed to put it out, but the rest of the building was saved.

Still, the damage to that part of the house was severe. The servants were most unhappy with the Lady, since they could easily have perished, if the fire had gotten out of hand.

Lady Catherine had marched up to the main house and demanded to be accommodated, since her home was uninhabitable.

Unfortunately for her, the servants had already communicated to Miss de Bourgh the circumstances of the fire.

Anne intercepted Lady Catherine at the main entrance. 'Lady Catherine, I have told you before that you are not welcome in my house.'

'You would let your mother be homeless. You would deny me a roof over my head?'

'There is a perfectly good roof on the Dower House.'

'A fire has gutted the house. I have nowhere else to stay. You would not turn me out into the cold? Your own mother?'

'Lady Catherine, the only room damaged was the drawing room. If you did not like the furniture, you could have sold it and purchased different items. You did not have to burn the furniture, especially not in the middle of the night, and not while it was still in the house.'

'Are you implying that I set fire to my home?'

'I am not implying anything. I am stating that you are not welcome in my house, since I do not trust you not to try and burn my home as well. You will have to return to yours.'

'But everything smells of smoke. It is ghastly.'

'If you do not like the smell of smoke, you should not have fires. You had better send for tradesmen to check and fix any damage to the structure.'

Lady Catherine grumbled. 'Very well, I shall call them and have them bill you.'

'No, you will not have them bill me. Since the damage is to your house, it is your responsibility to fix it. Which means you pay for it.'

'I cannot afford to have the house fixed.'

'You should have thought of that before you set fire to it.'

'But...'

'Good night, Lady Catherine.' Anne shut the door in her face, and ignored the pounding on the door.

<div align="center">~~~ooo0Ooo~~~</div>

Miss de Bourgh was well satisfied with her achievements.

She was also most happy with her own improvement. Although she would always be a little delicate when it came to her health, the fresh air, exercise and regular activities had brought about a marked increase in her stamina.

Anne had hired masters to help her learn to dance as well as to play the pianoforte, and had also found time to practice diligently. While she was not yet proficient, she had learnt to play several pieces of music which she enjoyed.

When she wrote to her aunt that she considered a season in town, Lady Matlock sent her a lady to instruct her in court protocol for her presentation. Miss de Bourgh could now curtsy with poise and grace.

She had even made friendly overtures to her neighbours, which, after an initial shock, were happily reciprocated.

Everything was coming up roses for the Mistress of Rosings Park.

Except for one thing. She was lonely, even though she was very much in love, because the object of her love was unaware of her feelings, and considering how he had ignored her hints, she was certain that he would never approach her.

~~~oo0Ooo~~~

Coincidentally someone else in the neighbourhood was feeling rather lovelorn.

Mr Collins had become rather fond of the lady, but she was Miss de Bourgh, Mistress of Rosings Park, and he was merely a humble clergyman.

He was in his garden, intending to cut some flowers, but became lost in contemplation of the many fine qualities of the lady, when she interrupted his thoughts by arriving at the parsonage.

After polite greetings, Miss de Bourgh stated, 'Mr Collins, I need your help yet again.'

'Miss de Bourgh, you know that I am always at your disposal to assist in any way that I can.'

'Excellent, Mr Collins. Although this matter is a little more personal. You see it has occurred to me that while Rosings Park now has a competent Mistress, even if I do say so myself, the estate also needs a Master. Therefore, I have decided that I must marry, and I hope you will assist me in finding the perfect partner.'
~~~

This was the day he had been dreading. Miss de Bourgh was looking for a husband, taking her forever out of his reach. Although he did not delude himself that she would consider himself as a match, while she remained single, he could dream of winning the lady's affection, beyond the friendship they enjoyed.

'Have you looked amongst your neighbours? I am certain that you will find many willing to accommodate you.'

'I have, but I have given much consideration to the kind of man who would be suitable not only for the estate, but for myself. I would like a man who is intelligent, but not such a mental giant that I feel intimidated in conversing with him. He must be kind and caring toward all, including my tenants and staff. He must give respect where it is due, and be the kind of man who is respected in return.'

'In addition to those qualities, I would like a young man, about my own age, and one who is pleasing to look at. I should also mention that I am enough of a romantic that I wish for a marriage of mutual affection. Therefore, most importantly, he must care about me, rather than my wealth, since I am not interested in a fortune-hunter.'

Anne looked at Mr Collins expectantly.

'That is quite a list of requirements, Miss de Bourgh. I can think of a number of men who would meet three or even four of the criteria, but I cannot think of one who meets them all.'

'But you agree that if I find a man who meets all those criteria, he would make a suitable husband for me, and a good Master for Rosings.'

'Certainly, any man fortunate enough to have all those qualities would be most suitable. Shall you require me to interview potential candidates from the area, and advise you of their suitability?'

'That will not be necessary. I already know one man who meets all of my requirements, except that I am not certain how he feels about me. I think he cares for me, but I am uncertain if it is enough for him to make such a commitment.'

'Miss de Bourgh, any man would feel privileged if you were to choose him.'

'Do you feel privileged?'

'I? Why should I… you cannot mean…'

'Mr Collins you have been my good friend and support since you arrived here. I have come to care for you deeply…'

Anne stopped, her carefully rehearsed speech fled from her memory as she blushed.

William Collins looked at her with a gentle smile bordering on awe, as he raised a hand to caress her blushing cheek with a delicate touch of his fingers. 'I think that you are the most wonderful lady of my acquaintance. I too care deeply about you. But I never thought that you would, or even could, reciprocate those feelings.'

At those words, Anne's spirit lifted and she glowed as she asked, 'in that case, Mr Collins, would you do me the very great honour and be my husband?'

'The honour is all mine, Miss de Bourgh. It would give me the very greatest pleasure to be your husband.'

Since his fingers still rested on her cheek, Collins leaned forward and very carefully touched her lips with his.

The slight tingling sensation generated by this kiss made Anne sigh in pleasure.

~~~ooO0Ooo~~~

Once the couple calmed down from their early euphoria, they considered practical matters.

'What kind of a wedding would you like? Is there anyone in particular whom you would like to perform our marriage ceremony, since obviously I cannot do so?'

'I rather like your mentor, Bishop Parkhurst, if he is willing. It will also circumvent mother from creating an uproar.'

Collins politely ignored the unflattering reference to Lady Catherine. 'I will need to write to him to inform him of our plans, and I am hoping to ask his advice for the best way to deal with this situation.'

'Personally, I think a common licence is the best option, because, if you read the banns for us, mother will object.'
~~~

'The question I had was whether it would be better to allow her to object publicly or only in private.'

Anne considered it for a moment and came to an unpleasant conclusion. 'In the long term, letting her make a fool of herself in public would be best, as long as we can confine it to Hunsford.'

~~~oo0Ooo~~~

Over the next few weeks, a flurry of express riders were kept busy between Hunsford, London and Meryton, carrying letters from the couple to their families and the bishop.

Anne de Bourgh had enjoyed the previous Christmas with her Fitzwilliam relations. It occurred to her that combining their wedding with a family Christmas would be a perfect solution. Lord and Lady Matlock realised that Anne was trying to make up for years of isolation and happily agreed with her plans.

Since three of her daughters were looking forward to spending their first Christmas with their new husbands, Mrs Mortimer and Lydia were going to be on their own for Christmas. It was a simple matter to invite them to Rosings for the double celebration.

On the Tuesday before Christmas, several carriages arrived at the church at Hunsford, which was nearly overflowing with the tenants of Rosings and the people of Hunsford.

Bishop Parkhurst had declared himself delighted to perform the wedding ceremony.

The Earl of Matlock was proud to stand in for Sir Lewis de Bourgh, to walk his niece down the aisle.

Mrs Jenkinson, as Anne's closest female friend, was honoured to be the Matron of Honour.

There was only one detail that struck the congregation as rather unconventional, although it took them a while to work it out. Mr William Collins had asked his closest friend and relation to stand as his witness.

Lydia Mortimer was tickled pink to have been asked to fulfill the role of *Best Man*. In honour of the occasion, she even dressed the part, wearing an elegantly styled cut-away coat, over a shirt and waistcoat,
~~~

complementing the pantaloons and hessians. Even her cravat was perfectly tied.

When she met Collins before the ceremony, he burst into delighted laughter. 'Cousin Lydia, with you beside me, no one will notice any outbursts from Lady Catherine.'

~~~oo0Ooo~~~

He was proven to be almost correct.

During the ceremony, when the bishop said 'speak now or forever hold your peace', Lady Catherine, who had invited herself to the wedding, tried to object. She was first shushed by the people of Hunsford, but when she persisted, two of Lord Fitzwilliam's footmen removed her from the church.

The incident caused barely a ripple in the flow of the wedding ceremony.

It was not long before the bishop was pleased to present Mr and Mrs Collins – de Bourgh

~~~oo0Ooo~~~

Christmas was a very relaxed and festive family affair at Rosings that year.

The newly married couple settled into their new life with relative ease. The bride had been given excellent advice by Mrs Jenkinson, who had thoroughly enjoyed her own brief marriage. For a clergyman, Collins proved to be surprisingly amorous, and delighted in pleasing his wife.

The staff and tenants at Rosings Park were happy that their Mistress had chosen a man who was respected by all who knew him.

They were even more pleased that Lord Fitzwilliam had used Lady Catherine's outburst during the wedding, which was obviously approved by himself and Bishop Parkhurst, as an excuse to remove her from Rosings. She now lived in a small cottage, with the few staff still loyal to her after the fire, on the grounds of the Matlock estate.

But, as usual, Lydia had to have the last word. One evening when Lord Fitzwilliam commented on her role and dress at the wedding, she quipped, 'it is widely known that the Best Man for a job is a woman.'

The rest of the family just shook their heads.

~~~ooO0Ooo~~~

Early in the new year, a new parson took up residence at Hunsford.

He was Collins' old schoolfriend who had advised him on the best approach to Lady Catherine. The appointment was made after a long discussion between Mr Collins and Mr Fallows.

Fallows was initially dubious when Collins informed him that the position was dependent on one condition. When Fallows learned that he had to agree to preach respect for ladies, he became enthusiastic.

'I have three older sisters. Believe me when I say that I learned to respect them. They would have soundly trounced me if I did not.'

Bishop Parkhurst was pleased to confirm the appointment.

~~~ooO0Ooo~~~

20 Launch

The Darcy, Mortimer and extended Fitzwilliam families went to London to attend the 1813 season with two single and two married debutantes.

Georgiana had gained enough confidence that she had decided that she was ready to face and conquer the *ton*.

Lydia, although still irrepressible, had learned when to keep quiet, smile, and voice her comments so that only her family could hear.

Since Kitty had married before being presented, she joined her sisters for the event.

Anne Collins–de Bourgh completed the excited group.

When he heard about the coming out of Lydia and Georgiana, Charles Mortimer had volunteered to be their escort for the season. Charles had been completely smitten with Miss Darcy since the day he met her. But knowing she was young and had not had a chance to meet other men, he had been acting as a friend. He hoped that eventually she would choose him, after having the opportunity to peruse the marriage mart.

Patrick happened to have business in town as well and he too offered his services as protector.

~~~oo0Ooo~~~

Once Anne, Georgiana, Catherine and Lydia were presented at court by Lady Matlock, Mrs Darcy, Mrs Mortimer and Viscountess Middlebrook respectively, Lord Matlock held a coming out ball for all of them.

Lord and Lady Matlock undertook to introduce all their nieces, by blood or marriage, to the assembled company.

When the dancing started, Lord Matlock danced the first set with his wife, since Anne insisted on being partnered by her husband.
~~~

Darcy partnered his sister, after ensuring that Elizabeth reserved the supper and last sets for him.

James led Kitty to the floor, and since Georgiana was unavailable, Charles partnered Lydia.

Patrick who was also in attendance, turned to Mrs Mortimer and asked with a mischievous smile, 'since the boys have once again given me the opportunity to ask the loveliest lady for a dance, would you do me the honour...' He held out his hand in invitation.

Mrs Mortimer laughed. 'I see that you still indulge in outrageous flattery. But I fear that I am just as susceptible to sweet words as I was in my youth.' She took his hand and allowed Patrick to lead her to the floor.

~~O~~

All the ladies caused quite a stir.

There were rumours about their large dowries, which caused consternation amongst the gentlemen in the market for a wife, since only two of them still remained single.

Lady Sherrington commented to her old friend, Lady Matlock, 'how clever of you to only introduce them to society after they are safely married. The cries of agony and the gnashing of teeth amongst the penurious second sons is excessively entertaining. Although the fact that Georgiana and Lydia are still single has mollified them somewhat.'

She looked around and noticed a gaggle of swains clustered around Lydia. 'But you have your work cut out for you, to ensure that they are not forced into a marriage against their wishes.'

That comment raised a peal of laughter. 'I pity the man who tries to make Lydia do anything she does not wish to do.'

When Lady Sherrington raised a questioning eyebrow, Lady Matlock informed her, 'that man will never have heirs.'

'Oh dear. Then the rumours I heard that Stephanie engaged an arms-mistress for her daughters are true?'

When Lady Matlock confirmed the rumour, Lady Sherrington broke into a delighted chuckle, 'it is about time that someone taught those rakes that they cannot have everything their own way. I just hope that the girl is not planning on marrying any time soon.'

'She is planning to enjoy at least three seasons.'

'I am excessively pleased to hear that. I wonder if we should start a pool, to see how many hearts and bones she will break by the time she marries.'

'My dear Cecilia, that would not be sporting.'

Lady Sherrington sighed dramatically. 'I suppose not. But it would be fun though.'

~~O~~

Lady Sherrington asked Elizabeth, 'pray tell, how did you manage to snare the most eligible and elusive bachelor? Everyone in the *ton* has been agog and envious at your achievement.'

Elizabeth smiled at her inquisitor. 'It was truly very simple. I did not chase him. Most ladies seem to be unaware that men are hunters. They prefer to hunt rather than *be* hunted.'

Darcy confirmed his wife's words. 'It was refreshing to be treated as a person, rather than prey. I also enjoy that my wife has a mind of her own, although I am aware that not all men feel the same.'

The lady laughed at the response. 'I will keep your advice in mind, and inform my granddaughters when it is their turn.'

~~O~~

Opinion was divided about who was the belle of the ball.

Both Georgiana and Lydia were tall, blond and blue eyed, and although both were slim and graceful, Lydia was physically stronger, due to her training with Miss Martin.

Georgiana's direct connection to the Fitzwilliams' proved rather enticing to the titled families. Although Georgiana had come out of her shell since she met her new sisters, she was still reserved. She was grateful for the presence of Lydia to take some of the focus off herself. And, although he had not said anything, Charles Mortimer's attention also helped to relax her, to the point that she actually enjoyed most of the evening.

Unlike Georgiana, Lydia had enough confidence for a roomful of debutants. Knowing she was loved by her family and that her substantial dowry made her financially secure, even if she did not marry, she was disinclined to rush into an attachment.

As she had told her family, since she was barely seventeen years of age, she was too young to make a choice for life. She planned on having at least three seasons to evaluate the offerings of the marriage mart.

Her confidence and bright personality drew a score of gentlemen to her side, who were all determined to win her.

One young man tried to stake his claim by asking her for a second set. He did not appreciate Lydia's response. 'I would be delighted to dance with you again… another time. But I promised my guardian that I would only dance one set per ball with any gentleman during this season.'

He tried to pressure her to dance with him by loudly declaring that if a lady refused to dance with a gentleman without a good reason, she could not dance for the rest of the ball.

Lydia looked him up and down and replied with a saccharine smile and in equally ringing tones, 'that is perfectly satisfactory to me, since you, Sir, are no gentleman.'

Everyone within hearing range seemed to suffer an inexplicable coughing fit.

Unsurprisingly to everyone but the gentleman, invitations to important balls became scarce after this incident. No parents wanted to risk their daughters being importuned by a fourth son. Particularly one who had three nephews already.

~~O~~

To her amusement, even Mrs Mortimer was the recipient of male attention.

Although she had turned fifty a few months earlier, she was still a remarkably handsome woman, with a body kept trim by practising with Julia Martin. Although, that practice was not generally known. Many ladies ten years or more her junior, eyed her with envy.

Word had spread that not only was she a widow, she was an exceedingly *rich* widow.

There were several mature gentlemen in attendance, who would have been quite happy to capture the lovely widow, not to mention her riches.

Mrs Mortimer enjoyed the attention and the dancing, but was not inclined to encourage any of them.

~~O~~

There were of course people who were not as pleased with Georgiana and particularly with Lydia.

'She is only Mrs Mortimer's ward. That woman will take in any kind of stray.'

'She may only be a ward, but she is the daughter of a gentleman, and her sister is Mrs Darcy. Another one of her sisters is married to Richard Fitzwilliam. Which means she has the backing of the whole Fitzwilliam clan.'

'How did her sisters catch those men? Half the women of the *ton* made a try for Darcy but he ignored every one of them, and even their attempts at compromise failed.'

Lady Sherrington, who was sitting at the same table, commented, 'they did not fawn over the gentlemen,' earning her looks of utter disbelief and chagrin.

~~O~~

'Why does she have to be so excessively spectacular? She is beautiful, moves with a grace I have never encountered before, seems to be intelligent and I hear that her dowry puts most of the daughters of the *ton* to shame,' grumbled the daughter of an Earl, in her second season.

'What is even worse, is that she has no respect for rank. Earlier I tried to put that mouse Georgiana Darcy in her place, but that chit ended up putting me on the back foot. I still cannot see how she did that. She should be deferential to me, but Miss Mortimer is no push-over,' the Duke's daughter commiserated with her best friend.

'And all our brothers are fawning over her...'

'What qualities does she possess that we do not?'

'Grace, intelligence and exquisite manners,' came the voice of Lady Matlock, who was passing the group.

~~O~~

'Have you seen Anne de Bourgh? Or, I suppose I should say Collins – de Bourgh. I had always heard that she did not attend town because she was sickly. But she is positively glowing.'

'I wonder if the change was caused by her coming into her inheritance, or whether her husband has anything to do with it.'

'I have heard that her husband helped her regain her health before she came into her inheritance.'

'Ohhh...'

'Not in that way, you naughty woman. He simply supported her against Lady Catherine. That woman was keeping her daughter sickly by not allowing her to do anything. But look at her now.'

'She is lucky to already be married. If she were still single, she would have every fortune hunter in town chasing her. What do you know about her husband? Did he marry her for her fortune?'

'Not at all. Would you believe she had to propose to him...'

'What is it with that family? They used to be predictable, but now they are all becoming quite unconventional. Even Darcy is smiling and being affable.'

~~~ooO0oo~~~

Even Kitty and James came in for some gossip. Although in their case it was about James' talent.

After Richard's wedding, Lady Matlock had seen James' painting of Kitty, and insisted on him painting portraits of herself and her husband.

Both pictures now hung side by side in the ballroom and were being admired by the guests. When the guests discovered who the artist was, several of them enquired if he was available to produce portraits for them.

By the end of the evening, James secured several commissions.
~~~

~~~ooO0Ooo~~~

The day after the ball, Darcy and Patrick met for luncheon at White's. They opted for an unobtrusive table to listen to the gossip. While both of them despised to gossip, they knew the necessity to keep informed of gentlemen's intentions.

While they heard nothing distinctly untoward, they were treated to some amusing snippets of conversation.

'Did you see the Mortimer ladies last night? They were quite lovely, just like their older sisters. You must remember them; it must have been three or four years ago. Especially the oldest. What a face...' Horace Carstairs said dreamily. 'It is a pity that Mrs Mortimer did not bring them back to town, and now all but the youngest are married.

His friend Lord Sinclair remembered something else from that time. He turned to Lord Neville Banning. 'I remember you showing quite an interest at the time. It was too bad that you broke your ankle and could not follow through with her. It was a pity that she never came back to town.'

'Yes, and now I heard that Fitzwilliam has snatched her up. The number of connections between the Fitzwilliams and the Mortimers is growing. Would you believe that Collins fellow who married Miss de Bourgh is a cousin of the Mortimers,' commented Lord Neville.

He huffed. 'I wonder how he managed to catch Miss de Bourgh. If I had known she was in the market for a husband, I would have been happy to volunteer.'

Lord Sinclair teased, 'maybe that was why Lady Catherine kept her mewed up at Rosings, claiming she was sickly. She did not look sick to me.'

'No, she did not. But did you see her cousin?' Miss Darcy is certainly worth the effort. Lovely looks, quiet demeanour and a hefty dowry.' Carstairs enthused. 'I could certainly use that money. You really missed something by not being at the ball last night, Banning.'

Lord Sinclair chose to disagree. 'I suppose it depends on what you like. I prefer my bed-mates to be more lively. Miss Lydia Mortimer fits that bill to perfection. And her dowry is reputed to be just as good.'
~~~

'She may be lively, but I suspect she would not take kindly to your philandering ways. After all, you can never settle for any one woman, Sinclair.'

'Hmmm. You have a point. Maybe Miss Darcy would be the better option. I doubt she would say boo to a goose.'

'She might not say boo to a goose, but she would never have the bad taste to fall for a rake like you,' said Darcy standing up to his full height and giving the gentleman a hard look.

'Darcy... I only meant... that is to say...'

'I know what you meant. Spread the word. Her family will not stand for any disrespect.'

'*Both* their *whole* families,' agreed Patrick.

<div align="center">~~~ooO0Ooo~~~</div>

21 Protector

While Darcy's words were heeded by many, some men chose to ignore the warning.

At a soiree, given by Lady Axingham, Lord Neville Banning, who had attached himself to a group of friends to gain admittance to the function, was trying his best to get Georgiana into a situation from which she could not escape, but they were intercepted by the youngest Miss Mortimer, who had kept an eye on her sister.

'Miss Darcy, would you kindly introduce me to your friend?' Lydia asked sweetly.

Georgiana complied, relieved to have Lydia's support, but was confused as to her intentions.

'Miss... Mortimer?'

'Indeed, Lord Neville. I admit to curiosity to meet you. My sister Jane has often spoken about you. She hoped that the illness which overtook you at Gunter's was but a passing faintness. I will be happy to report to her that you look to be in the pink of health... at present. I certainly hope there is no chance that it will recur.' While it appeared that Lydia demurely lowered her eyes, Lord Neville was convinced that she eyed his ankles, before looking up again. Lydia gave him a sweet smile, while her eyes promised severe injury, and not just to his pride.

'But you must excuse us. I was sent to fetch my dearest sister,' she indicated Georgiana with a nod, 'and we must not tarry, no matter how great the temptation.' She again glanced at his ankles, before looking back up and giving him another brilliant smile.

'Your sister?'

'By marriage. My sister Elizabeth is married to Mr Darcy.'

Lord Neville, who had been alerted to danger at the mention of the name Mortimer, understood the warning. He was afraid that his ankles could not recover from another break, and Miss Lydia Bennet radiated animosity, unlike her older sister, whom he had so badly misjudged.

He had equated serenity and politeness as weakness, and had been unprepared for the result. This younger sister, while exceedingly polite, was vibrant and not someone he was going to underestimate.

He decided that discretion was the better part of valour.

'I see. But I must not keep you. It has been most... enlightening to meet you.'

'Likewise, Lord Neville. I hope you enjoy the rest of your evening.' Lydia smiled sweetly, although the smile did not reach her eyes. She took Georgiana's arm and started to lead her away, while Lord Neville beat a hasty retreat.

Lydia heard faint clapping and a murmured, 'brava.' When she looked in the direction of the sounds, she saw a young man stepping out from behind a pillar, sporting a big grin as he bowed to her. But he did not approach. Instead he stepped back behind the pillar.

Georgiana suppressed a chuckle and most of her smile. 'It seems you have an admirer.'

'Apparently so. Do you know who he is?'

'No, I do not. But I suppose I could find out. I am certain someone will know the owner of those striking green eyes. But tell me, who sent you to fetch me?'

'No one. I just thought you wanted an excuse to get away from that man.'

'Thank you, Lydia. He made me most uncomfortable.'

'I am not surprised. He is the man who tried to compromise Jane in her first season.'

'He did what? How did Jane get away from him?'

'She kicked him in the ankle,' Lydia replied. She then proceeded to quietly, but with great relish, tell the tale. Georgiana was all admiration for the way that Jane had handled a potentially disastrous situation, although she was undecided whether she should be horrified or amused.

Eventually she giggled. 'I wondered why you kept looking at his ankles.'

'I hoped he would be bright enough to understand the message, and it seems that he was.' Lydia, pleased with her success, smiled broadly behind her fan.

~~~oo0Ooo~~~

Lord Duncan, Viscount Ashby was a young man of medium height with a slim but wiry build, unlike the other men in his family, who tended to be tall and stocky. He considered himself fortunate to take after his mother's family.

Lord Ashby had been sent to London by his father, ostensibly to get some town bronze, but mostly to remove him from the presence of his grandfather, the Duke of Pennock.

The Duke, while in his seventies, still had an eye for the ladies, and in the case of staff, was not inclined to take no for an answer.

Lord Duncan, still young and idealistic, was known to directly obstruct his grandfather's pleasures. The last time that happened ended with a broken arm for Lord Duncan, since the Duke brooked no interference with what he considered to be his rights, and had used his walking stick to devastating effect.

The Marquess, concerned for the safety of his only son, decided to remove him from the potential area of conflict, particularly because the Duke favoured his younger sons and their male offspring.

Although the Duke's third son, Lord Neville Banning was something of a disappointment, since he had been unable to procure a wealthy bride on whom to sire more sons. Lord Neville had spent most of the last ten years in town in the pursuit of a bride, but the family's reputation went before him, and parents were reluctant to let him approach their daughters.

Since the Duke, for all his faults, would not allow his sons or grandsons to gamble, the men of the family confined their vices to drinking and womanising. The exceptions were only the Marquess and his son, who treated all females with respect and were moderate in their habits.
~~~

~~~oo0Ooo~~~

Lord Ashby had been pleased to accept an invitation to the soiree held by Lady Axingham. He had met her younger son at Oxford and the two had struck up a friendship.

Part way through the evening a new party arrived accompanied by Lord Neville Banning, who had attached himself to the group, since Lady Axingham had not seen fit to extend an invitation to him.

Lord Ashby, had not seen the man in ten years. since Lord Neville considered his young nieces and nephews beneath his notice, and once Ashby was old enough, he had usually been away at school. He immediately recognised the family resemblance, and was concerned by his presence, since the function was attended by many young debutants. He resolved to keep an eye on his unwelcome relative.

He was right to be concerned. Within the hour, Lord Neville had secured an introduction to a young woman and immediately tried to get her into an untenable position.

Ashby was on his way to intercept the young lady and offer his assistance, when his chivalrous intentions became unnecessary. As he approached the couple, who had been joined by another young woman, he overheard the conversation taking place. It seemed that Miss Mortimer, the second young lady, had the measure of his uncle, and was not in the least intimidated by him.

Loath to miss any of the conversation, Lord Ashby stepped behind a conveniently located pillar, and listened with growing respect and delight as Miss Mortimer threatened his uncle with physical mayhem. In the most polite and veiled terms, of course.

When Lord Neville departed abruptly, Ashby could not resist but to applaud the performance.

As he stepped back, he determined to find out more about this charming spitfire.

~~~oo0Ooo~~~

As the season progressed, Georgiana and Lydia became favourites with many matrons of the *ton*. While both girls enjoyed the entertainment and the dancing, it became obvious that neither was seriously looking for a husband. At least not this year.

Since they were not in competition with their own daughters and nieces, the ladies were favourably disposed towards them and happily invited them to their own functions.

The only exception was Miss Devenish. As soon as she met him, she set her cap at Charles Mortimer. He was young and handsome, and although he was a younger son, gossip had it that his older cousin was not interested in marriage, since he had never paid the slightest attention to any of the young ladies presented to him. Mr James Mortimer, the other potential contender for the estate, was only interested in painting.

She often engaged Charles Mortimer in conversation, and realised to her chagrin that he only had eyes for Miss Darcy.

When Miss Devenish discovered that Miss Darcy did not like performing in public, she formulated a plan to demonstrate to Mr Mortimer that Miss Darcy was not as perfect and accomplished as he thought.

<div style="text-align:center">~~~ooO0Ooo~~~</div>

Miss Devenish's opportunity came when both ladies were invited to a musical evening at the home of Lady Sefton, and Mr Mortimer was also in attendance. She enlisted the help of her friend, Miss Harman, to enthuse about Beethoven's Piano Sonata No 14, the *Sonata quasi una fantasia*.

When everyone listened, Miss Devenish turned to Georgiana. 'Miss Darcy, did I not hear you mention that you are familiar with this piece?'

When Georgiana admitted that she had practiced the Sonata, Miss Harman gushed. 'I have heard that you are an excellent performer on the pianoforte, Miss Darcy. You simply must play the Sonata for us. I long to hear it performed by an expert.'

Georgiana tried to demur, but was eventually overruled by her hostess, when Miss Devenish offered to turn the pages for her.

Charles Mortimer, knowing how nervous Georgiana was about performing in public, offered his arm to escort her to the instrument. He ached for the lady he loved, being caught in such an uncomfortable position, and tried to think of a possible solution for her. 'Miss Darcy, you know that I am your friend.' When she nodded, too nervous to speak, he quietly suggested. 'Play for me. Only for me.'

She gave him a startled look, and he smiled, a smile full of love and encouragement. 'I have complete faith in you.'

'Thank you, Mr Mortimer,' she said with a tentative smile, as she settled herself at the pianoforte.

Miss Devenish sat down next to Miss Darcy and produced a specially prepared score which she placed on the instrument, opened at the first page.

Charles Mortimer chose a chair close to the instrument and in direct line of vision of Georgiana.

Georgiana placed her fingers on the keys, ready to play the first notes and took a deep, calming breath. She glanced briefly at the score, and started to play. Although she knew the music by heart, she kept glancing at the score, between stealing looks at Charles.

Miss Devenish's spirits soared, she only had to turn one more page and Miss Darcy would be undone, since the centre pages of the music had all been turned upside down, and were sure to confuse the hapless girl.

Meanwhile, Georgiana paid less and less attention to the music before her, and only looked at Charles.

By the time that Miss Devenish turned the fateful page, Georgiana was completely engrossed in the music and the look Charles Mortimer was directing at her.

She felt his love and protectiveness intertwine with the music she played, and suddenly realised that he was not just a friend, but the man she trusted above all others, and that she was completely in love with him.

That realisation translated into her performance as she poured all the love she felt into the music, until the final crescendo. The power of the performance held her whole audience spellbound, including Miss Devenish, who was so caught up in listening, that she forgot to turn the pages.

After the final note faded, Miss Darcy came out of her trance to roaring applause from her audience.

Lady Sefton was the first to approach, to congratulate Georgiana on her spectacular performance. 'I have rarely heard a piece of music performed with such virtuosity, Miss Darcy. You are truly gifted.'

Lady Sefton smiled at Georgiana, who recovered enough to thank her hostess. Lady Sefton then glanced at the score which was still open at a centre page.

'What an amazing piece of music,' she said, picking up the score and flicking through it. 'I presume it is your personal copy, Miss Devenish?' she asked the young woman, who had been so disconcerted by the failure of her ploy that she had forgotten to close the book.

Miss Devenish blushed as she realised that she had been caught.

'Yes, I thought so. I would like to keep this, if you do not mind, since I would like to learn this sonata as well.' Although Lady Sefton smiled, by the look she received, Miss Devenish was afraid that she had just made the biggest mistake of her life.

This was confirmed when Lady Sefton informed her, 'you know there has been an awful crowd at Almack's lately. I suspect a lady with your delicate constitution would find the crush too much to bear.'

~~~ooO0Ooo~~~

Neither Georgiana Darcy nor Charles Mortimer noticed the drama unfolding. As soon as Lady Sefton turned from her, Georgiana had risen and met Charles coming to congratulate her. 'You were a wonder. I am completely in awe of your ability.'

'I have you to thank. I could not have done this without your support. It meant everything to me. You mean everything to me,' Georgiana replied without considering the words gushing from her. The moment she realised what she had said, she clapped her hand over her mouth, blushing furiously. Fortunately, only one person had heard her.

Charles, who heard her declaration. was elated. 'May I speak to your brother, Miss Darcy?' he asked quietly and obliquely, to be answered by a blushing smile and a nod.
~~~

The rest of the evening they pretended that, apart from her stellar performance, nothing out of the ordinary had occurred.

<center>~~~oo0Ooo~~~</center>

22 Meetings

The following morning, Georgiana broke her fast with her brother. They had the dining room to themselves, since Elizabeth had been feeling unwell the last few mornings, and preferred to stay in her room until it passed. Georgiana waited until her brother had finished his first cup of coffee, before she broached a delicate subject.

'William, you know that yesterday I attended Lady Sefton's musical evening?'

'Yes, I know, and I was grateful that Anne and Collins were prepared to chaperone you.'

'You also know that Mr Charles Mortimer was present as well.'

'As a matter of fact, I did not *know*, but I surmised as much, since he is usually in attendance wherever you are. Is any of this relevant?'

Georgiana blushed and Darcy became fully alert. 'Pray tell, what happened last night?'

'The other guests and Lady Sefton asked me to perform, and I could not find any way to refuse. You know that performing in public still frightens me, although I now quite enjoy playing for family and close friends. Mr Mortimer knows that, and asked me to play for him. Only for him...'

Georgiana twisted her napkin, while trying to find the right words.

Darcy had a suspicion where this was leading. While part of him was sad that his little sister was growing up, he was pleased that she had the good sense not to fall for any of the rakes, who had pursued her.

'Go on...' he encouraged, patting her hand gently.

'I played Beethoven's Piano Sonata No 14. It is a lovely piece of music and I focused on playing it for Mr Mortimer. I forgot about all the other people in the room… But then… I mean… Ahh… When I played and looked only at Mr Mortimer, I realised that I love him with all my heart.'

Darcy sighed. 'I thought you might. While he was pleasant company at Pemberley last summer, I did notice that he was always watching you.'

'But you do know that he always behaved with the utmost propriety.'

'Naturally. Otherwise I would not have tolerated the attention he was paying you.'

Georgiana gave a weak little chuckle. 'Considering my previous experience, he was so restrained and subtle that I did not even realise he was paying attention to me. He was simply pleasant company.'

'As I said, that was why I permitted it. Of course, it helped that Aunt Stephanie vouched for his character.'

'I think he is the best of men.'

'I am pleased that we agree. Is that all or do you need to tell me anything else?'

Georgiana blushed even more. 'When I finished playing, I wanted to thank him for his support, how much it had meant to me. I accidentally let slip that…'

'That you love him.'

'Not in those words exactly, but you are correct in essence,' Georgiana admitted.

'I see. I presume that I am to expect his visit at some time.'

'He will call on you this morning.'

'Thank you for the warning. It is better for my continued health not to receive any shocks.'

'Do you approve?' she asked anxiously.

'I will let you know after I speak with the gentleman.'

<center>~~~oo0Ooo~~~</center>

Darcy went upstairs to check on his wife. When she had first started casting up her accounts, he had been concerned that she had consumed some tainted food, but she had reassured him that the cause might be something much more pleasant. Joyful even.

Since then he had breakfasted without Elizabeth, although he had initially offered to have a tray sent up, so that he could at least keep her company. She had vehemently refused, claiming he would only make things worse for her.

Now he wanted to see that she was again recovering, and to impart the news to her.

When he walked into her room, and seeing her much improved again, he smiled at Elizabeth and announced, 'I owe you one pound.'

Elizabeth beamed. 'So, I was right after all. You should allow that I know my cousins better than you do.'

'But how did you know? Did he say anything to you?'

'No, but ever since he met Georgiana, Charles has looked at her with the exact same expression, you sport when you look at me.'

Elizabeth went to her husband and let him enfold her in his embrace. 'Since you claim that you love me, I had to surmise that Charles loves Georgiana.'

She snuggled against his chest and turned her face up to him. 'Yes, exactly the same expression,' she said with a smile.

'I do love you,' whispered Darcy, before kissing those tempting lips.

<p style="text-align:center">~~~oo0Ooo~~~</p>

Darcy received Charles Mortimer in his study. He wondered how the younger man was going to deal with the situation. He did not have long to wait.

Immediately after the greetings, Charles said, 'Mr Darcy. I love and respect your sister very much. I ask your permission to marry her.'

'Short and to the point,' Darcy said approvingly. 'But before I make a decision, we will need to discuss a few things. You might as well make yourself comfortable.'

When they were seated, Darcy asked, 'can you support my sister? I know you come from a wealthy and supportive family, but I do not want Georgiana to live on charity.'

'I have a small inheritance. I mean small by the standards of my family. It was thirty thousand pounds, left to me by my grandfather.'

Darcy was stunned. He knew that Elizabeth's family was well off, but if Charles thought that thirty thousand pounds was a *small* inheritance, how much was the family worth? Admittedly, Georgiana's dowry was also thirty thousand pounds, but that was considered to be a *large* sum.

Charles noticed the stunned expression and explained. 'At the time of grandfather's death, both James and I were in our teens. Grandfather owned two large estates and two townhouses. The estates went to his sons, who each expected to leave them to Patrick and Gerald respectively. The family townhouse went to Patrick's and James' father, the other to his wife. Grandfather wanted James and me to be provided for as well, and set monies aside which we would receive on our majority.'

Darcy nodded in understanding. He too wanted to leave all his future children well provided for.

'Initially my inheritance was invested in the four-percents, although for the past eight years, it has been invested with Mr Gardiner and has more than tripled. In another year, I expect to have enough money to buy a small estate. I realise it is not up to the standard of what Miss Darcy is used to, but I will do everything in my power to improve on it. I want her to have the best of everything, but most of all I wish to make her happy.'

'Mr Mortimer, Charles, I too, first and foremost, want my sister to be happy. Considering the ties between our families, I am inclined to give my consent.' He held up his hand to stop Charles from interrupting.

'But... Georgiana is still full young. I would like you both to wait another year. You may court her, and, if a year from now you both still feel the same way, I will agree to your marriage. By that time, you may even be in a position to support Georgiana properly. But in the meantime, you might as well call me Darcy.'

Charles smiled and heaved a sigh of relief. That had been easier than he had feared, since he knew how protective Darcy was about his sister.

'Can we tell Miss Darcy now?'

Darcy laughingly agreed and led the way to the morning room where Georgiana paced restlessly.

'I may court you for a year. If you still want to marry me then, your brother will give his consent,' Charles blurted out as soon as he entered the room.

Georgiana blushed and broke into a relieved smile, but could not resist a small tease. 'What if you should change your mind?'

'That will never happen.'

Darcy was pleased by the certainty in the young man's voice.

~~~oo00oo~~~

Lord Duncan, Viscount Ashby, had been to see his father's man of business and requested his help in finding out about Miss Mortimer. He had been surprised, when Mr Barkley said, 'I presume you mean Miss Lydia Mortimer, since she is the only one of the sisters who is still unmarried.'

'Tall, blond, and fiery.'

'Yes, that would be Miss Lydia Mortimer.'

'You know her?'

'I know *of* her, as I do about the whole family.' Mr Barkley then proceeded to enlighten Lord Ashby about what was generally known about the Mortimers. He was surprisingly well informed, and Ashby said so.

'Lord Ashby, that is my job. Much about business is knowing the people involved. The Marquess relies on me to know about anyone of consequence.'

'Since it is your business to be well informed, can you find out which functions the lady is likely to attend, and obtain invitations for me?'

While Barkley raised an eyebrow, he did not question the instruction, only agreed that he would do what he could to assist. He
~~~

also determined to write to the Marquess about the young man's interest. Although, considering the family, their reputation and connections, he expected the Marquess to be pleased.

The Duke and the rest of the family, were probably going to be less enthused.

~~~oo0Ooo~~~

Lord Ashby attended yet another ball. This time he looked forward to the function, since he hoped to meet a certain blond spitfire. Mr Barkley had been efficient, and provided him with a list of functions, as well as invitations. As the grandson of a Duke, particularly one as well reputed as Lord Ashby, he was welcome everywhere.

This time he was in luck, since the son of his hosts was an old acquaintance from Oxford. Michael Lindhurst was happy to introduce Ashby to some of the other guests.

'Lord Ashby, may I introduce our neighbours from Kent, Mr and Mrs Collins – de Bourgh. Mr and Mrs Collins, I would like you to meet my friend from Oxford, Lord Duncan, Viscount Ashby.'

The couple were pleased to meet the Viscount, and introduced him to the rest of their party. Miss Darcy, Mr Charles Mortimer, Mr Patrick Mortimer and Miss Lydia Mortimer.

Georgiana and Lydia exchanged a look during the introduction. Mr Green Eyes now had a name – Lord Ashby. Georgiana was exceedingly pleased, Lydia's admirer seemed to be the son of an Earl, and a friend of Mr Lindhurst, whose parents had become good friends to Anne and Collins.

Ashby exerted himself to be charming. 'Mrs Collins – de Bourgh, I have heard wonderful things about Rosings, and the improvements you have made. I wonder, was it difficult to be taken seriously by your tenants?'

'Not at all, Lord Ashby. They are most cooperative. I find that discussing plans with them rather than giving orders makes working relations much smoother.'

'I learnt the same from my father,' Ashby agreed, before requesting dances from Georgiana and Lydia.
~~~

Georgiana was happy to grant him her fourth set. Since word of their courtship had spread, some gentlemen were not as eager anymore to dance with her. Instead of being upset by this neglect, Georgiana was pleased, since it gave her a chance to chat with Charles.

Lydia, on the other hand, was still in high demand. Since her more forceful proclivities were unknown to most, gentlemen flocked around her. She was young, pretty, wealthy and well connected. All the attributes that the gentlemen of the *ton* looked for, although young and pretty were of lesser importance.

She therefore had to disappoint her new admirer. 'I am exceedingly distressed, Lord Ashby, but my dance-card is already full. Only the eighth set is not spoken for to a gentleman, since I reserved that for myself to rest.' Lydia was curious how Ashby was going to respond. Whether he was going to be pushy or accept her choice. She was pleasantly surprised, since he did neither.

'In that case, Miss Mortimer, since I would not wish to deprive you of your rest, would you allow me to sit with you and converse?'

Lydia was impressed. Lord Ashby was the first man, outside her family, who wanted to talk with her.

'I shall look forward to our conversation.'

~~~oo0Ooo~~~

Both Lydia and Ashby thoroughly enjoyed their discourse, while Patrick sat with them to ensure that they observed most of the proprieties.

Ashby found out quickly that Lydia was not looking for a husband in the foreseeable future, and adjusted his conversation accordingly.

As a result, they explored their respective interests. Rather than flirting, they enjoyed discussions about politics, history and literature. Ashby was impressed by the breadth of knowledge Lydia possessed, while she enjoyed the fact that he was prepared to have a serious discussion. Although they did find considerable humour in some of the books they discussed, since Lydia could not resist but parody some of the views expressed by the heroines.
~~~

Although they had one somewhat awkward moment, when Ashby said, 'please do not hold it against me, but Lord Neville Banning is my uncle.'

'And yet you applauded…'

'With the greatest respect, I assure you.'

Lydia gave him a long look, before she allowed, 'we cannot choose our families, I suppose.'

Once they had overcome that hurdle, they both looked forward to meeting again at future events.

~~~oo0Ooo~~~

A few weeks later, at a ball given by Mr and Mrs McNally, Lydia was on her way to the ladies' retiring room, when she heard a commotion in a screened alcove, and a young female voice pleading, 'let go of me.'

When she peeked behind the screen, she saw a man grappling with a young girl. Since his back was to her, Lydia decided not to argue with the man. Instead, since there was no convenient coffee pot or even a vase, she withdrew her favourite dagger from underneath her skirt and hit him with the pommel.

As he collapsed, he ripped the sleeve of the young girl, who looked at Lydia in a mixture of relief and horror. Her rescuer put away the knife, grasped her arm and instructed, 'you had better come with me so that we can fix your sleeve.'

To their relief the retiring room was deserted as they entered.

The emotions caught up with the girl and she burst into tears. 'What am I to do? I have been compromised by that rake. And now you have rendered him unconscious. I…'

'Who says that you have been compromised?'

'But you saw…'

'All I have seen is a distraught young lady in the retiring room. I suppose her distress is due to an accident which ripped the sleeve of her exquisite gown.' Lydia gave her a mischievous grin. 'I quite understand that you are distressed over the damage. It truly is a lovely gown. But I am certain we can fix it.'
~~~

Lydia looked around, and, as expected, found a sewing kit, which had been supplied in case of accidents, since hems were often stepped on and needed repairs.

'But...'

'It was not your fault... that the sleeve was ripped.' Lydia said as she started to fix the small tear, which fortunately was along a seam.

'But, what about... him...'

'He will not dare say anything. Simply avoid him in the future. But we have not been introduced yet. I am Miss Lydia Mortimer...' Lydia briefly looked at the girl with an encouraging smile, before going back to her stitching.

'I am Miss Clarissa Tate. I am pleased to meet you Miss Mortimer,' Miss Tate responded hesitatingly.

'I too am pleased to make your acquaintance, Miss Tate.' Lydia cut the thread and put the needle away. She smiled at Clarissa. 'See, you cannot even tell that you had an accident.'

Miss Tate looked at her sleeve and managed a small smile. 'Indeed, Miss Mortimer. You are all kindness. I am excessively grateful for your assistance... with my sleeve.'

'You are most welcome; it was my pleasure. But if I might suggest, you really should learn to defend yourself.'

'But such things are not taught to ladies. How come you know how? And did I truly see a knife?'

'My...' Lydia was about to say guardian, when she suddenly realised that Mrs Mortimer had become her true mother, due to the love, encouragement and protection she had gifted to Lydia. 'My mother encouraged my sisters and me to learn to defend ourselves against unwanted attention. She even went so far as to hire an arms-mistress for us. Perhaps your parents could do the same.'

'I will ask. Thank you, Miss Mortimer. For everything.'

<p style="text-align:center">~~~ooO0oo~~~</p>

23 New additions

While they were in London, Mrs Mortimer received regular letters from Jane and Mary. So did Elizabeth, in addition to missives from Charlotte Bingley, who was now happily settled in Derbyshire, not thirty miles from Pemberley.

One after the other informed their correspondents of the joyful events they were expecting later in the year, which was the main reason each of them had foregone the season in London.

Mary's first child was due at the end of June, with Jane not far behind in July. Charlotte wrote that she was expecting Master or Miss Bingley in July as well. Eventually Elizabeth confirmed that Pemberley would also see an increase in the family in October.

Of the married sisters, only Kitty was exempt from the population explosion. She admitted to feeling relieved, since she was not yet ready to be a mother.

Elizabeth was torn between her desire to be with Mary and Jane during their confinement, and the need to be with Charlotte.

Mrs Mortimer pointed out that she, as well as Lydia, would be on hand for Mary and Jane, and with Elizabeth's own confinement approaching, it would be better for her to be with her friend in Derbyshire, rather than travel extensively.

Elizabeth reluctantly agreed.

~~~oo0Ooo~~~

'I was so sorry for Miss Tate,' said Lydia apropos of nothing at dinner one night.

She and Mrs Mortimer had returned to Brook Hall, at the end of May, and were enjoying some peace and quiet, and a chance to relax after months of going from one entertainment to the next.
~~~

Mrs Taylor and Miss Martin made up the rest of the company. The two ladies had become such an integral part of the family, that at home they were automatically included.

'I have given that some thought,' replied Mrs Mortimer. 'From what I can tell, there are many young women, mostly the daughters of wealthy businessmen, who end up being married to men whom they do not like, and who would not have been chosen by the family. Part of the reason is because society has many rules which work against women.'

'You know my thoughts on compromise. But I thought that if those heiresses could learn to look after themselves, they would have a little more control of their futures.'

'How could they do that? I know that I have been lucky to have Miss Martin to teach me, but there are not many ladies who can teach her lessons.'

'True, but what if we set up a school, with Mrs Taylor in charge of teaching young ladies their accomplishments, and Miss Martin to teach self-defence?' Mrs Mortimer looked expectantly at her dinner companions.

They all looked excited at the prospect.

'I confess I have been concerned about my continued usefulness in this household.' Mrs Taylor admitted. 'With all the girls except Miss Lydia married, you do not actually need me anymore.'

'I admit that I have been wondering about you as well. While I consider both of you more as family, rather than employees, I know you well enough to be aware that you are too proud to accept, what you consider to be, charity. Which you would consider living in this house without having anyone to teach.'

Mrs Mortimer was pleased to notice two relieved smiles. 'Having spent the season in London, crystalised my ideas. I am planning to buy Netherfield. The tenant farms can become part of my own estate, while the Manor House and gardens could become a school. This school is to be run jointly by the two of you. Do you like this plan?'

'You know that I love teaching. I can even deal with difficult cases.' Mrs Taylor gave Lydia a pointed look, but then smiled and winked.

'I would be pleased to teach those heiresses how not to be importuned.' Miss Martin cocked her head in thought for a moment. 'If it became known that the ladies can defend themselves, there might even be fewer attempts at compromise.'

'Especially if they learn what they should protect themselves from. Which the parents usually think they are too delicate to learn about prior to their marriage.'

'I could even find you candidates.' Lydia offered enthusiastically. She had made a number of friends in town, many of whom could benefit from such a school. Or, more likely, their younger sisters.

<div align="center">~~~ooo0ooo~~~</div>

One other person was ecstatic about their early return from town.

Joshua had become a regular visitor at Brook Hall. Once each week, Mr Phillips would take Joshua with him when he left for work.

That work took him to Brook Hall to spend time with Lydia when she was in residence. She played games with Joshua and taught him to ride properly.

When he asked how she had gotten strong enough to lift him onto a horse, she had explained about her physical training. Joshua became enthusiastic about the idea that he could learn to defend himself if anyone should try to pick a fight with him. Miss Martin, as the expert, guided the training.

Another time, when Lydia made a comment about Jane being interested in strategy. Joshua promptly parroted the prevailing male attitude about girls not being able to learn such things, since it would be wasted on them. 'After all, girls cannot join the army, what good is knowing anything about strategy.'

Lydia pointed out that in dealing with fashionable society, a knowledge of strategy was even more useful. It would allow Jane to succeed in navigating the *ton*.

Once he realised that there were practical applications to the things which Mr Phillips wanted him to learn, he started to apply himself. Mrs Taylor was happy to assist.

But with Lydia being in London for months, Joshua had pined for her company. Mrs Taylor and Miss Martin had continued his education, but they were not as playful as Lydia.

While he was happy that Lydia was back, he was upset that she would have to leave again soon.

~~~oo0Ooo~~~

Patrick suggested to Charles, 'I know that you have been shadowing your father and Gerald for years, learning to run an estate. But I think it would be good for you to broaden your experience. Why not spend the next year at Bridgewater?' He grinned when he added, 'it is also closer to Pemberley.'

Charles accepted the offer with alacrity.

While he visited Pemberley on a regular basis, he also learned of the improvements Patrick had made to the running of his own estate. He felt the experience would stand him in good stead when it was his turn to manage an estate of his own.

~~~oo0Ooo~~~

When Mrs Mortimer arrived in Cambridge to support Mary through her confinement, she also found Jane in residence.

Jane justified her presence by pointing out that while the veterinarians around Meadowbrook were excellent, the midwives had not impressed her with their competence. Cambridge on the other hand, had any number of competent midwives and doctors.

Richard divided his time between attending his wife and his duties at his estate. Once the time for Jane's lying in approached, he planned to stay until their child was delivered.

The difference between the two sisters could not have been greater.

Cool, calm and intellectual Mary was in a tizzy about the birth of her child, while Jane was quite relaxed about the process. Their husbands, of course, were the opposite.

Richard, who had been on hand to assist in the birth of any number of foals, worried about the process where his wife was concerned.

Harrison on the other hand remained calm and steady. He kept telling Mary that the odds of a good outcome were heavily in her favour.

'I am aware that the greater percentages of women going through childbirth survive the experience, but 7 out of every one thousand still die,' Mary worried.

'Doctor Carrington, is up on the latest discoveries, and insists that by observing stringent cleanliness in himself and any of his assistants, the number of infections can be dramatically reduced,' Harrison patiently explained for the fourth time that day.

Eventually Lydia told her sister, 'stop fretting. You are not doing your baby any favours by running yourself down with worry. If you were going to worry this much, you should have worried before you started this process. Now it is too late to change it.'

Mary, confounded by Lydia's blunt speech was shocked out of her downward spiral of worry. She sat speechless for a full two minutes before she commented dryly, 'out of the mouth of babes...'

Lydia, momentarily surprised by the comment, laughed, 'you are learning, dear sister, you are learning.'

<div style="text-align:center">~~~ooo0Ooo~~~</div>

As it turned out, the optimists in the family were right. Within two weeks of each other, Mary delivered a healthy girl, while Jane gave birth to an equally healthy boy. Both mothers survived the ordeal with minimal problems.

Mrs Mortimer was moved, almost to tears, when she was introduced, first to Stephanie Harrison, and then to Stephen Fitzwilliam. Both young mothers shared an almost identical look of mischievousness which would have done credit to Lydia.

Mary, immediately following her successful delivery, sent an express to Elizabeth, informing her not only of the fact that she was now an aunt to baby Stephanie, but of Doctor Carrington's strictures about cleanliness during childbirth.

A week after the birth of Stephen Fitzwilliam, she received a note from a grateful Charlotte Bingley, to inform her of the birth of Charles

Bingley Jnr. She attributed her own speedy recovery to the advice Elizabeth had shared with her. She also explained that the enclosed note from her husband expressed his effusive thanks for the same advice.

Opening the second note, justified Charlotte's explanation, since most of the words were made illegible by numerous inkblots.

~~~oo0Ooo~~~

It was pure accident that Mrs Bennet found out that she had two grandchildren and another one on the way, when Mrs Phillips asked her how it felt to be a grandmother.

'I am a grandmother?' she asked in astonishment.

'Dear me, did you not know? I would have thought that you would have been told.'

'No. I only gave those girls life, but Mrs Mortimer gave them a *life*.' She sighed. 'I have had much time to reflect lately. All the things I used to be concerned about. All the things I used to consider important. My mother taught me that men want a pretty and lively wife, who agrees with them and never contradicts them.'

She shook her head in musing. 'All my girls were educated to a greater degree than most of the gentlemen in this area, and yet they all made better matches than any of the lively girls in this neighbourhood. Look at Mrs Long's nieces. They are both very pretty, and yet they are still single. Mr Darcy, Mr Bingley, Colonel Fitzwilliam. They all married intelligent, well-educated girls. Maybe my mother was wrong...'

Mrs Bennet went to her room to consider the latest news.

~~~oo0Ooo~~~

Mrs Mortimer and Lydia had been back at Brook Hall for two months when they received a letter from Lady Matlock, who had attended Elizabeth during her lying in.

At that point, Mrs Mortimer was reminded of a Darcy family tradition, when her friend shared the news of the birth of Mortimer Elias Darcy. Both mother and son were well, and even Darcy had survived the birth, but apparently it had been a close call.

~~~oo0Ooo~~~

Mrs Mortimer sent out invitations to the family to spend Christmas at Brook Hall. All her daughters and their cousin accepted the invitation.

This time, her daughters did not use their former rooms. They were all quartered on the guest floor, since the guest rooms were located next to the nursery, which was made ready for its first visitors since Mrs Mortimer moved to Meryton.

William Collins was pleased with the opportunity to show his wife the place he considered home, until he moved into Rosings. 'After my mother died, I never had a proper home until Mrs Mortimer took me in.' They were the last to arrive, and after taking one look at Anne, Mrs Mortimer told Mrs Kirby, 'We have a change in plans. Freshen up the Mistress' suite for Mr and Mrs Collins – de Bourgh.'

She turned back to her guests. 'You really should have informed me of your condition. If I had known, I would have had the rooms ready for you. Instead, you will have to come into the parlour and have a nice cup of tea and relax.'

When they were seated and sipping their tea, they chatted pleasantly for a few minutes, until Mrs Kirby informed them that their suite was ready.

~~~oo0Ooo~~~

For Jane and Mary, this was the first opportunity to meet their cousin Anne. The lady surprised them by commenting to Jane, 'please forgive me for saying so, but I expected Boadicea to be more intimidating.'

'Boadicea?'

'Knowing my cousin Richard as I do, and from the things my husband has told me about you, I expected to see a warrior queen, not an exquisite lady of fashion.'

All eyes went to Lydia, even before she said, 'do not let her looks fool you.'

That comment broke the ice, and soon all the young ladies were chatting. The new mothers shared their experiences with Anne, while Lydia and Georgiana took seats away from them, to discuss the upcoming season and their hopes and plans.

Meanwhile the husbands all retreated to the library, where they horrified Collins with their own experiences.

~~~oo0Ooo~~~

The families attended Christmas services. Afterwards most of them left quickly to prepare for their celebration.

Collins and Anne lingered, because he wanted to introduce his wife to his former mentor. While they chatted, they were carefully observed by a member of the congregation.

Mr Stewart had gone back into the church, and Collins was leading his wife to their carriage when he was accosted by Mrs Bennet.

'Have you come to see if Longbourn needs an heir again? I am sorry to disappoint you. As everyone can tell you, I have a son, who will be the Master of Longbourn.'

Anne, feeling a little out of sorts due to her condition, defended her husband. 'Madam, my husband has no need for a paltry estate like yours. He is the Master of Rosings Park, one of the largest estates in the country.'

Collins gently squeezed Anne's hand. 'Thank you my dear. But it is not necessary for you to defend me, although I appreciate your care.'

William turned to Mrs Bennet and said gently, 'Mrs Bennet, I am truly sorry what you suffered because of my father, but I am not him. I am happy that you now have the security you always craved.' He bowed and led his wife to their carriage.

Mrs Bennet looked after him in bewilderment. She wanted to be vexed, but could not quite work out why.

Eventually, weeks later, she realised that she had spent so many years terrified of the future, that she always expected the worst.

~~~oo0Ooo~~~

24 Surprise

Mrs Mortimer had brought Lydia to London for her second season, where they met up with Georgiana who was staying at Darcy House.

Today Elizabeth was taking the girls to her favourite modiste, where Georgiana was to arrange for her wedding dress to be made, even though she was not yet officially engaged. Elizabeth believed in being prepared. She did not want another last-minute rush as for Kitty.

Since she was not needed, Mrs Mortimer opted for a quiet day at home.

She was comfortably ensconced in the library, enjoying a book and a cup of tea, when she received an unexpected visitor.

'Patrick, what a pleasant surprise. I did not know that you were in town,' Mrs Mortimer greeted him pleasantly.

Patrick greeted her pleasantly and explained that he had come to town on business, when he discovered that she was also present. 'Naturally, I could not miss the opportunity to visit.'

They chatted for a while about inconsequentials, when Mrs Mortimer, whose mind was obviously on weddings at this time, asked a fateful question.

'Patrick, do you not think it is time you found a wife too?'

'Possibly, but I cannot tolerate the idea of a marriage of convenience,' he explained reluctantly.

'Has no woman ever touched your heart?' Mrs Mortimer was saddened that Patrick was still alone. While she loved all her adopted family, there was something special about Patrick.

He gave her an inscrutable little smile. 'Only one, but I have never had the courage to tell her.'

'Whyever not? You have so much going for you. I am convinced that any woman would be delighted to find out that you cared for her.'

'Do you truly think so?' He asked, still with that enigmatic little smile.

'Of course I do. You are a wonderful man.'

Patrick decided to throw caution to the wind. 'I love you,' he said simply.

Mrs Mortimer was startled at the declaration, but forced a cheerful smile. 'What a nice thing to say. I love you too. You are the best of Gerald's grandsons.'

He briefly closed his eyes as if in pain. 'Do you always have to think of me as your late husband's grandson?' he asked in frustration.

'You cannot mean...' Mrs Mortimer could not believe the direction this initially innocuous conversation was taking. She was desperately trying to think of something to say to change the conversation, but her mind had gone blank.

'You are the woman I have loved all these years. I tried to deny it even to myself, but when I looked for a wife, I compared all those women to you. None of them was ever as good. Eventually I realised that I was in love with the original. I did not want a copy.'

'But you need an heir.' She fought a rear-guard action.

'Charles can be my heir. James prefers London because of his work.' Patrick said casually. 'And Charles would work out well, since Bridgewater is close to Pemberley. It would make it easy for Georgiana to visit with William and Elizabeth.'

He seemed to have an answer for everything. 'But...'

'Stephanie, I will never marry any other woman. I love you and want only you as my wife.'

'But...'

'Can you not say anything other than but?

'But our relationship... my age...' she tried to protest.

He shrugged. 'We are not related by blood. Not even legally. Do you not remember that Gerald Mortimer Junior was my mother's second husband? The only reason we are family is, because, shortly after I was born, you married my adopted father's father. Which would seem ridiculous to some people, since he was thirty years your senior. If a thirty-year age difference did not bother you then, why do you now quibble about seventeen years?'

'Heirs,' she repeated.

'Bridgewater is not entailed and as I said, Charles will be good for the estate.'

'Compared to you, I am an old woman,' Mrs Mortimer said in a last-ditch effort to bring Patrick to his senses, even though she was fully aware that she only looked marginally older than his age.

'You are a beautiful woman and since you have always been active and not let yourself go, you are in better shape than many women half your age. But more importantly, I love your mind, your personality and your experience. You know who you are and what you want, and I have loved you for more than a decade.'

Stephanie Mortimer was nearly in tears at his passionate words.

'Tell me, is the idea of remarriage distasteful to you because you loved grandfather so much that you cannot entertain the thought of being with another man? Are you afraid that you are being disloyal to him?'

She could not lie to him. 'No. As a matter of fact, Gerald hoped that I would marry again...' She rose from her chair in agitation and started pacing.

'Then why did you remain single?' Patrick asked. He too had risen and now stood in front of her.

'As soon as I came out of mourning for my husband, I adopted the girls. Then I was busy with them, and simply forgot about it.'

'Did you not wish for any happiness for yourself?'

She sighed, bracing herself for the seemingly inevitable. 'I did, but it seemed an impossible dream.'

'Why?' It was a simple question, but the answer was anything but.

Stephanie Mortimer looked at Patrick for a long minute while he waited patiently for her answer. She was at last allowing herself to acknowledge that impossible dream, which she had suppressed for so long, by forcing herself to think of Patrick as her grandson. Or at least her husband's grandson. As the barriers she had so carefully crafted over these past ten years crumbled, she reached up, brushing her hand over Patrick's cheek and rested it on the back of his head.

Adding just a little pressure she pulled his head towards her and kissed him. Not a gentle kiss appropriate for family, but a deep passionate kiss into which she poured all the longing she had suppressed for years, and which initially shocked him with its intensity.

After his momentary surprise, Patrick pulled Stephanie close and returned her kiss with equal ardour. Stephanie moulded herself against his body and enjoyed the sensation caused by the heat being generated between them. The couple stood for long minutes, lost in the heady feeling of achieving their desire.

As enjoyable as the kiss was for both participants, eventually they separated enough for Mrs Mortimer to speak. 'You were the impossible dream. But I never allowed myself to dwell on it, since I could not acknowledge, even to myself, that I lusted after my husband's grandson. And he thought of you as such, even though you were adopted.'

'Lusted… hmmm… that sounds promising.' Patrick smirked.

'What can I say. You are an attractive man, and you have improved with age.' Now that she had at last admitted her secret, she was relaxed about her feelings.

'Does that mean that you will marry me?'

'Yes. Although under the circumstances we might have to go to Gretna Green.'

'How soon can you be packed?'

~~~oo0Ooo~~~

In the end they did not travel to Scotland.

Mrs Mortimer and Patrick went to see her old friend Bishop Parkhurst.
~~~

'Have you come to see me to ask if I would officiate at Miss Darcy's wedding?' he asked pleasantly.

'I have come about a wedding, but not Georgiana's… mine.'

'That is wonderful news. I presume you are the lucky man?' the bishop asked Patrick.

'Yes, I am.'

'Congratulations, when are you planning to marry?'

'There is a slight issue. Which is why I have come to you for advice.' Mrs Mortimer replied nervously.

'I would not have thought you would need any advice on marriage,' he teased.

Stephanie blushed at the innuendo, but went on to explain the relationship between her and Patrick.

When she stopped speaking, the bishop still looked at her expectantly. 'Please continue. What is the problem?'

'The church and society frowns on certain marriages between relations…'

'But you said yourself, that you two are not related. Even if Mr Mortimer had been formally adopted, the rule of father's father's wife does not apply.'

'So, you think we can get married?'

'Of course, you can. It is good to see a couple who wish to marry for affection rather than wealth.'

'Even though Kitty, my adopted daughter is married to his half-brother?'

'There is no reason why not.'

Patrick interjected, 'in that case, can we get a licence. I would like to marry her before she changes her mind.'

'I would like you to wait a few minutes while I think about this,' the bishop said blandly and left the room.

Mrs Mortimer and Patrick were starting to fidget, when Bishop Parkhurst re-entered the room with two other men. 'This is Archbishop Canters,' he introduced the older man.

'I will marry you now, if you so wish,' the Archbishop smiled at their shocked faces. 'Not so sure, are we now?' he teased.

Patrick and Stephanie looked at each other, and both broke into identical grins. 'We would very much like to get married now,' said Stephanie. 'If you have the time, that is...'

'Excellent, I have not married anyone in years. Since we have the required witnesses, shall we...'

~~~oo0Ooo~~~

Twenty minutes later, the very happy but bewildered Mr and Mrs Mortimer exited the bishop's residence and entered their carriage.

'I just wanted advice that it was legally possible for us to be married in England,' the new Mrs Mortimer laughed weakly. 'When I woke up this morning, I did not even know that you cared for me, and now I am married to you.'

'We can go back and have the marriage annulled, if you have changed your mind,' Patrick offered teasingly.

'Do you want to have this marriage annulled?'

'Good heavens, no! I waited long enough for you...'

Mrs Mortimer did not waste time with words. She pulled her new husband into another passionate kiss. 'I think I like being married.'

When they arrived back at Mrs Mortimer's townhouse it was still early, and she did not expect the girls back till late afternoon.

When Patrick found out about the timing, he asked with a suggestive smirk, 'what shall we do for the rest of the afternoon? Do you have any suggestions?'

His new wife had several, and he enjoyed all of them.

~~~oo0Ooo~~~

Patrick had gone back to his own house, to arrange to have his things moved into Mrs Mortimer's home. Since she had Lydia with her, it seemed the easier solution.

Stephanie Mortimer nervously awaited the return of her daughters. When Kitty, who had gone along on the shopping trip, and Lydia returned, Mrs Mortimer procrastinated by arranging tea for them all, after the girls' long outing.

But eventually she came to the point.

'Girls, there is something you should know,' she started. 'There is someone whom I have loved for a long time, and I just found out that he loves me too.'

'That is wonderful.' 'Will you get married?' 'You deserve to be as happy as we are.' The girls were enthusiastic about the news.

'Since you have loved him for a long time, it has to be someone we know,' speculated Kitty.

'I am glad that you are happy for me. But we will not be getting married...'

'If you love each other, you must get married.'

'We already did.'

This statement caused another babel of questions.

'What?' 'When?' 'Who is your husband?'

'That would be me,' said Patrick as he walked into the room.

Stunned silence greeted this announcement.

He walked to his wife, bowed and kissed her hand.

'Patrick?' whispered Kitty.

'Are you going to congratulate me that I have managed to convince your mother to give me a chance?'

Lydia burst out laughing. 'You went from being my nephew, to being my brother due to James' marriage to Kitty, to being my father.' She whooped with laughter. 'Wait till James finds out. You are now both his brother and his father...'

'Oh dear. I had not considered that aspect,' sighed Mrs Mortimer.

'I am afraid it is too late. James will simply have to learn to live with it,' replied Patrick pragmatically. He turned to his new wife and smirked. 'Lydia raised a valid point though. You realise that Kitty is now not only your daughter, but also your sister.'

'This is getting too complicated,' Mrs Mortimer said in consternation.

'Seriously though, Aunt Stephanie, I am exceedingly happy for you. Patrick is one of the better men I know. He is handsome, rich and has a sense of humour. You did well. And even better, after all these years, you do not even have to change your name.'

She chuckled evilly. 'Best of all. You will confuse and seriously annoy all those old biddies of the *ton*, any time you show up anywhere with Patrick.'

~~~oo0Ooo~~~

Once Kitty had gone home and Lydia retired tactfully to her room, Mr and Mrs Mortimer discussed living arrangements and marriage contracts. Patrick insisted that since he had enough wealth of his own, his wife's wealth should remain hers.

'Are you still determined to make Charles your heir?'

'Yes I am. Why do you ask?'

'If Charles is to take over Bridgewater, would it not make sense for him to start managing the estate now, rather than later?'

'And where would we live?'

'At Brook Hall of course.' Mrs Mortimer smirked. 'Or at Netherfield, if you prefer.'

'Netherfield? Why Netherfield.'

'Because I bought it last year. I have plans for it, but it would work just as well if we lived at Netherfield.'

'I have seen Netherfield. I prefer your house. What are your plans for Netherfield?'

'I combined the estate with Brook Hall, which coincidentally makes the estate about the same size as Bridgewater. You might consider it a
~~~

wedding present to you, if you are prepared to live at Brook Hall. But the Manor House would make an ideal school.'

'Since when do you want to start a school?'

'Since the girls are grown up and won't need a governess or an arms-mistress, I thought that Netherfield could be turned into a school for heiresses. Mrs Taylor and Miss Martin can be the primary teachers.' She smiled. 'Admittedly, I also thought that it would give me a purpose, since I did not expect you to turn my life upside down.'

'I agree, those two did an excellent job on your girls, although I think that your influence was a strong contributing factor. But, other than those reasons, why do you want to start such a school?'

'Last year I saw several of the girls forced into marriages with most unsuitable men. I felt sorry for them. If they had known how to defend themselves, they could have found better matches.'

'I suppose Miss Tate was lucky that Lydia was on hand to help her. I understand that others were not as lucky.'

'I happen to know of three instances where a girl was forced to marry against her will. But I am also angry with society for putting the blame on the girls for being victims. I think it is about time to redress the balance.'

'I gather that you will be sponsoring the school?'

'Yes, I will. Do you have a problem with that?'

'Not at all. As a matter of fact, I am all in favour of your plan. As I said before, I like the way all your girls turned out. And it will be amusing to watch all those fortune hunting rakes being foiled. Although, how are you going to attract students?'

'Lydia has taken it upon herself to find recruits. I know that the younger sisters of the ones who were forced to marry will be her first choices.'

'Wise decision.' Patrick complimented his wife. He raised her hand to his lips and asked, 'now that we have agreed on our future living arrangements, how shall we spend the rest of the evening?'

~~~ooO0Ooo~~~
~~~

25 Gossip

Mrs Mortimer invited all the family to dinner the following evening, to share her news. Kitty and Lydia had been sworn to secrecy until then.

The timing was perfect, since Mary and Harrison, as well as Jane and Richard had arrived in town for a visit. The Harrisons were staying with Mrs Mortimer, while the Fitzwilliams were being hosted by Darcy.

Everyone was curious about the reason for the unexpected invitation, but had to wait until all the guests were assembled in the drawing-room.

Mrs Mortimer stood up and addressed her audience, 'my dear family and friends, I have an announcement to make...' She paused for effect, before continuing. 'Yesterday I was married.'

Except for Lydia and Kitty, everyone looked at her in stunned surprise, before looking around the room to discover her husband.

When they could not discern a stranger in the room, there ensued a babel of voices, all asking the same question, 'WHO?'

Mrs Mortimer held up her hand in a request for silence. When her family quieted, she announced with a pleased smile, 'Mr Patrick Mortimer.'

The gentleman stepped up to stand next to his wife and took her hand with a pleased and proud smile.

Again, the room erupted in a babel of comments. This time, mainly consisting of congratulations, although some wondered about how long they had kept the secret of their attachement.

'No wonder you were always so cagey about answering questions in whom you were interested,' laughed James. 'Congratulations, brother. Now I do not have to worry about you being left on the shelf, and moping around Bridgewater by yourself.'

The ladies, once they overcame their shock and had a chance to see the look of happiness on the faces of the new couple, rushed to embrace Mrs Mortimer.

Lady Matlock voiced the sentiments of all, 'You have devoted the last fourteen years to your girls, and you did a wonderful job raising them, but now it is about time you had some fun in your life.'

'But it was a pleasure to raise these wonderful young women,' protested Mrs Mortimer.

'It is not the same and you know it. Do not deny that you have missed the attention of a husband.'

'You can hardly expect me to answer that in front of my daughters.' Mrs Mortimer fought valiantly not to blush like a young girl.

'That is answer enough. But, be that as it may, I for one am thrilled for both of you.' Lady Matlock added with an evil chuckle. 'I cannot wait to hear the reaction of the *ton* when this news gets out.'

'You had better listen carefully tomorrow, since the announcement of our wedding will be in the papers in the morning.'

<p align="center">~~~ooO0Ooo~~~</p>

Over dinner, the couple revealed some of their plans. Charles was stunned again when he found out that Patrick was making him the heir of Bridgewater. Although it did not take him long to realise the benefits of the arrangement, and exchange significant glances with Georgiana, who was delighted at the prospect to remain close to her family.

For Patrick the decision to hand over Bridgewater to Charles had been easy. While he had grown up as a Mortimer, he knew that he had no family claim on the estate, other than that the only father he had ever known had willed the estate to him. Gerald Mortimer had loved Patrick and James equally, as the sons of his beloved wife, even though Patrick had a different father.

When it became obvious that James had no interest in managing an estate, Mr Mortimer had trained Patrick to succeed him, although he had made substantial provisions for James. And despite what James had told Kitty, he did not actually have to paint to earn a living. He simply enjoyed it. Also, pretending to be a poor painter, had kept fortune-hunters away from him.

When Stephanie had confessed that she had no wish to live at Bridgewater, because she associated the estate with her first husband, Patrick was happy for Charles to take over. This way, another Mortimer would become Master of the family's main estate.

And the combined estates of Brook Hall and Netherfield would keep him comfortably busy.

Darcy was pleased about the situation for several reasons.

While he had always hoped that Georgiana would marry well, he also wanted her to be happy. He liked Charles Mortimer and knew that the couple loved each other.

Darcy knew that Bridgewater was a substantial estate, and since Charles would not have to pay for it, he would be able to keep his financial buffer. Adding Georgiana's dowry to that, the two would be very well set up indeed.

Of course, another reason was Bridgewater's distance from Pemberley, which was an easy day's travel. Georgiana would not be cut off from the support of her family. Even Matlock was not that much further.

And it would be obvious to everyone that neither of them were fortune-hunters, since they would be well matched.

Elizabeth was delighted that she would have her sister close at hand, since they had formed a strong bond over the last two years.

The family then spent a considerable part of the evening discussing Mrs Mortimer's plans for the school at Netherfield.

<div style="text-align:center">~~~oo0Ooo~~~</div>

The following morning the news of the wedding between Mrs and Mr Mortimer was discussed in drawing rooms all over the fashionable areas of London.

A number of young ladies, who had met Mr Mortimer, had thought him rather dashing, especially ladies who were well into their twenties.

The discussion of the wedding by Miss Lever with her cousin, Miss Pacey, in the drawing room of their aunt, Mrs Everett, was representative of the general reaction. 'Can you believe it, he married Mrs Mortimer. That woman must be at least four or five years older than he is.'

'Yes, I know. But have you seen her? She is still rather stunning I have to say. I suppose there is no accounting for taste.'

'But what does she have that we do not?'

'Intelligence, grace, style, exquisite manners, and her figure is much better than yours,' her aunt answered the rhetorical question. 'But you are wrong about her age.'

'You mean she is younger than nine and thirty?'

'No, she happens to be older,' Mrs Everett, who believed that her nieces thought too highly of themselves, was delighted to inform the pair. 'Two years older than I am, as a matter of fact.'

'But you are fifty years old,' exclaimed Miss Lever. 'That would make her...' Words failed her as she stared in consternation at her aunt.

'I am pleased that you can at least do simple arithmetic.'

~~~ooO0Ooo~~~

The reaction amongst mature ladies, at least the ones who did not have daughters or nieces in search of a husband, was much more complimentary to Mrs Mortimer.

'That lucky woman. If I had realised that Mr Mortimer would consider a woman older than himself, I might have set my cap on him myself.'

'I suppose it must be a love match. After all they are both wealthy enough that they do not have to marry for financial considerations.

~~~ooO0Ooo~~~

At the gentlemen's clubs the conversation was along similar lines.

'Mortimer is certainly a dark horse,' commented Lord Sinclair. 'For years I wondered whether he was interested in women at all. But I never heard any rumours that he might be a molly either.'

'Damn. I had not even considered the mother when I tried for the daughter,' lamented Lord Neville. 'And I am closer in age to her than Mortimer is.'

'Well, you missed the boat now.'

'Pater tried his luck with her last season,' commented Mr McGrath, who was inclined towards corpulence like his father. 'He said she is charming and intelligent, but she simply was not interested. I would not have minded her as a step-mother. But I suppose Pater cannot compare to Mortimer. That man actually looks good in pantaloons.'

'You do not suppose that is why she married him?'

'Well, she certainly does not need the money. But then, neither does he.'

The gentlemen were confounded. The only thing that made any kind of sense was that it must be a love-match. But it was a pity that both their estates were consolidated within the family.

~~~ooo0Ooo~~~

Society had been waiting to see if Mr Charles Mortimer's courtship of Miss Darcy was still ongoing. After nearly a year, the expectation was that if it continued, an engagement would soon follow.

Reaction to yet another match between the two families was predictable.

'What is it about that Mortimer family that they keep snatching up all the prizes of society. First there was Elizabeth Mortimer, who married Darcy, then Jane Mortimer was snatched up by Fitzwilliam. Admittedly, as a second son I can understand that he wanted an heiress. But then that insignificant parson, who is a cousin to the Mortimer ladies, landed himself in the position of Master of Rosings. And now yet another Mortimer is courting Miss Darcy. I suppose since he too is a second son, he was interested in her dowry.'

'Did you not hear? It is Miss Darcy who will be making the advantageous match. I am told that Mortimer's cousin has just named him the heir of his estate. While it is not as large as Pemberley, it is still quite substantial.'

'Are there any in the Mortimer family who are still unattached?'
~~~

'Only the youngest daughter, Miss Lydia Mortimer.'

'I have met her. She is a real beauty. I wonder what it would take to convince her to marry me?'

'I expect she requires intelligence, good character and a man free of disease. Do you match all of those qualities?'

'Damn. Not even one.'

~~~ooO0Ooo~~~

Despite their lack of success in charming Miss Lydia Mortimer, gentlemen flocked to her wherever she went. The combination of youth, beauty, wealth and connections was irresistible to the gentlemen of the *ton*.

She had her pick of partners at balls, she was a popular dinner partner and occasionally a gentleman even enjoyed her conversation on topics other than gossip.

This of course, caused envy amongst some of the young ladies, despite the fact that Lydia was obviously not interested in forming an attachment any time soon.

'What has she got that I do not?' was an oft repeated question by many of the debutants.

Some ladies, and even some gentlemen, were unkind enough to reply – 'everything'.

But Lydia did make a number of friends amongst the youngest ladies, who looked up to her for her fearless attitude towards the gentlemen.

Foremost amongst her friends was Mrs Clarissa Sedgeman, formerly Miss Tate. The previous summer, the young lady had fallen head over heels in love with Mr Martin Sedgeman, the oldest son of a minor gentleman. She claimed that she owed her current happiness to Miss Lydia Mortimer.

Lydia warmly congratulated her friend on her felicitous match, but could not help but ask, 'what of your sisters? Did you not say that you had two younger sisters?'

'You remember exactly. I told my parents how you helped me, and they are most grateful to you. Because of that they are currently looking
~~~

for someone who can instruct my sisters, but they have not been able to find an appropriate teacher for them. I admit, after my experience, I worry for them.'

'How old are your sisters?'

'They are twelve and ten. Which means they have a little time yet, but still...'

'In that case, I may have a solution for you. My instructors will be setting up an Academy for Young Ladies, to help ladies who could be potential targets for rakes. It will probably be another year before the school is ready, but then your parents might consider their school.'

'The ladies who taught you are going to teach others? That is wonderful news. Just wait until I tell my parents and all my friends. I suspect they will have their choice of students.'

Lydia was pleased with her success. While it was only a start, it was the first step in the right direction.

~~~oo0Ooo~~~

Lord Ashby mostly remained on the fringes of Lydia's admirers. Instead of asking her to dance, he would often sit and converse with her when she was resting for the one set, which she always reserved for that purpose. He enjoyed those conversations. Miss Mortimer charmed him because she did not try to do so.

She made it quite clear that she was not prepared to settle down to the life of being a second-class citizen. 'I will never let any man dictate to me what I can think or do. If that means that I have to remain single all my life, so be it.'

Miss Mortimer seemed to be unaware that her attitude spoke to the hunter in Lord Ashby. Like most men of his time, he did enjoy to hunt, and this game was proving to be exceedingly elusive. But unlike many other so-called gentlemen, his intentions were honourable.

~~~oo0Ooo~~~

As the season came to a close, the long-anticipated wedding between Miss Georgiana Darcy and Charles Mortimer took place. Since all her family were in town, it seemed logical for them to be married in

London, before moving to Bridgewater after a brief wedding trip of one month.

Having waited a whole year, Georgiana was now eager to be married, and become Mistress of her own home. That Bridgewater was close enough to Pemberley for frequent visits, was a great comfort to her.

Charles, while he felt confident that he knew about the running of an estate, was also pleased when Darcy offered his assistance, should Charles ever have need of it.

Lydia was thrilled when Georgiana requested her to be the bridesmaid, while Patrick again stood up with the groom. Mrs Mortimer noticed that this time, there was no wistful expression on his face.

Darcy, of course, had mixed feelings, handing his sister over to the care of another man. But he overcame his misgivings, after prompting from Elizabeth, and placed Georgiana's fate in the hands of the man she loved, and just as importantly to Darcy, who loved her in return.

<p style="text-align:center">~~~ooO0Ooo~~~</p>

26 Compromises

Life settled back to normal when they returned to Brook Hall.

Or at least as normal as life can be for a newly married couple who are both used to having their own way and being in charge.

While Mrs Mortimer had been happy with the idea of her husband running the estate, the reality was considerably more confronting. After all, she had been in sole charge of her home, including the estate, for fifteen years.

On yet another day when she had automatically given orders about a tenant, Patrick took her aside for a discussion.

'Stephanie, I love you dearly and I respect your ability to run an estate. But what do you expect me to do? Sit around like a pampered lapdog while you do everything?'

When his wife looked upset, he went on to assure her. 'I understand that you have developed the habit of running the estate, but I too am used to being useful.'

Her shoulders slumped. 'I did not think it would be this difficult to adjust. When I was married to Gerald, he ran the estates while I looked after the house. Although of course, I did visit the tenants, since the women preferred to speak to me rather than my husband. I was busy and content with the situation.'

She pulled a frustrated grimace. 'You are correct. When I moved here, I had to learn to be the Master of the estate, and I admit I enjoyed being in sole control. Now I am used to people coming to me with their problems and expecting me to solve them.'

Patrick took her hand and kissed it. 'For me, part of your attraction is your competence, but I too had not realised how difficult the adjustment would be for us. How can we come to a compromise?'

'I need something to do that will keep me too busy to interfere with the running of the estate.'

'What about getting Netherfield ready to be a school? You were talking about doing that next year, but why not start now?'

'Why not, indeed.' Stephanie broke into a relieved smile. 'Overseeing the remodelling will keep me out of the house and away from the temptation to give orders about things that are now in your purview.'

'Thank you. Although I hope that since you know the estate better than I do, you will offer advice.'

'Advice it is.' They sealed their bargain with a lingering kiss.

<center>~~~oo0Ooo~~~</center>

The adjustments to the marriage were not confined to the couple. Even the servants struggled a little.

The suite Mrs Mortimer had been using had always been known as the Master's suite. Now that there was a Master in residence, using what used to be known as the Mistress' suite, they had to adjust the terminology. The decision was made to call the combined suites the Master suite.

The former Mistress' suite was to be remodelled, to turn the bedroom with the dual aspect into a study for Mr Mortimer's use, since the couple were emphatic about sharing the east facing bedroom, which Mrs Mortimer favoured. And as long as the room contained Mrs Mortimer, and he could share it, Mr Mortimer was content.

This caused a small upheaval between his valet, Reeves, and Mrs Mortimer's maid Tilly on the first morning they were in Brook Hall.

'Where do you think you are going? You cannot enter my lady's bedchamber,' Tilly called out to Reeves, who had his hand on the doorhandle to the bedroom of the Master suite.

'I was about to open the curtains in my master's room, like I do every morning,' the man said in an officious manner.

'You can go and open the curtains in your master's rooms, but you most certainly will not intrude in my lady's bedchamber,' huffed Tilly.

'Those are now my master's chambers,' declared Reeves.

'No, they are not. My lady may have granted your master the estate, but this is her house and these are her chambers,' Tilly defended Mrs Mortimer by stepping between Reeves and the door, her voice rising.

Before the argument could escalate further, the door opened and Mr Mortimer's head appeared in the small gap. 'Reeves, please open the curtains in the other rooms, but I will not allow you to lay eyes upon my wife unless she is fully dressed.'

Tilly gave Reeves a triumphant look, as the man bowed stiffly and murmured, 'certainly, Sir. I should have realised.'

Tilly turned to enter the room, when she caught sight not only of Patrick's mischievous smile, but also of a bare shoulder. 'Mrs Mortimer asks that you return in an hour,' he said as he closed the door in her face.

Tilly was grateful that no one was present to see her blushing.

<div align="center">~~~ooO0Ooo~~~</div>

Mrs Mortimer sent word to Mrs Nicholls that she expected to spend the following day at Netherfield. In the morning she invited Lydia to accompany her for the day.

Since it was a beautiful day, they chose to ride. Once they were on their way, Lydia asked, 'why are we going to Netherfield for the whole day? Aunt Stephanie, please tell me that you and Patrick did not quarrel already.'

Mrs Mortimer chuckled. 'Not at all. I am simply removing myself from the temptation of interfering with Patrick's management of the estate.'

'But it is your estate.'

'Not any more, since I gave it to Patrick as a wedding present.' 'According to the law, it would have been his anyway, but he wanted me to keep my possessions.'

'But why did you do that? He has his own estate. I thought you more independent than that.'

'Patrick intended to bequeath his estate to Charles, but with our marriage, it seemed more sensible to hand Bridgewater over to Charles now, rather than wait, and try to run two major estates. Either Bridgewater or Brook Hall would suffer, or we would have no time together.'

She shrugged. 'I did not wish to live at Bridgewater. Since Patrick was prepared to give up his home, it seemed only fair that he became the Master of Brook Hall. He needs to have something useful to do. I have seen the state of Bridgewater, and heard from others how good he was at managing the estate. I am perfectly happy for him to do what he is good at.'

Mrs Mortimer smiled at Lydia's dubious look. 'As it is, everything is working out perfectly. I had put off remodelling Netherfield, because I did not have time to spare. After the season in town, I expected that I would need to spend time catching up with estate business. Now that Patrick has taken on that task, it leaves me free to set my plans for the school into motion.'

Lydia looked relieved at the explanation. 'I was worried that you were prepared to become a second-class citizen.'

Mrs Mortimer whispered conspiratorially, 'if I wanted an estate, I have more than enough money to buy one.'

She added more briskly, 'I am fully aware that according to the law, as a married woman I have very few rights. But the trick with marriage is to find a husband who values and respects you. Then the law is mostly irrelevant. I trust Patrick to run the estate, which gives me time to pursue my own interests. We cooperate and compromise when needed.'

Lydia rode the rest of the way in a thoughtful mood.

<div align="center">~~~oo0Ooo~~~</div>

When they arrived at Netherfield, Mrs Nicholls had tea and their favourite pastries ready.

Mrs Nicholls was surprised but gratified, when Mrs Mortimer asked the lady to join them for a discussion.

'You may have heard by now that I am planning to turn Netherfield into a school for young ladies. Or to be more precise, heiresses. I have seen too many young women forced into marriages by rakes who were only after their dowries, and I plan to curtail their depredations.'

'You will have Julia, I mean Miss Martin, teach the girls?' Mrs Nicholls looked pleased at the prospect.

'Indeed. Today I would like to have a look at the house to see how many bedrooms we can allocate to the girls, and still have enough rooms for teachers. I also want to see what and how much maintenance is required, as well as arrange for redecorating. And I wish to see if there are any rooms suitable for an experiment.'

'What kind of experiment?'

'I would like to install those new flushing toilets, and bathtubs which can be filled from cisterns and a boiler via pipes, rather than have to have all the bathwater heated in the kitchen and carried upstairs in cans by servants. I am certain they have better things to do.'

'How many girls are you planning to accommodate?'

'How many bedrooms are there?'

'Including the Master's and the Mistress' suite, there are twenty-four bedrooms. Some are larger than others.'

'If we plan on two girls per room, then probably around thirty.'

'To feed that many people, you may need to consider expanding the kitchen,' Mrs Nicholls offered tentatively.

'Mrs Nicholls, you know this house and you know what it takes to look after that many people, students and teachers. Please, I would like to hear your opinions, which is why I am talking to you. I expect you will need extra staff as well. Provide me with a list of everything you can think of. Some things we may need to negotiate. But I need to know the exact requirements and the costs, to set the appropriate fees.'

The housekeeper smiled in relief. Mrs Kirby, the housekeeper at Brook Hall had always been complimentary about Mrs Mortimer's management style, but it was pleasant to experience for herself having a sensible employer, rather than a screeching termagant like Miss Bingley had been.

'There is one more thing I need to know. Are you willing to serve as housekeeper in this school?'

'Who will be in charge of the school?'

'For day to day administration, Mrs Taylor will be in charge. For anything extraordinary, she will speak to me. Miss Martin will teach the girls self-defence and assist Mrs Taylor. I expect you will have significant autonomy. If there is a problem that cannot be resolved between the three of you, I expect any or all of you, to speak to me.'

Mrs Nicholls was astonished by the amount of trust Mrs Mortimer was placing in her, but the servant's grapevine worked both ways. Mrs Mortimer too had made enquiries, and was satisfied with the reports she had on the competence of Mrs Nicholls.

'I would be delighted to remain as housekeeper,' Mrs Nicholls informed her employer.

They spent the rest of the day touring the house, inspecting everything, from the servants' quarters in the attic to the kitchen and storerooms in the basement. In the library they had even found a plan of the house, which Mrs Mortimer took with her to study in detail.

By the afternoon, Mrs Mortimer had a tentative plan how to arrange the house.

<p style="text-align:center">~~~ooo0Ooo~~~</p>

The following day, Mrs Mortimer was ensconced in her study at Brook Hall with the plan of Netherfield and several sheets of paper where she was making notes.

That was where her husband discovered her. He greeted her with a lingering kiss. 'I wondered if you were here or had gone to Netherfield again.' He looked at the plan and the notes on her desk, and asked, 'what are you working on?'

At her invitation he pulled up a chair next to her, and Stephanie had just finished enthusiastically outlining her plans, when they were interrupted by Mr Kirby. 'Mr Lindsay is here to see you.'

'Will it disturb you if I speak to him in here?' asked Patrick. 'I believe your knowledge might assist…'

When his wife agreed, 'I could use a break from staring at that plan,' Patrick asked Mr Kirby to show the tenant into the study.

Mr Lindsay greeted them both politely, and then addressed Mrs Mortimer. 'My lady, I have come with a request.'

'Mr Lindsay, any issue with the estate you need to address to my husband. He is now in charge.' Mrs Mortimer smiled easily.

Patrick surreptitiously squeezed her hand under the desk, and asked the tenant, 'what is your request?'

'Well, Sir. it is like this.' He went on and explained long-windedly how he wanted to improve one of his fields.

When Lindsay finished, Patrick asked his wife, 'Mrs Mortimer, you are more familiar with the field which Mr Lindsay is talking about. What do you think?'

She suppressed a pleased smile as she asked, 'Mr Lindsay, correct me if I am wrong, but I seem to recall that seven years ago, you already tried and failed at that experiment.'

'Ah… well. I thought I give it another go.'

Now it was Patrick's turn. 'Mr Lindsay, are you planning to do anything differently this time?'

Since the man was not going to make any changes, Patrick declined his request.

When they were alone again, he kissed her hand. 'Thank you, my dear. Your knowledge was invaluable. Based on his reasoning, I would have been inclined to grant his request, which would have been a mistake.'

'Any sensible man listens to his wife,' she teased him.

'Provided that his wife is sensible. Fortunately for me, you are eminently so.'

Both were relieved that their adjustments were becoming easier.

<center>~~~oo0Ooo~~~</center>

27 Changes

The rumour-mill in Meryton was in full swing. The juiciest bit of current gossip pertained to Mrs Mortimer. The fact that she had returned from London with a new husband, when there had never been even the slightest inkling of such an event, set tongues wagging.

While Patrick had visited Brook Hall on a few occasions, he was unknown in the neighbourhood, since his visits had been brief, and only the loyal staff at the house had seen him. The fact that he reputedly was rich, handsome and younger than the lady, caused considerable envy in some quarters.

The first Sunday after taking up residence in Brook Hall, the couple, accompanied by Lydia, attended services in Meryton. They caused a stir, when Mrs Mortimer entered the church on her husband's arm.

Patrick, perceiving the interest, was overtly solicitous of his wife's comfort throughout the service, earning himself a look of suppressed amusement from both ladies.

When they exited the church, several local ladies and their husbands lay in wait for them. Mrs Mortimer, with casual aplomb, introduced her husband and mentioned that he was distantly related to her late husband.

Sir William Lucas, bluff and good natured as always, was the first to offer his hearty congratulations. 'It is capital that you have managed to convince this wonderful lady to marry you. Someone as alive as she, should not bury herself in duty all the time. It is about time she had some fun.'

Lady Lucas added, 'I hope that you will be free to come to dinner one night this week. Would Wednesday suit you? You too, of course, Miss Lydia.'

Patrick rather liked the bluff gentleman, and by mutual consensus, they were happy to accept the invitation.

Mrs Goulding was less than subtle. 'It was such a surprise to hear that you had married. You sly thing, you never let on that you were being courted.'

Patrick took up her challenge by replying blandly, 'it has taken me years to convince Mrs Mortimer to take me seriously. She kept telling me I was too young. I am grateful that she did not spread the story and make me look like a lovesick puppy to her friends.'

After chatting pleasantly with a few of their neighbours, they boarded their carriage to return to Brook Hall.

As soon as they were out of earshot of the gossips, the ladies burst out laughing. 'Oh, Patrick, that was brilliantly done. The way you pulled that old biddy's fangs,' gasped Lydia between guffaws of laughter.

'I spoke nothing but the truth,' replied Patrick innocently. 'I cannot help it that your mother did not realise that she was being courted.' His twinkling eyes gave the lie to the statement.

<div style="text-align:center">~~~oo0Ooo~~~</div>

The next item of gossip to make the rounds of Meryton was that Netherfield was to be turned into a school for young ladies.

The next time, Lady Lucas called on Mrs Mortimer, she was full of questions about the kind of students she would be accepting, and about the subjects which would be taught. She vacillated between shock and amusement, when Mrs Mortimer explained that the young ladies would receive the same education as her daughters had received.

'Are you planning on a revolution? Sending educated young women, who cannot be forced to keep their place, out into society. Will that not make them unmarriageable?'

'You have met the men my daughters married. Personally, I think they have chosen well. I am convinced there must be more men like them in the country.'

'What about Miss Lydia? She is nineteen and still single.'

'By her choice. She decided before her coming out that she was in no rush to marry.'

'But will any man be interested in a young woman as strong and independent as she is?'

Mrs Mortimer laughed. 'I am sorry, my dear Lady Lucas, but you should have been in London this past season. You would have been highly amused. The more Lydia rebuffed the gentlemen, the more eager and persistent they became. There were at least six, who were seriously interested in her, despite the fact that she never pretended to be anything other than what she is.'

'But we were always taught to be demure, quiet and agreeable. Not to be forward and flaunt ourselves.'

'Lydia does not actually flaunt herself. She acted with propriety and decorum at all times. She does not put herself forward, but she also does not back down. She has a self-confidence which seems to be irresistible.' Mrs Mortimer smiled fondly. She was very proud of her daughter. Despite her difficult start, she had turned into a wonderful young woman.

Lady Lucas answered that smile with one of her own. 'You have taught her exceedingly well. That is a quality you both share. I suspect it is also the reason for your husband's attraction to you.'

'Perhaps,' was all Mrs Mortimer would say.

Lady Lucas decided it was time to return to her original question. 'Will you only teach boarders, or will you take on day students?'

'I had planned to only have boarders, since the young ladies I want for my school will need Miss Martin's tutelage.' Mrs Mortimer went on to explain her reasoning.

'You truly are trying to start a revolution. Teaching girls to think, and to decide what is best for them. And then giving them the skills to enforce that decision.' Lady Lucas chuckled. 'I could almost feel sorry for the rakes. They will not be able to get their way, either with words or actions.'

'Will it not be terrible; some of those gentlemen might have to sink so low as having to find paying employment. and possibly having to get their hands dirty,' Mrs Mortimer said dramatically.

'This will truly be a revolution. Gentlemen having to work for a living, because they cannot find a wife to support them,' laughed Lady Lucas.

~~~ooO0Ooo~~~

The ladies were in conference at Netherfield to finalise the plans for the proposed changes. Since Lydia was interested in the school, she had come, along with Mrs Taylor and Miss Martin.

The two new head teachers were pleased when they found out that Mrs Mortimer planned for them to use the Master and Mistress suites respectively. The large sitting room joining the suites, was to become their study and office, while they still had private sitting rooms as well.

Two small suites, on each of the upper floors at the back of the house, were to be turned into bathing rooms.

Mrs Nicholls was shocked. 'You are planning to install those bathing rooms on the servant level as well?'

'Naturally. I like servants to be clean, since I find that it quite ruins my appetite, if the footman serving me has not bathed for a month. It spoils even the most delectable aroma of the food.'

'Mrs Kirby has mentioned your penchant for cleanliness, but she never explained why.'

'Possibly because she never asked for an explanation. Now, as you can see, on the first floor we can set up another four suites for use by teachers. On the second floor the larger rooms at the front of the house will do nicely for two girls each, while the smaller ones at the back can be single rooms. Which means we can comfortably accommodate twenty-four students.'

'Not all the girls will be happy about having to share rooms,' Lydia pointed out.

'But it will teach them to compromise and make friends, even if only to make their stay more pleasant. And if we find that two girls are truly incompatible, we can switch them around. I think it will be a comfort to most of the younger girls to have someone with them.'

On consideration, the other ladies agreed with her reasoning. Then the subject of teachers was raised.

Mrs Taylor suggested, 'I think we should hire ladies who can all teach the basics, but each with different specialities, such as languages, music and drawing. Maybe include one or two bluestockings to focus on
~~~

academic subjects. although for some specialised subjects we may need to hire temporary masters.'

'We do have access to experts in a number of fields, and if they are not available, I am certain they will be able to recommend substitutes,' suggested Lydia. When Mrs Taylor and Mrs Nicholls looked perplexed, she added, 'my sisters… and their husbands.'

'Have you considered hiring male teachers?' asked Miss Martin out of curiosity.

'I have considered that option as a last resort, if we cannot find a woman to teach a particular subject. But I would give preference to ladies, since they have fewer options to earn a living.'

They went into more detail discussing the accomplishments the teachers should have. Then Mrs Nicholls asked for changes to the kitchen and scullery, before requesting additional staff.

On the subject of footmen, Mrs Mortimer suggested they should be hired for ability not looks. 'I do not wish the young ladies to have too many distractions or temptations.'

<p style="text-align:center">~~~ooo0Ooo~~~</p>

While the ladies were busy with the changes to Netherfield, Patrick established himself as the Master of Brook Hall. Thanks to his wife's cooperation, it was not long before the outdoor staff and tenants approached him for advice and decisions.

Although the indoor staff, while providing him with excellent service and promptly obeying his orders, always went to Mrs Mortimer for instructions.

The estate flourished. While the tenants had all gotten used to Mrs Mortimer being in charge, most of the men were relieved to be dealing with a gentleman again, especially the ones dealing with animal husbandry. Some subjects were simply too uncomfortable to speak about to a lady.

Despite being preoccupied with Netherfield, each week Mrs Mortimer and Lydia visited the tenants. In the process, they found many volunteers amongst their daughters, to work at the school. The mothers in particular were in favour of their daughters working in what they considered a safe environment.

~~~oo0Ooo~~~

Lydia, as the only sister left in the house, enjoyed being such an integral part of Mrs Mortimer's life, and learning about the complexities of being Mistress of an estate.

One day, after another one of Joshua's weekly visits, she pondered the difference between Mrs Bennet and Mrs Mortimer. Lydia wondered about the kind of life she would have had, if her mother had not rejected her after the birth of her brother.

She realised that Mrs Bennet had unwittingly done her a favour. She remembered her mother pushing fifteen-year-old Jane at any single man who crossed their path, and berating her sister for not being flirtatious enough. Her only concern had ever been to marry her daughters off as soon as possible, irrespective of the gentlemen's suitability.

Lydia shuddered to think that she might have ended up being a brainless flirt without any accomplishments, only interested in pretty clothes for herself, and incapable of even such basic things as managing a house. Considering Mrs Bennets predilection for beauty, Lydia suspected she would have judged the worth of a man by a handsome face and pretty manners, without consideration whether he had character or the means to support her.

Instead, she had been given the opportunity to learn about the world and herself. While she was not as accomplished in the different areas of expertise in which her sisters excelled, she had learned enough of each to be considered accomplished by society's standards. While it made her an excellent marital prospect at a level Mrs Bennet could only have dreamt about, she was not ready to become a second-class citizen, no matter what anybody said.

Only one thing terrified Lydia. The sensation which the memory of a certain pair of expressive green eyes caused in the pit of her stomach. She fought valiantly to suppress those feelings.

~~~oo0Ooo~~~

At breakfast the following day, Lydia's mind was still on Mrs Bennet. Now that she had had her epiphany, she remembered her outburst at the woman at their last meeting with shame. While her words had been true, they had also been cruel.

She begged off from going to Netherfield yet again, to go for a ride to Longbourn.

'You are going to see your mother?' Mrs Mortimer was all astonishment.

'I am going to make peace with Mrs Bennet. I realised how much I have gained and she has lost. I do not expect us to ever be friends, but I want both of us to have closure.'

Lydia was stunned by the look of pride and love directed at her by her guardian. 'You were the one I almost despaired about when you first came to live with me. And now, look at you. You are the only one of your sisters who has enough charity to forgive.'

Mrs Mortimer enfolded Lydia in a fierce hug as she whispered, 'I am so very proud of you.'

'Thank you, Mother,' replied Lydia without thinking, nearly causing the lady to lose her composure.

<div style="text-align:center">~~~ooo0Ooo~~~</div>

An hour later, Lydia was knocking at the front door of Longbourn. The door was opened by Mrs Hill, who exclaimed in surprise, 'Miss Lydia!'

'I wonder if I could speak to Mrs Bennet for a moment, if she is available.' Lydia suddenly felt much less certain if she was doing the right thing. Was it presumptuous of her to come here like this?

Her dithering was cut short when Mrs Hill ushered her into the parlour, where Mrs Bennet sat on her own, mending what must be a pair of Joshua's breeches.

The lady looked up and cried in astonishment, 'Lydia...'

Lydia curtsied and blurted out, 'I just came to tell you that I forgive you. And to thank you for giving me the opportunity to grow,' she stopped and swallowed the rest of the sentence, *beyond what you could have taught me.*

She watched in consternation as Mrs Bennet burst into tears, clutching her sewing to her chest, and whispered, 'thank you... thank you... thank you...'

Lydia managed to mumble, 'you are welcome,' before she fled, feeling unequal to deal with Mrs Bennet's reaction.

But brief as her visit was, she left behind a woman, who felt as if the weight of the world had just been lifted off her shoulders.

~~~oo0Ooo~~~
~~~

28 Proposal

The season in London was underway again. Since the remodelling of Netherfield was nearly completed, Mrs Mortimer, accompanied by her husband, as well as Lydia, Mrs Taylor and Miss Martin came to town.

Mrs Mortimer and Mrs Taylor planned to interview prospective teachers, while Lydia hoped to enjoy the entertainments London had to offer.

Mr Mortimer and Miss Martin came along to provide companionship and protection.

As in previous years, Lydia was exceedingly popular with the gentlemen. Her dance-card was full at every ball she attended.

But there was one difference. One gentleman, who for the last two years had been content to enjoy only her conversation, asked her to dance.

Lydia was reluctant. 'If after all this time I dance with you, people will have expectations.'

'Have you never danced with friends before, Miss Mortimer?'

'I have, but they had been friends all my life, Lord Ashby.' Lydia did not want to admit that she dreaded dancing with him, because they would constantly be touching, and she found the sensation too disconcerting. 'I am sorry, but I simply cannot.'

At least, since he had asked for the last dance, she did not have to miss out on all the rest, and she still enjoyed her conversation with him.

Lydia encountered Lord Ashby at every function which she attended, which made her wonder at the quality of his spies.

~~~ooO0Ooo~~~

Lord Ashby bowed and asked politely, 'Miss Mortimer, may I have the honour of the last set.'
~~~

'I am sorry, Lord Ashby, I am already engaged for the last set.'

~~~ooO0Ooo~~~

Lord Ashby bowed and asked politely, 'Miss Mortimer, may I have the honour of the last set.'

'I am sorry, Lord Ashby, I am fatigued, and wish to rest.'

~~~ooO0Ooo~~~

Lord Ashby bowed and asked politely, 'Miss Mortimer, may I have the honour of the last set.'

'I am sorry, Lord Ashby, I have no wish to dance the last set.'

~~~ooO0Ooo~~~

Lord Ashby bowed and asked politely, 'Miss Mortimer, may I have the honour of the last set.'

'No, Lord Ashby, I do not wish to dance.'

~~~ooO0Ooo~~~

Lord Ashby bowed and asked politely, 'Miss Mortimer, may I have the honour of the last set.'

'No, Lord Ashby.'

~~~ooO0Ooo~~~

Lord Ashby bowed and asked politely, 'Miss Mortimer, may I have the honour of the last set.'

'No.'

~~~ooO0Ooo~~~

Lord Ashby bowed and asked politely, 'Miss Mortimer, may I...'

'No.'

~~~ooO0Ooo~~~

'Why do you keep refusing to dance with Lord Ashby? I thought the two of you had become good friends,' asked Mrs Mortimer

Lydia mumbled an incomprehensible reply.
~~~

'Is he the reason why you were so concerned about me becoming a, as you called it, second-class citizen? Are you worried that could happen to you?'

'It has crossed my mind.' Lydia blushed and nodded. 'Aunt Stephanie, what does it feel like to be in love? I know how the novels describe it, but if they are right, then I am not in love, but I think I may be.'

'I do not believe that everyone feels the same way. One person can even feel differently in different situations. What I felt for my first husband is very different to what I feel for Patrick.'

Lydia looked disappointed. 'That is not very helpful,' she complained.

'There is one common factor which I have noticed whenever I have loved someone. And I mean not just my husbands, but also you and your sisters. Their and your happiness is important to me, even more than my own.'

Lydia sat quietly absorbing the information. At last she said softly, 'I think I am in love.'

But she also admitted, 'it terrifies me.'

~~~ooO0Ooo~~~

Lord Ashby bowed and asked politely, 'Miss Mortimer, may I have the honour of the last set.'

'No, and please stop asking.'

~~~ooO0Ooo~~~

Lydia looked around the ballroom. She had already danced four sets, but it seemed that Lord Ashby had taken her words to heart. He was usually one of the first guests to arrive, but tonight she could not see him.

The supper set was about to start when he suddenly stood before her. Lord Ashby bowed as the music started, took Lydia's hand, and before she could gather her wits and object, he led her to the floor.

Lydia hissed, 'what do you think you are doing, Lord Ashby?'

'I am following your instructions, Miss Mortimer. You said that I should not ask you to dance… I did not ask,' he replied blandly, but with a suspicious twinkle in his brilliant eyes.

Lydia looked at him for a moment in stunned disbelief at his audacity… and his cleverness. Coming to a decision she suddenly smiled impishly. 'Lord Ashby, do you always do as you are told?'

'In your case… usually. Did you have anything specific in mind?'

'Yes… Marry me.'

'It will be my pleasure.' He gave her a brilliant smile, which she returned in equal measure.

~~~ooo0Ooo~~~

Word about Lydia's proposal was spreading throughout the extended family. Mrs Mortimer was discussing the situation with her old friend, Lady Matlock.

Her surprised response was, 'oh Lord, there goes the aristocracy… or maybe she will be the making of them.'

'Are you aware that you sound just like Lydia?' asked Mrs Mortimer.

Lady Matlock looked startled and then grinned. 'My point exactly.'

Mrs Mortimer shook her head and sighed, 'I suppose you are correct. This is the beginning of the end.'

~~~ooo0Ooo~~~

The end… for now

Unconventional Ladies

Author's Note

Some readers commented that the education of the girls in the previous book was too unrealistic.

If you too consider some of the education the girls received to be too out of character for the time, you might find this article by Barbara W. Swords interesting.
http://www.jasna.org/persuasions/printed/number10/swords.htm

The self-defence aspects may be a little exaggerated, but girls in the country were often taught to shoot. Pocket pistols were also called muff-pistols since ladies carried them in their muffs, and were quite prepared to use them. Life was cheap in those days.

Angelo's Fencing Academy did in fact allow female students.

And the girls in my stories do not engage in full-scale brawls. They go for kicks to the ankles and the shins, or stepping hard on someone's foot. All very simple and plausible techniques, which any sensible mother, or even a brother, would teach the girls.